When We Were Widows

ALSO BY ANNETTE CHAVEZ MACIAS

Big Chicas Don't Cry

Too Soon for Adiós

When We Were Widows

a novel

ANNETTE
CHAVEZ MACIAS

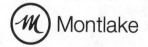 Montlake

Text copyright © 2024 by Annette Macias
All rights reserved.

Published by Montlake, Seattle

www.apub.com

Amazon, the Amazon logo, and Montlake are trademarks of Amazon.com, Inc., or its affiliates.

ISBN-13: 9781662521492 (paperback)
ISBN-13: 9781662521485 (digital)

Cover design by Caroline Teagle Johnson
Cover image: © Santi Nuñez, © Melissa Milis Photography / Stocksy;
© Levente Bodo, © 200519865-001, © Cavan Images, © Thomas Barwick / Getty

Printed in the United States of America

For my mom. I'm proud to be your first daughter.

CHAPTER ONE
ANA

There were only four things or people in this life that my mother loathed with every morsel of her soul:

The man who killed my father.

The Los Angeles Dodgers.

Cuca Padilla.

And being late to Sunday Mass.

The first one—well, that was a given. My father was shot during a robbery at our neighborhood liquor store when I was only eight years old. The second target of her hatred was rooted in a traumatic childhood memory she refused to talk about even to this day. And her nemesis, a.k.a. Cuca Padilla, had earned my mother's scorn by betraying her in one of the worst ways possible.

The last one stemmed from her belief that if you were late to worship God, then you risked him being late to answer your prayers.

"I don't play when it comes to praying," she once told me.

That's why I didn't push the snooze button on my alarm when it blared at 5:30 on a Sunday morning. In order to be on time for the 7:00 a.m. service, we needed to leave the house no later than 6:40. And I needed at least an hour to take a shower, get dressed, do my makeup, and finish my first cup of coffee.

I'd also built in ten minutes to my routine to wake up my mother, who was now asleep in her room across the hallway. Electronic alarms were no use on her—the woman could sleep through an earthquake. And had. Many times.

No, I was her alarm, so that meant I needed to get out of bed and make sure she was wide awake before I took my shower.

So I groggily sat up in the dark, pulled my sheet off my body, swung my legs over the side of my queen-size bed, and stepped onto the carpet of my bedroom.

Squish.

A cold and wet sensation zapped me fully awake, and I instinctively yanked my feet back onto the safety of my bed. I turned on the lamp sitting on my nightstand, and my tired eyes scanned the floor. At first, I didn't see anything unusual. But as my eyes began to adjust more and more to the light and my brain started to turn on, I realized the normally light-beige carpet looked darker. A lot darker.

I twisted my body until I could gingerly touch the floor with my index finger. Disbelief made me touch it a second time with all five fingers on my right hand.

My stomach dropped. Yet still my mind tried to find a rational explanation as to why the carpet seemed wet. My eyes flew to the glass sitting next to my alarm clock, with the hope of finding it on its side or missing from the nightstand altogether. But nope. It was still there and still filled halfway with water.

A long, fearful sigh filled the room as I forced myself to get off the bed and confirm what was beginning to be my dreaded suspicion.

With the room now filled with light, I could see my flip-flops sitting next to the bed and slid my feet into them and stood.

Squish.

I cringed as water kissed my toes. The carpet wasn't just wet. It was soaking wet.

As if it would make a difference, I tried to tiptoe across the room toward my bedroom door. Every step made me cringe.

"Please, please, please," I prayed out loud as I stepped into the hallway.

Squish.

The carpet outside my room was just as drenched. Panic thundered inside my chest, and tears filled my eyes. Then I did the only thing I could think to do in that moment.

I yelled for my mother.

◆ ◆ ◆

"Well, do you want the good news or the bad news first?" Gene said as he took a seat at the kitchen table. Mama promptly served him a cup of coffee and placed the sugar bowl and a spoon in front of him.

"Thank you, Imelda," he said with a nod.

"I always want the bad news first, Gene," I said with a groan. "You know that."

After dumping two heaping spoonfuls of sugar into his mug, he explained what he'd found.

"Well, it looks like the toilet in the hallway bathroom was overflowing all night. Besides that bathroom, Imelda's room, and the hallway, half of your room and the inside of your closet are also wet. Other than getting a new toilet, you're going to need to replace all the flooring in those areas and probably most—if not all—of the drywall."

It was just as bad as I'd expected. Although a tiny part of me had hoped it wouldn't be.

Suddenly, an uneasy suspicion erupted in my gut.

I looked over at Mama. "Did you flush your tissues after wiping off your face cream again?" She'd clogged the toilet a few other times that way, but I'd always fixed it with the plunger.

"No," she insisted as she shook her head. "I throw them away in the trash can now, like you told me to."

Gene cleared his throat.

My eyes narrowed as I leaned closer to her. "Mama?"

3

Guilt reddened her cheeks, and I knew she had in fact flushed the tissues again. And now I had a river inside my house.

"Ay, Mama!" I said and covered my face with my hands. "Didn't you hear the water running at all?"

My mother pursed her lips together and shook her head. "I close the bathroom door. I close my door. Plus, I don't hear anything because you always have the air-conditioning on, even though I keep telling you it's too cold in my room."

I tried to stamp out my frustration by blowing out a long, hard sigh. "I have the air on because I have night sweats, Mama. Just put another blanket on the bed if you're so cold."

"I already have dos cobijas, and one of them is the heavy black-and-white San Marcos with the tiger. We're going to have to go to Tijuana and buy me another one if you insist on keeping the temperature in here like a meat locker."

"Mama . . ."

I heard Gene clear his throat again.

My mouth clamped shut. The poor man had only come to help, and now he was being forced to hear our usual back-and-forth bickering.

Mama must have realized the same thing because she jumped up and offered to get Gene a piece of pan dulce to go with his cafecito.

"So, what's the good news?" I said after a heavy sigh.

Gene took a long sip of his coffee before answering. "It doesn't look like Benny's office or the living room or kitchen were affected. If you hadn't called me when you did or hadn't turned off the water like I'd told you to, you could be looking at a lot more damage. It's a good thing you got out of bed when you did."

I guess not being late for God had saved part of my house, at least. "All right, Gene. How much is this all going to cost me?"

The white-haired man waved his arms at me. "Oh no. I can't fix this. This is way too big of a job. You're going to have to hire a contractor."

My heart stilled. "A contractor? But I don't know any contractors. I only know you."

Gene had been our family's go-to handyman for over twelve years. He lived next door and had once owned a hardware store just a few blocks away. His sons had taken over the business a while ago, but instead of retiring fully, he'd continued to work by doing odd jobs for everyone in the neighborhood. I trusted him to do whatever needed to be done and knew he'd be honest about the cost and the time. When he'd shown up at the house just as the sun was rising, I felt like it was a sign. A sense of peace had washed over me for the first time that morning because I knew he would make everything all right again, just like he always did. I didn't want to hire anyone else—especially not a stranger.

For the millionth time since he'd died five years ago, I silently cursed Benny for leaving me to deal with things like flooded houses and hiring contractors.

"I could recommend someone," Gene offered. "But first you need to call your homeowner's insurance. They'll send out an adjuster and maybe even their own contractor. You do have insurance, right?"

Although I knew Gene wasn't trying to be condescending, I still bristled at the question, since it seemed more like an assumption that I didn't.

"Yes, of course," I answered.

"Good. That's good, Ana. You'd be surprised at how many widows don't know if they have insurance or not because it was their husbands who always handled things like that."

I nodded my head in understanding. Gene didn't need to know that the only reason I still had homeowner's insurance was because Benny had set up the automatic payments years ago, and I'd never had the time or urge to figure out if I should cancel it and shop around for another company.

Gene stayed only long enough to eat his bread and finish a second cup of coffee. After he left, Mama and I sat at the kitchen table in silence for a few minutes.

Finally, she spoke. "I'm sorry, Mija. I didn't mean for this to happen."

I wanted to tell her that *this* wouldn't have happened if she hadn't been so stubborn about her face tissues and had listened to me in the first place. But I knew it wouldn't do any good. She was my mother. I was her daughter. And even though I'd taken care of her for decades, I was always going to be the child in this house, and she would always be the mother who knew better.

"I know you didn't," I replied instead.

"So, what are we going to do now?"

I ignored her use of the word "we" because we both knew this was all going to be on me to figure out. "I'm going to call the insurance company, like Gene said. Hopefully, they'll just refer me to one of their contractors, and we can get the repairs going sooner rather than later."

"And where will we stay?" she asked.

The question threw me. I hadn't even considered the fact that my house—the home I'd lived in for over thirty years—was now unlivable. My throat tightened with a combination of fear, sadness, and frustration. But I refused to cry.

Once I trusted myself to speak, I said, "We'll go to a hotel, I guess."

Mama nodded, but then seemed to consider something else. "What if it's going to take a few weeks or even a month? We can't afford that, can we?"

Again, I ignored the royal "we." My mother's tiny Social Security check would barely cover one night at the local motel.

"I'll figure it out after I talk to the contractor."

She cleared her throat. "Why don't we stay with Yesica? She's all alone in that big house now. When she bought it, she told me there was a room on the first floor I could stay in whenever I wanted."

It was true my daughter did have enough rooms in her home. But we lived in Bell Gardens, and she lived over twenty miles away in Santa Monica—a drive that could take nearly forty minutes *without* traffic.

And while I was sure she would welcome her grandmother to stay with her, I wasn't as confident that she'd extend the invitation to me.

It wasn't that we were estranged—not in the usual sense of the word. But we weren't close or even affectionate with each other. Yesica had always been closer to her father, and after he died, she'd only grown more distant. Unlike her younger brother, Alejandro, who now lived in Colorado, my daughter only seemed to call or visit me out of obligation. I never got the feeling that she wanted to spend time with me outside the holidays—and even those visits had grown fewer and farther between.

So, yes, I had my doubts about living with her. Even if it would be only temporary.

I wrung my hands in worry. "Like I said, I'll figure it out once we know how long everything is going to take."

Mama didn't say anything, but I knew her expressions well enough to know there was some concocting and planning going on inside her head.

I waved my finger at her. "Do not call Yesica. I will call her myself . . . if I have to."

She shrugged. "Okay."

Her hesitant tone triggered an alarm bell in my head. "Mama?"

"I said okay," Mama said as she stood up from the table. "I need to take my pills. And I might as well make us some huevos, since we missed Mass. Maybe we can go tonight?"

"We'll see, Mama," I said with a shrug. "We have a lot of cleaning up to do. I'm sure God will understand if we miss one Sunday."

She didn't agree, but she also didn't argue as she shuffled out of the kitchen.

I stayed in my seat after she'd gone. A million questions ran through my head. Why hadn't I been more firm with my mother about flushing her tissues? Why did we still have so much carpeting in the house? Why wasn't my husband here to deal with this mess?

I didn't touch my own cup of coffee or the plate of eggs and beans my mother served me a little later. My stomach was in knots as I thought about everything that had happened and everything that was going to need to happen later. It was all too much.

But I had to admit that some of that worry had to do with the fact that deep down, I couldn't trust my mother.

Whether it was flushing face tissues down the toilet or calling my daughter whom I was barely speaking to these days, Mama was going to do what she always did: whatever she wanted.

CHAPTER TWO
YESICA

In my defense, I hadn't meant to break the damn window.

And, also in my defense, I'd already had a pretty crappy Monday, and it was only 9:00 a.m.

So, when Damien called me into his office later that morning, I was still annoyed.

"Well?" I'd said as I plopped down on the leather sofa in his corner office.

"Well, what?" he said, arching a silver, expertly trimmed eyebrow in my direction. Damien Rojas was a senior vice president of M&T, the consulting firm I'd worked at for the past four years. He was thirty years older than me, which explained why I was starting to feel like I'd been summoned to the principal's office. Or worse, to my dad's.

My stubbornness, however, quickly won out over any apprehensiveness, and I sat up straight. Damien loved me—not in a creepy, inappropriate way, though. I was his star employee, his top performer. I'd made more money for this firm than any other associate. Maybe it was wrong to think that Damien would never really fire me over a onetime loss of control—but that was what I'd decided to think.

My intuition told me this was just a formality. He had to prove to the others in the office that I wasn't going to get any special treatment just because I was his favorite and helped to bring in the money that allowed them to get those hefty Christmas bonuses every year.

I waved my hand in his direction. "Go on. Do the whole 'This is unacceptable' speech. Shake your head disapprovingly at me, and then let me get back to work."

"This is unacceptable," he said tersely.

I couldn't help but wince at his unexpected tone. His disappointment was obvious, and guilt made me sink deeper into the couch, as if I could hide from his disapproving glare. The last thing I ever wanted was to be on Damien's bad side. He was the one who'd hired me, and our bond had only deepened over time. He was more to me than just my boss.

At first, our regular lunches and late nights in the office had fed the watercooler chisme about a supposed May–December romance. It still made us both laugh when we got looks while walking down the hallways together. Had the gossipers bothered to ask, I would've happily shared that Damien had become a trusted mentor and friend. And his wife, Connie, was like an eccentric and spirited aunt who loved to go shopping and gossip about anything and everything. The parents to five sons, they both said I was like the daughter they never had.

I was also his protégé. Damien was planning to retire next year and had told me a few months ago he was going to recommend me to replace him. I deeply respected Damien. So it stung to realize that he was most likely embarrassed by what I'd done. My stomach sank.

Truth was, I was embarrassed too.

The team meeting that morning was supposed to have been a run-through for a huge client presentation happening the next day. It was supposed to be only a formality before we began the next official steps toward our client merging with another company. But just as I was about to head into the conference room, the client called me. He was furious after reading online news reports about the other company's stocks nose-diving due to an early-morning raid at the CEO's home by the FBI.

"How in the hell did you miss this?" he'd barked through the phone. "Isn't this the exact reason why I hired your firm in the first place?"

Under normal circumstances, I would've talked him off the ledge and eventually convinced him that all was not lost. But nothing in my universe was normal anymore. It hadn't been for six months.

So, instead, I apologized and asked if he'd give me until the end of the day to figure out what had happened and come up with a new plan. He didn't really agree and only said that if he didn't answer my call later, then not to call again. Ever.

I should've walked back into my office right then and there to cool down. I should've told my assistant to tell everyone who was waiting for the meeting to start that I'd be there soon. But I didn't. It didn't help that I already felt like the universe was playing some sick joke on me. I was fed up with everything and everyone. With my face heated to a thousand degrees and my irritation level at a million, I walked into the conference room and blew up at everyone.

"Do you all know how bad this makes the firm look? How bad it makes me look?" I'd screamed. "We should've seen this coming weeks ago. How did you all miss this? I have worked too damn hard to get to where I am. I will not go down for a mistake one of you made."

The berating probably lasted a good five minutes before I decided I needed to get some air. I gave everyone their marching orders and told them they had until noon to come up with alternative merger options for our client. Then I'd stormed out of the conference room.

Once I was back in my office, I slammed the door behind me. Just then, my phone pinged with a calendar reminder. I glanced at the screen and saw it was for an appointment that afternoon with my fertility doctor. An appointment I'd canceled months ago but never removed from my Outlook.

Rage, frustration, and grief threatened to swallow me up. And I lost it. I spun around and hurled my phone at the beige couch in my office as if I was throwing a fastball into the glove of an imaginary catcher. But because I was never good at sports or any other type of coordinated activity, my aim was skewed, and my phone hit the window next to my office door. I'd gasped and slapped my hand over my mouth as a spiderweb crack appeared across the glass.

I noticed now that Damien looked more ashamed than angry, and that scared the shit out of me. Because I realized in that moment that glass might also now represent my professional career at M&T. I ran my hand over his office sofa's exquisite Italian leather and sighed. I had been thinking about whether to replace it and the matching chairs when I was officially named to fill his Armani loafers. Would my tantrum cost me the symbolic shoes and the very real office?

"I'm sorry, Damien," I told him as sincerely as I could. "It won't happen again. I will go apologize to the team and pay for the damage to the window, of course."

I stood up, believing the conversation was over. I was wrong.

"Sit down, Yesica. We need to talk."

After taking a seat again, I squared my shoulders to brace for the scolding headed my way. But they slumped after Damien just said in a soft voice, "I'm worried about you, dear."

By now I should've been used to hearing those words. After all, I was a young widow—something that was still considered an abnormality in this world. It made people uneasy. Disturbed even. It concerned them and prompted questions about how I was managing this life with a dead husband. I thought I'd gotten used to the fretful gazes or unspoken words of pity.

But not from Damien.

I wanted to tell him there was no need to worry, but he could always see through my bullshit.

Jason had died six months ago in a car accident. And although his death was tragic and sad, I didn't want it to define me. I wanted to be thought of as more than just a pitiful young widow.

But as determined as I was to show others I was dealing with everything just fine, there was one thing I couldn't shake. It held on to me like a rabid wild animal—refusing to release its grip so I could move on fully.

It wasn't grief. No, this beast was fury.

I sighed and folded my arms across my chest. "All right," I said. "I guess I'm in the 'anger' stage of my grief. I admit I've been a little irritated."

"A little?"

I ignored the prick of annoyance at his sarcastic remark. Flying off the handle was the last thing I needed to do in front of Damien. "Yes. A little. In fact, I think I've done a pretty damn good job of not going off on a few people who rightly deserved it."

People like the client who had just berated me over the phone. As much as I had wanted to yell right back, I'd kept my cool. Well, at least until I'd walked into the conference room.

He leaned back in his chair and sighed. "That's the problem then."

Confusion caused me to arch my eyebrows. "It's a problem that I've been acting like a professional and not some raving psycho?"

"Yes, because you've been holding a lot in, Yesica. You came back to work only two days after Jason's funeral."

"And?" I said defensively, unsure why my mourning period was a subject to be criticized. Where on earth was this conversation coming from? In some ways, a scolding would've made me more comfortable. "What's wrong with wanting to do something productive instead of moping around my house feeling sorry for myself?"

The concern reflected in Damien's eyes only made me more uneasy. "I don't think you've allowed yourself to grieve . . . fully. You need to talk to someone. Maybe someone who loved Jason as much as you did. What about your father-in-law, Henry, or even your mother-in-law?"

The snort I made seemed to surprise Damien, and he raised his eyebrows in a question.

"You already know there is no way I'm talking to Celeste about Jason. And I've heard Henry isn't doing that well, unfortunately," I explained.

My mother-in-law, Celeste, had never liked me. I didn't know what she hated more. The fact that I was Mexican or the fact that I was probably the first woman Jason had dated who wasn't afraid to disagree with her. Jason was her only son, her only child. And it had probably killed her that he hadn't married someone like the country club debutantes she always seemed to invite over to lunch whenever she knew Jason would be visiting without me. But now that their son was gone, it was the excuse Celeste needed to finally push me out of her family.

My father-in-law, on the other hand, had always been kind to me. Henry and I would sneak outside after Christmas dinner to smoke cigars and drink his favorite whiskey. Henry had always loved me. And I truly loved him. Sadly, he'd been diagnosed with dementia a year ago, and I hadn't seen him in a while. It broke my heart whenever I allowed myself to wonder if his disease would eventually make him forget me.

"How about your mom?" Damien pressed. "You told me your dad passed just before you started working here. She probably understands what you're going through."

Maybe, I had to admit. But the last thing I wanted was to ask my mom how she'd gotten over losing my dad. It was a sore subject, to say the least. My body still winced every time I thought about her phone call telling me he'd died from complications after suffering a stroke a few days earlier. I hadn't even known he'd been sick or in the hospital. She had robbed me of being able to say goodbye to him, and a part of me still couldn't look at her the same way because of it. It didn't matter that it was five years ago.

"Yeah, we talk about it sometimes," I lied. "But I don't like making her sad."

"That's understandable. There are other options," he said.

My phone vibrated in my hand. Luckily my very expensive protective case had done its job, and except for a new crack in the corner, the phone had escaped pretty much unscathed. I glanced down quickly to see it was my grandma calling. A little irritation pinched my chest at her awful timing. I knew she couldn't have known what I was in the middle of. Well, logically I knew that. Though sometimes I wondered about her uncanny ability to call during the most inopportune times, with usually the most random questions or requests. Experience had taught me that my grandma's calls were never about anything really important. The big stuff, though? She didn't seem to think I ever needed to know about those kinds of things.

When she couldn't remember the name of the restaurant I had taken her to for her birthday last year, she called me three times during a huge client presentation.

When she passed out during Mass last Easter because of a low blood sugar episode, I didn't hear about it until a few weeks later.

Sorry, Mama Melda, your nonimportant question will have to wait until after I find out if I still have a job or not.

I tapped the red "Ignore" button and looked up at Damien.

"I know this doesn't look good. But I swear to you I didn't mean to hit the window. I admit I lost my cool and I threw my phone at my couch. It really isn't my fault that my aim sucks."

I had hoped the last sentence would at least squeeze out a smirk from him. But I was wrong.

Damien let out another long sigh. He stood up and walked over to sit next to me on the couch. "Yesica, I believe you didn't mean to hit the window. But there are others who might not be able to be convinced. Especially given the other things."

His words triggered a full-on emergency alert in my head, and my mouth went dry. "What other things?" I asked suspiciously.

"There have been a few complaints about your, um, attitude."

"My attitude?" I could feel my face growing hot with fury. "Are you fucking kidding me right now?" He squinted at me disapprovingly. "Sorry," I added. "Can you explain?"

"Mainly, some people have noticed that you've had a quick temper, and you blow up at things that before might not have caused such a dramatic reaction. Of course, I've handled these few issues without having to get HR involved. And . . . I was able to talk with Steve a little while ago, and he agreed to let me handle this incident as I see fit without filing any official write-ups or disciplinary forms."

I made a mental note to thank Steve later. He was the director of the department and, luckily, a regular lunch buddy. My body sank into the sofa in relief.

"Thank you, Damien. I really appreciate . . ."

"I want you to take a six-week leave of absence."

My mouth slammed shut. I couldn't have heard what I had heard. "What?" I finally asked.

Damien shifted in his seat. I could tell he was uncomfortable, but I didn't care. I was the one whose career was now in jeopardy. I had already lost my husband. I couldn't lose my job too.

"You need a break, Yesica. Mentally and physically. You obviously have not fully processed Jason's death, and it's starting to affect your work. I can't risk another blowup. You can't risk another blowup because I won't be able to save your ass the next time. Steve and I agreed that a leave of absence is the best option."

I made a mental note to never ask Steve out to lunch again.

"Shut up! He didn't really say that, did he?" Evie, my best friend, yelled from the kitchen.

"He most certainly did," I muttered and took another swig of my beer. Then followed it with a bigger swig of tequila. Straight from the bottle.

"So not only are you on a forced leave of absence, but he's making you go to a grief support group?"

The forced leave of absence was bad enough. When Damien had sprung the therapy requirement on me, though, I'd nearly thrown my phone again.

"He seems to think I'm having anger issues because I haven't allowed myself to fully grieve Jason," I yelled from my spot on my den's couch.

How I was able to function after that meeting, I still didn't know. It was humiliating to have to send out emails notifying my staff and clients that I was taking a delayed bereavement leave. Damien had offered to do it for me, but I'd insisted. Maybe I was being forced to leave, but I still wanted to be in control of the narrative. My professional reputation depended on it.

After the emails had been sent and I'd packed up the few things I wanted to bring home with me, I walked out of my office with my head held high and a huge fake smile on my face. I wanted everyone to see for themselves that I wasn't broken. I wasn't sneaking out in shame.

I was still Yesica Diaz-Taylor, dammit, and I was going to be back.

But as soon as I was inside my car and was sure no one could see or hear me, I called my best friend in tears and asked her to meet me at my house after she got off work and to bring several bottles of alcohol, a package of Oreo cookies, and two cans of Cheez Whiz.

We'd already eaten half the package of cookies, and now Evie was searching my cabinets for some crackers for the cheese. Apparently, bad day or not, she was not going to allow me to simply squeeze it straight into my mouth.

"So, what else did Damien say?" Evie returned from her hunt and handed me a bag of plain rice cakes and sat next to me on the couch. "What? It's all you have," she answered in response to my arched eyebrow.

I shrugged and grabbed the can of Cheez Whiz. "You know Damien. He's still my biggest fan. He says he still wants me to replace him when he retires next year and that I don't have anything to worry about."

"There you go, then," Evie mumbled through a mouthful of Oreos.

I couldn't decide if I was sad about the dry rice cake in my hand or if I was just sad period. My friend's hopefulness was not contagious. "It's not that easy," I explained. "If the promotion was only up to Damien, then I'd feel more confident. But the partners get the final say. Damien is only going to recommend me—he can't offer me the job outright.

And it's going to be hard to come back after six weeks and catch up. I hate being out of the game that long. People have short memories in my world. What if they don't remember how good I am at what I do?"

My friend nodded knowingly. Then Evie scooted closer and put her arm around my shoulders. "Go ahead. Squirt the cheese in your mouth. You deserve it."

I laughed for the first time that day. What would I do if I didn't have Evie? I hugged her back. It was moments like these that I thanked God for bringing her back into my life. We had been friends for most of high school. But when I'd left to attend college at the University of Michigan, my visits home became more sporadic. And she didn't have the money to keep flying out to see me. Evie did make it to my wedding, but by then we were more acquaintances than friends. And then, eventually, we weren't even that.

Then the accident happened.

We hadn't spoken in years, yet I'd still felt compelled to text her after making the obligatory calls to his family and mine.

Jason died was all I wrote.

Within seconds, she'd replied with, Send me your address. I'm on my way. And now she was sitting on my couch feeding me Cheez Whiz.

Just the other day, we were talking about finally taking a trip to Hawaii this summer. Evie, who worked as a music teacher at one of those fancy prep schools where celebrities sent their kids, had been saving for months. And I figured I should take a vacation soon because once I got the promotion, I'd be working even longer hours than I already was.

Now, Hawaii and everything else in my life was up in the air. I blew out one of those "all is lost" sighs I'd learned from my mother.

"Unfortunately, this just may be the first time Cheez Whiz can't fix my problems," I told my friend after a couple of squirts.

"Don't say such things! Cheez Whiz always makes things better."

We both giggled for a minute or so before Evie reached out and grabbed my hand.

"It's going to be okay, you know? You are the fucking best at what you do. Just keep remembering that. This break could be a good thing for your mental health. These next six weeks are going to fly by, and you'll march yourself back into that office stronger than ever."

I couldn't help but tear up again. Evie always seemed to know what I needed to hear.

"Thank you, Evie," I told her now. "Thank you for being my friend."

She smiled at me. "You're welcome. You know I'll always be here for you. Do you need anything else right now?"

I almost opened my mouth to tell her my secret. The one I'd been keeping since the day Jason died. But I thought better of it. Today had already been an emotionally draining day. I wasn't ready to tell her the truth about everything. I wasn't ready to deal with the repercussions it would have on my life. Not yet.

So I just smiled back at her and said, "Cheez me, you beautiful lady, you!"

Evie had just squeezed another good-size dollop into my mouth when my phone rang. I reached to grab it from the coffee table and showed Evie the caller ID.

"Hi, Mama Melda," I answered. "I'm so sorry I didn't call you back sooner."

I wasn't the only grandchild who still called my grandma "Mama Melda." Since she was only in her forties when I was born, she insisted she was too young to be an abuela, or grandmother. And no way did she want to ever be a "nana." Her real name was Imelda, but since I couldn't pronounce that as a toddler, "Melda" it was. And it stuck. For pretty much everyone else in the family too.

"It's okay, Mija," Mama Melda said. "I know your job keeps you very busy."

Not for six weeks, it won't, I thought to myself. "Is everything okay?" I said instead.

She sighed. "Well, not really. That's why I'm calling you."

The Cheez Whiz from earlier clashed with a sudden sensation of dread. My stomach cramped and I sat up straight. "Oh no! Are you okay? Is Mom okay?" I rushed.

"Yes, yes we are okay. But the house is not."

My grandma then proceeded to spend the next ten minutes explaining how she's been following the same nightly routine for years, including using tissues to wipe the cold cream off her face. The explanation also included how she usually used Pond's, but Mom had bought her a store brand last time, and she didn't like it as much because it was greasy and she had to use twice as many tissues to get it off.

"So, really it's not my fault the tissues caused the toilet to overflow. If your mom had gone to Target to get my cream instead of the market, then this wouldn't have happened."

As usual, my grandmother's long, drawn-out storytelling did nothing to convey the real story at all. "Mama Melda, what happened, exactly?"

"The toilet flooded the house yesterday," she partly yelled and partly cried. "Well, part of the house, and now me and your mom have to go live somewhere else until the insurance company's contractor fixes the floors and walls."

It took me several seconds to digest my grandma's words.

Toilet.

House.

Go.

Live.

Somewhere.

Else.

"Oh." It was all I could say. If my life experience as Mama Melda's granddaughter had taught me anything, it was that these individual words were about to add up to a big request.

Mama Melda continued. "The contractor is coming tomorrow morning to give your mom an estimate. But the man she talked to at the insurance company today told her it could be anywhere from two to six weeks. Maybe even two months. It just depends on how bad the damage is."

"Wow." From the corner of my eye, I could see Evie inching closer to me on the couch. My one-word answers had definitely piqued her curiosity. And the more words that came out of Mama Melda, the more my stomach roiled with anxiety.

Mama Melda had never been subtle about anything. So I knew the reason—the real reason—for her call was about to drop.

"Anyways," she said after a long sigh. "We were thinking we could stay with you while the house gets fixed."

And there it was.

"Oh," I said again.

"You're all alone in that big house anyway. And you told me I could stay in the guest room on your first floor whenever I wanted, so it's perfect. Yes?"

I looked over at Evie in disbelief. She raised her hands and mouthed, "What?"

The pain in my stomach traveled all the way up to my temples, and I had an instant migraine.

"Well, what do you say," she asked after I didn't reply right away. "And don't say, 'Oh.'"

What could I say? Mama Melda was seventy-five years old and as smart as they came. We both knew what my answer was going to be before I'd even answered the phone.

I inhaled a deep breath, reached out for Evie's hand in support, and said, "Of course you can both stay with me."

CHAPTER THREE
ANA

To those on the outside, my mother looked as sweet as sugar mixed with honey. Her four-foot, ten-inch frame, her kind, twinkling coffee-colored eyes, the salt-and-pepper hair she always wore in a long braid down her back, her cavernous cheek dimples, and her contagious laugh all concealed her true nature.

Mama was no timid little old lady pushover. She was a force to be reckoned with and the four-star general of our family. That was because she had to be. Mama never remarried after my dad was killed. She raised me and my younger sister and brother on her own, doing whatever it took to make sure we had food in our stomachs and a bed to sleep in. Sometimes that meant staying with relatives or friends from church while she worked nights at a factory or getting our groceries from the local food bank when needed.

My memories of my mom during those first couple of years after my dad's death weren't good ones. We were all dealing with our loss in our own ways, I guess. For my mom, that meant focusing on just surviving day to day, and that left little time for having fun. As a little eight-year-old girl grieving her dad, I was desperate for my mom's affection and attention, but it seemed hard for her to give me either. In fact, I remember feeling like my mom cared more about paying the bills than spending time with us. One memory that had always stayed with me was the time I began crying hysterically in the middle of a gas station store because she refused to buy me candy. She kept telling me that she only had enough money to fill up our car and nothing extra.

"You always say that," I'd yelled at her. "You always say we don't have enough money, but I don't believe you. If Daddy was here, he'd buy us whatever we wanted because he loved us. You don't love us. I wish you weren't my mommy."

Even now, I got a chill thinking about what I'd said and what she'd told me back: "Well, too bad. You're stuck with me."

Later that night, after we'd said our bedtime prayers, she'd sat on my bed and said that if I ever threw a tantrum like that again, I would be grounded.

"Life is hard and unfair, Ana," my mother explained. "I'm sorry you have to learn that now. But hating me isn't going to change anything or make it better. In fact, it'll just make it worse, because I'm the only one left in this world who's always going to put you first. All I ask is that you always do what I say and understand that it'll be because I know what's best. When you grow up and have kids of your own, then maybe you'll believe me."

And she was right, of course. Now, I understood why my mother was the way she was. It made me emotional to think about how she had lost the love of her life in the worst way possible, yet she couldn't really grieve him because she had us kids to take care of. She didn't have the luxury of staying in bed all day or crying every time something didn't go her way. I had come to realize that my mother wasn't being cold, or even mean, back then. She was just being strong. She did love us. And the way she showed that love was by sacrificing so our family could stay together.

Still, I would be the first to admit that Mama was far from perfect. I didn't always agree with her and sometimes lost my patience when she was being unreasonable or stubborn. But whenever I got angry because she was still treating me like a child, I tried to remember where it was coming from. It didn't matter that we were grown and had families of our own. Her instinct would always be to take care of her children and to say or do what she believed was best for us. The least I could do was take care of her in return and teach my kids to always give her the respect she didn't just deserve, but had earned.

That meant if Mama Melda asked them to do something, they always said yes. That's because the asking was just a formality. She was really *telling* them to do something.

Only fools and strangers dared to tell her no.

I knew that was the only reason why my mother and I left early on a Friday morning and began the drive to Yesica's house in Santa Monica.

Of course, I was furious when Mama told me she'd called Yesica and asked if we could stay with her while the house was under construction. And, of course, I was forced to call Yesica myself the next day and tell her we could rent one of those Airbnb houses instead. It wasn't that I didn't want to stay with her. It was just that it wasn't very convenient. My five-minute weekday-morning commute to my job at our neighborhood nursery in Bell Gardens was now going to be about an hour—if I was lucky. Plus, I knew my daughter liked her space and her independence. She'd always been that way. She'd moved out of the house as soon as she graduated from high school thanks to a full scholarship to the University of Michigan. Yesica had only moved back to California a few years ago because Jason's uncle had wanted him to take over the Los Angeles headquarters of his manufacturing company. They'd bought a beautiful home in Santa Monica close to the beach and had invited me and my mother over a few times for dinner.

And not once did she tell me there was a room at her home if I ever needed it.

So maybe it was a combination of bruised ego and inconvenience that made me try to give Yesica an opportunity to rescind the invitation she'd given to my mother. Either way, I thought I was doing her a favor.

I didn't realize it would start yet another argument between us.

"Do you really think you can afford an Airbnb right now, Mom?"
she said as if I was the child and she was the adult. "You don't know yet
exactly how much you're going to have to pay out of pocket for those
repairs."

My shoulders had stiffened in response. "I do know. The insurance
adjuster said I was only responsible for the thousand-dollar deductible,"
I said defensively. Yesica, like her father, always questioned whether I
understood certain things. Maybe I didn't have a college degree like her,
but I wasn't naive either.

"Does that include any furniture or other items you have to
replace?" she continued. "I'm sure other things were probably damaged
beyond just the flooring and walls, right?"

I didn't dare tell her I had no idea if the insurance was going to
cover anything else. I just said, "I'll know more once they're close to finishing. But don't worry about it. I will handle whatever other expenses
come up."

"So why add the cost of an Airbnb?" she asked. I didn't like her
accusatory tone.

I closed my eyes in an attempt to not sound as angry as I was
beginning to feel. "Look, I know it was Mama Melda's idea for us to
come stay with you. All I'm saying is we don't have to if it's going to be
an inconvenience."

"It's fine, Mom. I have the room."

I'd noticed she didn't say that she'd wanted us to come.

"Okay, then," I had reluctantly agreed. "We can stay here for a
few more days before they start the construction and then move in
this weekend." I should've known the conversation would turn out the
way it did. Whenever I thought I was doing something to help her, it
somehow always turned into a battle.

And now my mother and I were in my car, driving to Yesica's
house. I prayed silently to St. Joseph that the next several weeks
wouldn't trigger an all-out war.

Yesica lived in a neighborhood of Santa Monica called Sunset Park. Her street, Wilshire Place, was dotted with just a handful of newer luxury homes that boasted large lush yards and three-car garages. She said they'd picked the area because it was close to the beach and to a lot of restaurants and shopping boutiques. All I could think of, though, as we pulled into her driveway was how it seemed like a world away from my own home.

I'd lived in the city of Bell Gardens all my life. My mother used to say she liked the city, which was located in southeastern Los Angeles County, because it was close enough to living in LA without having to actually live in LA. Before I married Benny, me, my mother, my sister, and my brother had been living in a two-bedroom apartment off Garfield Avenue. My brother had his own room, and the rest of us were crammed into the other. At the age of nineteen, I'd never had my own bedroom. So when Benny—who'd inherited a house from his mother—offered to marry me after I told him I was pregnant, I said yes. Marrying Benny had taken me out of that tiny apartment and right into a life of my own. His name may have been on the title, but I was determined to make his house into a home.

And it made me sad to leave it, even if I knew it was only going to be temporary.

My mother opened the passenger door before I'd even turned off the ignition. She got out and headed toward the front of the house, disappearing behind a brick archway and tall shrubs.

"That's okay," I called after her. "I'll get our bags."

Before opening my own door, though, I pulled down the visor and checked my lipstick. I'd felt silly putting it on, but now I was glad I had. Yesica had once told me she never stepped out in public without at least some lipstick and mascara on. Part of me knew she would notice if I showed up to her house without wearing at least one.

After arranging my tote bag on top of my rolling suitcase and then doing the same to my mother's, I made my way to the wide-open door, pulling both behind me. I could hear voices echoing off the foyer and headed in their direction. I found my mother and my daughter standing in the middle of Yesica's kitchen.

It was so different from mine. The bright-white walls, marble granite countertops, and stainless steel appliances were a stark contrast to my faded lemon wallpaper, dingy brown cabinets, and mismatched stove and refrigerator. Benny's parents had bought the house in the eighties, and, just like all the other rooms, the kitchen looked much the same as the day I'd moved in.

Yesica was smiling and nodding when her eyes caught mine. "Hi, Mom," she said as she walked toward me. We hugged. It was more polite than bearlike. And lasted just a few seconds. Even her hugs now seemed to be done out of obligation rather than affection. And for the millionth time, I couldn't help but miss my daughter, even though she was standing right in front of me.

"Thank you again for letting us stay here," I said as I arranged the suitcases next to her kitchen table.

"No need to thank me," she replied as she walked back toward her spot by the kitchen island. "I'm glad I can help. Any news from the contractor?"

I sighed. "Nothing new. They're going to start the demo on the drywall on Monday. Once they open everything up, they'll get a better idea of how much needs to be replaced."

"It's good that Gene's going to be around to watch the crews during the day and watch the house at night."

"Yes. I was so grateful to him for offering to do that. He's been a lifesaver. Even when your dad was here, Gene always helped us out."

I froze after mentioning Benny. Somehow bringing him up always led to some sort of argument between us. Yesica had always been a daddy's girl. They were very close. So close in fact that I sometimes felt like the odd woman out. They had their inside jokes and favorite places that only the two of them could go to. She was living out of state when he'd died, so she hadn't been able to say goodbye. Somehow that was my fault too.

She didn't seem affected by me talking about him this time, though. Still, I decided to play it safe and changed the subject.

"I'm assuming Grandma is going to be staying in the downstairs bedroom, so I'll take her suitcase over there. Where did you want me to put my stuff? I think I remember there's a spare guest bedroom next to yours?"

There was no mistaking the surprised look that came over her. "No, not that room," Yesica said quickly.

The confusion I was feeling must have been etched all over my face, since she added, "I just figured you'd want to stay in the room down the hallway from mine, because it has its own bathroom."

"Sure, that sounds good. Having a bathroom so close will be nice," I said, trying to dismiss the sense of uneasiness at her first response. Her explanation did seem reasonable, and I didn't want to press the issue. I decided to change the subject yet again.

"And I get paid on Fridays, so just let me know how much I can give you for utilities and whatever else you need," I said.

She shook her head. "Don't be ridiculous, Mom. You're not going to pay me for staying here."

Again, I was only trying to help her. Why was it so hard for her to accept it?

"We're going to be using your electricity and water," I explained. "Your bills are going to go up, Yesica."

"I can afford to pay my bills."

My shoulders tightened, bracing for an argument. Why did she always twist my words around? "I didn't say you couldn't. I'm just trying to help. I don't want us staying here to be an inconvenience."

"It's fine," she said. "It won't be. I don't need help with the bills."

I knew there was no use arguing with Yesica. She was as stubborn as her father. "Well, at least let me do the grocery shopping and cook dinner every night," I offered. "I know you work late hours, so I don't expect you to eat at home, but at least I can put food away for you so you can eat later."

It might have been my imagination, but I thought I saw a pained expression cross her face. Then it was gone.

"Actually, I'm going to be taking some time off from work," she said.

"Are you going on vacation, Mija?" my mother asked in an excited tone. "Are you taking us with you? Are we going to Hawaii?"

I looked over at my mother and held up my hand. "Mama, stop. We are not going on vacation with Yesica."

Yesica sat down on one of the stools next to the island's counter. "I'm not going on vacation, Mama Melda."

"Oh," my mother said softly, although her disappointment screamed with just that one word.

I was confused. The one thing I knew for sure about my daughter was that her job meant the world to her. She was always working—nights, holidays, whenever and wherever. For her to take time off, something had to be wrong.

"I don't understand," I said. "How long are you going to be off? A few days? A week?"

"Um, more like six weeks." From the way Yesica was looking everywhere but at me when she said this, I knew she was hesitating about telling us the truth. Whatever it was, it had to be bad.

"Why?" I asked just as an awful thought came to my mind. "Yesica, are you sick?"

She shook her head furiously at me. "No, I'm not sick. I swear. I've just been working a lot lately, and I never really took any time off after Jason died. It's a little slow at the office right now, so I figured I might as well take a little break while I can."

I knew my daughter well enough to know she wasn't telling me the full story. But I also knew that the more I pressed her about it, the less she would tell me later. So I had to accept her explanation. For now.

"Taking a break is good. I'm glad," I offered, trying to sound more positive than I felt.

"Yeah, it will be good, I guess," she said and then stood up. "Well, I'll let you two get settled in your rooms. I already put clean sheets on both beds and fresh towels in the bathrooms. Let me know if you need anything else."

Before she walked out of the kitchen, I remembered there was one thing I wanted to ask.

"Yesica, if you don't have any plans already, I'd like to cook you a special dinner for your birthday tomorrow. Whatever you want. Just name it."

I had come prepared too. There was another suitcase still in the trunk filled with pots, pans, casserole dishes, Tupperware containers, spatulas, a molcajete, a big olla, and even my comal. My daughter had never been a big cooker like me or my mother, so I figured she probably didn't have a lot in terms of kitchen equipment. I'd planned to go through her cabinets and pantry tonight and make a shopping list for whatever else I thought we'd need during our stay.

But Yesica didn't even hesitate about answering my question. "You don't have to go to any trouble, Mom. We can just order takeout or something. I'm going out tonight with Evie, and then I have some errands to run tomorrow during the day. But I'll be home in time for dinner, and then we can decide what to order then, okay?"

I nodded, hoping the disappointment in my gut didn't show on my face. I had wanted to do something special for her—something to show my appreciation for letting us stay with her. There wasn't anything special about takeout.

At least you're getting to spend her birthday with her this year, I told myself. It was still a good thing.

Maybe I still had doubts about staying with Yesica. But I was determined to use the time to fix whatever had broken between us.

Even if she fought me every step of the way.

CHAPTER FOUR
YESICA

"Happy birthday!" Evie screamed.

"Happy birthday to me," I said before downing my Chocolate Cake shot.

The combination of the Frangelico hazelnut liqueur and vanilla vodka did its magic as it danced on my taste buds. At the moment, it didn't matter that I didn't understand the chemistry behind how the mixture of the two alcohols plus lemon and sugar could turn into a taste of chocolate cake. All that mattered was that it warmed my body and made me smile despite a nagging sense of disappointment.

In just a few hours, I would be officially thirty-three years old. The past year had been one of the worst of my life, so I should've been more excited to say goodbye to thirty-two. The problem was, as much as I tried, I couldn't find much to celebrate or even look forward to. My present life resembled nothing like the one I'd expected to have by now. Even my career—which usually brought me so much satisfaction and pride—was teetering on the verge of collapse.

Although I'd told Evie differently, there was nothing happy about this birthday at all.

"Okay, one more round and then we go dance!" Evie ordered.

I shook my head. "I'm not drunk enough, and I'm not going to be drunk enough tonight."

"But I like drunk Yesica," my friend whined.

I laughed at her puppy dog eyes. "I like drunk Yesica, too, but she'll have to take a rain check. Sober Yesica has a grief support group meeting in the morning."

Although I was steadfast in my determination to not get anything out of the group, even I knew it would be in bad form to show up hungover. It was kind of a bummer not to be able to fully celebrate my birthday with as many alcoholic beverages as possible, but I'd never really been into making a big deal out of the day. At least not in the last few years anyway. If I wasn't working, then Jason and I would go to dinner at our favorite seafood restaurant. He'd give me a piece of jewelry or roses, and that would be the extent of the celebrating.

This year, though, Evie had said I should do something different. And since she had a school concert the following night, she'd brought me here to this bar on the Westside for shots and dancing.

"You know you're allowed to let go and have fun," Evie said.

"I know. I do . . . sometimes," I said.

Truth was, it took a lot for me to let go. I'd learned early on that coloring inside the lines earned you praise and respect. Being responsible and professional opened doors, especially in the corporate world, for someone who looked like me. I never wanted to give anyone a reason to doubt that I had things under control.

Except for throwing my phone the other day, I thought.

Birthdays and other special occasions were typically the only times I didn't care about how much I drank. Although my mother and grandmother moving in with me probably would've been a good excuse.

Evie had promised me a night of dancing and drinking, and I had wanted both. I desperately needed both. But then Damien had texted earlier to let me know the support group was meeting at nine the next morning.

Happy birthday to me, I guess.

As we waited for the waitress to bring over our last round of shots, Evie reapplied her lipstick.

"Isn't it just going to come off again with the next drink?" I asked with a laugh.

"Not all of it. Besides, we need to take some birthday pics for Instagram," she said.

A few more seconds and one more application of lipstick later, Evie held up her phone and leaned over toward me. She took about five pictures before she was finally satisfied and went to work posting her masterpiece.

"Damn, girl, you look amazing in this picture," she said, still looking at her phone. "That dress is perfect on you. I'm so glad I convinced you to buy it. It's the perfect birthday dress!" She turned her screen in my direction so I could see what she was seeing.

I'd bought the dress last weekend—before everything. We'd done a girls' day out, starting with brunch and then shopping at Third Street Promenade in Santa Monica. I hadn't planned on buying a dress at all. But Evie had pulled me into a boutique she'd discovered last month in search of a new blouse she needed for the concert. As I walked through the small shop, I spotted a few items that interested me. But the only thing I pulled out to try on was the dress. It wasn't a style or color I usually went for. It was deep plum, with an even deeper neckline and cutout sheer billowy sleeves that exposed the top part of my arms. The bodice was tight, and the hem hit just a few inches above my knee. Evie had insisted I buy it for myself as a birthday present and that I wear it tonight.

So I'd done as she'd begged and accessorized it with a pair of black wedge heels that seemed to magically extend my legs even longer. To match the look, I wore my dark hair in loose wavy curls—a far cry from the sleek bun I usually donned for the office.

I had to admit I looked good. To the random Instagram follower, I even looked happy.

"We both look amazing," I told her as I studied the photo. "Text me that picture."

My phone buzzed a few seconds later, and I laughed when I saw the edited photo Evie had sent. It was a close-up that put my cleavage basically front and center.

"Really?" I asked and pointed to the girls.

"What?" Evie asked. "Your boobs look amazing. You need to remember how good they look, since you don't let them out that often."

I shook my head and decided not to post the photo on social media after all. College friends and coworkers didn't need to be reminded of my . . . assets. It was still a good picture of me and Evie, though, so I saved the photo on my phone anyway.

"I'm serious, Yesica," Evie continued. "You need to stop covering what God gave you. Those suits you wear to work are straight out of a retired nun's closet."

I gasped in offense. "Uh, excuse me. How dare you disparage Tahari like that? And I pay good money to expertly tailor every single outfit."

"Fine, not a nun then. But, come on. Don't you get tired of the pantsuits?"

"I don't, actually. Besides, you know what I do for a living. If I want to be taken seriously, I have to look serious. Not that it matters anymore. I'll be wearing yoga pants and T-shirts for the next six weeks."

Evie put her arms around my shoulders and pulled me toward her. "Aww, I'm sorry, hon. I didn't mean to bring up work. Let's talk about something else."

"Gladly!" I said, sitting up straight.

"Are your mom and grandma all moved in?"

I groaned. "I'd rather talk about work."

Evie laughed. "It hasn't even been one day. Is it really that bad?"

I thought about it for a few seconds. Moving away for college had given me the space I'd needed to carve out my own life—away from the expectations and obligations that came with growing up in a family who believed your business was everyone else's business too. To this day, I could still feel the burning embarrassment at having my tías and a handful of other female relatives I barely knew congratulate me on finally getting my period at the age of thirteen during my younger cousin's birthday party.

Nothing was sacred or off limits to Mexican moms.

When we'd moved back to Southern California, I made a point of not oversharing every little thing with my mother or Mama Melda for fear it would be a breaking news item in the family group text thread. But now that they were living with me, there wasn't much I would be able to keep to myself. Not to mention the fact that my mom and I didn't have the closest relationship—at least not like we did when I was a little girl. And after my dad died, it had just gotten rockier.

"No, I guess it's not going to be the worst thing in the world," I admitted to Evie. "It's just that my mom and I are like oil and water. You know we don't always mix. I have no idea why I agreed to let them stay with me."

"You agreed because you are the dutiful Mexican first daughter. You will always do what your mom—or what your grandma—asks of you. It's kind of heartwarming, actually."

"It's a cliché is what it is," I droned.

"Well, you're still a better daughter than I am. I think it's been a few months since the last time I saw my parents."

"Don't they still live over in Reseda?" I asked, referring to a city barely an hour away.

"They do. Them moving over there to live closer to my sister and her kids was the best thing that could've happened for our relationship. Now, they don't expect me to visit every weekend, since my sister basically takes care of everything for them. Being the baby of the family has its advantages. You, however, are the oldest daughter who happens to live in a big house with empty bedrooms. Of course you would say yes."

"I guess," I said after a long frustrated sigh. "I just thought I'd gotten pretty good at saying no. Like she no longer expects me at every single family party or holiday. I'd bet good money that she had Mama Melda ask me on purpose."

"I love your grandma," Evie said. "I can't wait to come over and talk smack with her about the Dodgers."

"'Los pinche Doyers,'" we both said in our best Mama Melda impressions.

We were still laughing when the waitress finally came over with our shots.

"To first daughters everywhere," Evie said and raised her glass.

"To first daughters and their very best friends," I added.

We stayed for another thirty minutes before calling it a night. The crowd had grown louder and drunker, and we both laughed when we agreed we were getting old, since we'd rather go home than deal with the chaos.

But after I got in my car and began to drive home, I couldn't help thinking about what Evie had said about doing something different this year for my birthday. My first as a widow.

I really didn't think going to my first grief support group counted.

That was the reason why instead of going straight home, I turned into the small parking lot of a bar several miles away from my house. I wasn't quite sure why, but as soon as I'd seen it, I decided to stop. It wasn't a place I would normally go to on my own. First of all, it wasn't even in my neighborhood. Second of all, it was called the Deck. It was boring and unoriginal. Evie would say it lacked personality.

I'll just have one drink and leave, I told myself as I pulled open the front door.

The place was dimly lit, as all bars usually are. I spotted a few tables filled with people, a stage, and a dance floor. I walked over to one of the empty stools at the bar.

"What can I get you?" the blonde bartender in a black tank top asked almost immediately.

"I'll take a Malibu and Diet Coke," I said.

I scrolled through my phone until my drink arrived. I took a sip and winced. She hadn't skimped on the rum, which meant it was probably a good idea to sip rather than down.

I scanned the room and couldn't help but wonder if this was the anointed bar for nearby Santa Monica College. Most of the patrons looked to be about that age. Old memories of my own college barhopping days flooded my mind. But once I'd graduated and gotten married, dive bars weren't really my scene anymore. Except for that one time. And that's when I knew why the place had called out to me.

I had come to a bar just like this one the night Jason told me he was leaving me. The first time.

It was the long Memorial Day weekend a few years ago, and I had canceled our plans to go out of town with friends in order to work. I'd told Jason to go without me, but he'd refused. Part of me believed he just wanted to make me feel guilty so he could use it against me later.

We had been married for only five years at that point, and things had been rocky. I'd only been at the firm for about a year and had been working my butt off to prove myself—and I hadn't gotten noticed by the partners yet. Jason, who worked at his uncle's manufacturing firm, had become growingly frustrated about my long hours and working weekends.

I'd come home from work late that Saturday night exhausted and still annoyed by problems at work. The contract I'd been working on was supposed to be signed by the end of the month, but we'd been inundated with challenges and setbacks for the past few months. For the first time, I had doubts about whether the deal would happen. Needless to say, I was in a horrible mood. I also knew Jason wasn't exactly overjoyed that I'd told him I was too tired to pick up dinner so he was on his own, and I'd just eat the previous night's Chinese food take-out leftovers.

When I got home, Jason was watching TV in the den. He didn't even acknowledge my presence. I knew he was upset.

I'd decided not to say anything and went directly to the kitchen to warm up my dinner. That's when I'd noticed the empty Chinese food containers on the counter.

"Did you eat the leftovers?" I accused.

"Yeah. I couldn't decide what to order, so I just ate what we had."

"But I told you I was going to eat them for dinner," I yelled from the kitchen. "You didn't leave me anything."

"Sorry," he said, still not looking over at me. "There wasn't that much."

I stomped over to where he sat and got in between him and the TV. "But why?" I asked.

He shrugged. "What's the big deal? Just eat something else."

I should've just let it go right then and there. Unfortunately for Jason, I'd run out of patience hours before. "It's a big deal because you always do this," I argued.

Jason turned off the TV. "I always eat your leftovers?"

"No, you find ways to punish me for working too much. Last month, you didn't talk to me for twenty-four hours because I didn't go with you to your parents' house for dinner in the middle of the week, even though we both know your mom didn't want me to go anyway. You stormed out of the house the other night after I told you I didn't have time to stop and pick up your suits before the dry cleaner closed. Tonight, you're pissed that I couldn't go away this weekend, so you ate my dinner!"

"You're being ridiculous . . . as usual. I'm going to bed." He threw the remote on the couch and began walking toward the stairs.

Anger prickled every nerve in my body. I was tired of always being the bad guy or the one being overly sensitive. It had become an exhausting pattern: Jason would get mad, I'd want to talk about it, and suddenly I was making something out of nothing and he'd shut down. Well, that night, I decided I wasn't done arguing. "And you're walking away as usual. How about instead of being so passive aggressive about everything, just be honest and stop pouting like a child!"

The moment I'd said it, I knew I shouldn't have. He turned around, and the expression on his face twisted my stomach so tight I felt nauseous.

"I'm not happy anymore, Yesica. I don't think this is working. We're broken."

Broken? "What are you talking about?" I asked.

"Everything you do lately revolves around your work. You're never here. We never do anything together anymore. I feel like I'm an afterthought in your life."

Yes, it was true that I'd been putting in a lot of time at the office. When I was home, however, I tried to be present and focus on him. But it was hard when he seemed to always be angry with me. I couldn't help but feel bitter. Didn't he know that everything I did, everything I was doing, was for us? The only reason we'd moved here was because of him, and it wasn't my fault I'd ended up finding a job that was both rewarding and demanding. How dare he use that against me? It wasn't like there hadn't been compromises on my side. I never questioned *his* late nights at the office or the random Saturdays where he'd announce out of the blue that he had to go in to work.

I tried to stifle my building panic, and my compulsive need to find a solution to a problem kicked in. Jason said we were broken, but I refused to believe we couldn't be fixed.

"Is this because we didn't go away this weekend? You know this deal is important to me," I said, and I threw my hands up in exasperation. "When the deal is done, we can go away—just the two of us. I promise. Please be patient, okay?"

"I have been patient, Yesica. There's always going to be another deal, and I'm tired of our marriage always taking a back seat to this obsession you have with having to prove yourself over and over again at work."

My mouth nearly hit the floor. "Obsession? It's not an obsession, it's a necessity. I'm a Latina, Jason. I always have to prove myself. You are a white, hetero man who comes from a wealthy family. You can't understand because you got handed a cushy job because your uncle is the boss."

Not having to worry about always having to be better and do more than your colleagues simply because of your gender or skin color was a privilege I had never enjoyed. And Jason, of all people, knew this.

He'd comforted me numerous times when I'd come home from work at my old firm back in Michigan upset at having been passed over for yet another promotion, or when my boss took credit for a deal I'd worked my ass off to get. I didn't understand why he was acting like this was something new.

He winced at my dig about his job. "I work hard too. I just know how to strike a balance so my job isn't my entire personality," he said. "But you don't know how to do that, and I'm tired of being the bad guy for trying to help you. I'm done."

My heart stilled. I knew things weren't perfect between us. But I'd never thought they were bad enough for him to give up on us. "What do you mean?" I asked.

"*I'm* not happy," he admitted. "I haven't been happy in months. Can you look me in the eyes and tell me you're still happy with me?"

I should've said yes right away. Honestly, I wasn't. But I guess I hadn't wanted to admit it to myself until the moment he'd asked the question. When I hesitated, he assumed my answer. Even in that lowest of moments, I wasn't prepared for what he said next: "I'm going to pack some stuff and stay at a hotel until I figure things out."

I gulped down the shock. "You're leaving me?" I asked, even though I didn't want to know.

He sighed. "I don't know. But we can't go on like this. We both deserve more."

After he'd left, I waited an hour, expecting him to walk through the door after having cooled off. When he didn't show, I left, too, thinking I'd drive around to see if he'd gone to his usual hangouts. Eventually, I gave up and landed at a bar like the Deck. Four tequila shots later, I had to call an Uber to take me home. And Jason still wasn't there.

He ended up coming back home a few days later, after I'd called him and told him I still wanted our marriage to work and promised to cool it on the late office hours. And things between us did get better—for a little while anyway. A year before Jason died, I'd even agreed that we could try to have a baby. Of course, that was an awful idea. I should've realized back then that a baby wasn't going to magically make things right between us. But once I'd set my mind to something, I was determined to achieve it.

My stupid uterus, however, had other plans.

One lone tear escaped from the corner of my right eye, bringing me out of my past regrets and back into the noisy bar. I took a long sip of my drink and winced. What had once been Malibu rum liqueur mixed with Diet Coke was now mainly watered-down Diet Coke. God, how long had I been in here anyway?

My eyes widened after glancing at the time on my phone. It had already been an hour since I'd said goodbye to Evie back at the club.

Time to stop hiding in this bar and get back to my life.

I pulled out a couple of dollar bills from my wallet and placed them on the bar. I slowly inched off the stool, wanting to make sure my legs hadn't forgotten how to walk while I was sitting and thinking about everything and nothing all at the same time. But just before I took my first step, music erupted inside the small bar. Within a few beats, I recognized the song as one of my favorites from the eighties.

That era made up most of the soundtrack of my Saturday mornings growing up. While Mama Melda preferred to play Mexican rancheras or mariachi classics whenever she controlled the stereo, my mom would blare new wave and alternative hits as she mopped floors or cleaned the bathrooms. Meanwhile, my brother and I would sing along as we folded laundry and vacuumed.

Even now, I always turned my satellite radio stations to the ones that played the eighties as I cleaned.

I looked up and saw a band performing on a small stage located near the back of the room. The guys on the stage were way too young to be the original group that had made the song famous, but they sounded pretty close to the real thing. I was impressed. So impressed that I stood listening until the very last note. And when they started a second song—another eighties hit—I sat back down on the barstool and ordered another Malibu and Diet Coke.

As I listened to the band play, I moved my eyes from member to member. The lead singer had jet-black shoulder-length hair, which made his pale skin look even more transparent. He wore a sheer black long-sleeve dress shirt, black leather pants, and black combat-style boots. His stark appearance fit the unique and soulful tone of his amazing voice. *He should be on the radio,* I thought.

The bassist and the keyboardist/backup singer were more average looking in their nondescript T-shirts and jeans. They didn't give off an artistic vibe like the lead singer did, yet they appeared to be just as talented. And judging by their contorted facial expressions and big, wide smiles, I believed they were just as impassioned by the music they were creating. They obviously loved being onstage. I wondered about their backstory. Maybe they'd once had dreams of selling out stadiums but were stuck with boring office jobs, and the band was their way of escaping the doldrums of everyday life?

My attention finally turned to the drummer. His dark-brown hair wasn't that long, just shaggy enough to whip in all directions as his head jerked in time with each beat. He was too far away for me to make out the color of his eyes, but I guessed they were probably dark, given his dark hair and tanned complexion. He wasn't pale like the singer. Instead, his skin carried that natural sun-kissed look—an obvious indicator of someone who spent a lot of time outdoors. Maybe he was a surfer? Santa Monica was filled with them. He wore a plain white T-shirt, and the rest of his body was hidden behind the drum set and other equipment.

I bet he's a blue jeans kind of guy, I thought.

I noticed that his smile was crooked, almost mischievous, as if he was thinking of ways to get into all sorts of trouble without getting caught. And that inspired a smile of my own.

He caught me staring at him, and heat rushed to my cheeks. His gaze dropped from my eyes to my nose and then lingered for a few seconds on my mouth. I swallowed thickly.

Before I knew it, I'd stayed for their entire set. The singer announced they'd be back in an hour, and then the DJ in the corner began playing a popular eighties dance hit.

"They're good, aren't they?" the bartender said from behind me.

I swiveled in my stool to face her. "They are. Do they always play here?" I asked.

"First and third Fridays of the month. George, the owner, keeps telling them they should do Saturdays, too, but they always say two nights a month is enough."

"What's enough, Jan?" a deep voice asked next to me.

My eyes went to the figure who had just taken the seat next to me. It was the drummer.

"You are. Always." The bartender laughed when he clutched his chest in feigned pain.

I couldn't help but smile. "Hello," the man said as he held out his hand.

"Hi," I said back without shaking it. And I purposefully didn't offer my name since he didn't share his. Maybe I'd been caught up in the looks he'd been giving me from the safety of several feet away. Now that he was so close, though, I didn't want him to think I had been flirting. I decided it was time to leave for real this time.

Jan, the bartender, handed him a bottle of water, and he downed it in just a few gulps.

"You're not going to stay for our second set?" he said after I stood up.

I shook my head. "Sorry. I have to get up early tomorrow."

"So do I. But I'm staying. Let me buy you a drink, and you can tell me why you hated that last song."

I stilled. How could he have known?

"You started looking at your phone about halfway through," he answered as if I'd told him.

I shrugged. "It's just not my favorite. Your singer did a good job, though."

"I'll make sure to let him know. Or maybe I won't because his ego is already big enough."

I couldn't help but laugh. I wasn't sure why, but this man both made me nervous and put me at ease. He had this way about him that triggered my interest. Suddenly, I was no longer in a rush to leave. So I sat back down.

We spent the next half hour or so talking about our favorite eighties bands and who we would go see in concert if they were still around. I learned that he and his friends had been playing together for a couple of years.

"I heard they want you to play more nights here. Why don't you?" I asked.

"This is just a way for all of us to let off some steam," he told me. "When we try to make it more than that, it's not really fun anymore. We used to play at another place on Sundays, but it became a hassle so we stopped. We don't even do birthday parties anymore."

"It's my birthday tomorrow. Well, technically, it will be my birthday in an hour," I said without thinking.

His eyebrows arched in appreciation. "Well, happy birthday. Now I really should buy you a drink. Jan," he yelled over to the bartender. "Can we get another water and whatever she was drinking before?"

"No rum this time. Just the Diet Coke," I told Jan. Not only was I driving, but something told me drunk Yesica might get herself in over her head with this flirty drummer.

"So tell me about the guy," he said. My eyes widened. "He's the reason you're here all by yourself on your birthday, right?"

Jan brought our drinks, and I took a sip since my mouth had suddenly gone dry. "I was out earlier with my friend at another club," I answered a few seconds later. "I wasn't ready to go home, so I stopped here."

"So the guy's at home?"

I almost said "the guy" was dead. But thought better of it. "No guy," I said instead, and I even waved my left hand to show my bare fingers. I hadn't worn my wedding ring since the day of the funeral. It was now packed away in one of the tubs in the garage, along with everything that had belonged to Jason.

He nodded, and it seemed like it was the answer he'd wanted. "Well, I hope you've had a nice almost birthday."

Nice? Yes, I guess the night had been nice. So why did I feel a pang of disappointment? Was it because I'd had years of "nice" birthdays with Jason already? Tonight was supposed to have been something . . . something more than that.

The DJ began to play another eighties song—this time it was a slow tempo, and the lyrics were about strangers dancing in the dark.

An idea came to me, and before I could talk myself out of it, I said, "How about a birthday dance?"

The drummer smiled, stood, and held out his hand.

When we reached the dance floor, he pulled me against him. I stiffened at the initial contact of our bodies. I couldn't remember the last time I'd been held like this on a dance floor, or anywhere else for that matter. It was as if I'd forgotten how to be. Slowly, he slid his hands down to grip my hips. He began to sway from side to side. But I froze.

"It's just dancing," he whispered in my ear.

I nodded and tentatively reached around his neck. We moved together, and eventually I let my body relax.

"This is a good song."

I tried not to react as goose bumps danced across my arms and neck. "So you're a Madonna fan?" I asked, trying to sound light and casual.

He let out a small laugh. "Isn't everyone? Well, maybe not her new stuff. But definitely everything from the eighties and nineties."

The drummer moved his hands to my lower back. Instinctively, I arched into him and closed my eyes. We didn't talk for a few seconds, and I allowed myself to enjoy the feel of being so close to another person again. It had been so long. I hadn't realized just how starved my body was for this kind of touch.

"This is nice," he said after a few more quiet moments ticked by. "You're nice."

"Do you do this a lot?"

"What? Dance?"

I inhaled a breath before answering. "No, I mean pick up strange women in bars."

Perhaps another man might have been insulted by the insinuation. Not the drummer.

"I don't always pick them up in a bar," he drawled. "Sometimes I meet them in the freezer section of my local grocery store."

I couldn't help but laugh. "Are all drummers this funny or just the ones who belong to eighties cover bands?"

"Just us. I hear the hair band guys are super boring."

The song ended, and I honestly was a little disappointed. He grabbed my hand again as we walked back to our seats at the bar. But I immediately let go of his grasp when a woman approached me. My stomach dropped at the same time.

"Yesica! I thought that was you!"

"Your name is Yesica?" I heard the drummer ask as the woman hugged me.

"Hey, Alice," I said. My heart was pumping so fast it was as if I'd just danced a salsa rather than swayed in place. Of all the bars in all the world, why on earth was Jason's former assistant at this one?

"How are you?" she asked softly and touched my shoulder. I called it the "pity tap." A gesture people did as if it gave more meaning to their hollow words. "I don't think I've seen you since the funeral. Which was beautiful by the way. It was a wonderful tribute to Jason."

I could feel the drummer's eyes on me, and a growing panic rolled through me. This was the reason I didn't go out anymore. Chance encounters with former friends and acquaintances brought up emotions I'd worked hard to push down into my own black oblivion. "Thank you," I said, wanting nothing more than to get out of this place.

Alice looked at the man next to me, and I could tell she was waiting for an introduction.

"Well, I have to get home. It was nice seeing you," I rushed out and then began to walk away.

Her eyes widened in surprise. What had she expected? We'd never been friends. In fact, I'd say we mutually tolerated each other because of Jason. When she'd been promoted to another position in the company, I'd bought champagne. I didn't pretend to be her bestie when Jason was alive. I had no reason to start now.

"Oh, okay. Let's do lunch sometime. I'll call you," she yelled after me.

I'd heard those words so many times after Jason died. People promising to keep in touch or meet up to talk. Most of the time they meant nothing. I knew that if I hadn't heard from Alice by now, I was never going to hear from her again.

Just add her to the list, I thought.

I'd just walked outside when I felt a hand grab mine. "Hey, hold up."

The drummer turned me around so I was facing him. "I have to go," I said. "Thanks for the drink and the dance."

His expression was no longer flirty and playful. He looked stunned. "Who's Jason?"

It was more of a statement than a question, but I answered anyway. "He's my husband . . . was my husband. He died six months ago."

I realized now why this birthday had been so important. For one night I had wanted to forget I was a widow. I just wanted to be me . . .

the birthday girl. But it seemed like strangers would always see me as the woman with the dead husband.

"Please don't leave," he implored. "I have to go back on in a few minutes, but stay until the next set is over. Let's talk. I *really* think we should talk."

I shook my head. The wonderful anonymity I had been feeling was gone. In other words, the clock was going to strike midnight, and my carriage was about to turn into a pumpkin.

The real world had crashed my party, and I wanted to go home. "No, I have to go. Sorry."

"Yesica . . . wait." It was strange to hear him call me by my name.

Before he could say anything else, I sprinted to my car and jumped inside.

CHAPTER FIVE
ANA

Yesica's sixth birthday had fallen on a Saturday. She'd asked for only two things that year—a bike and pancakes for breakfast. But the week before, Benny had decided we needed to also throw her a party at a nearby park so he could invite some of his friends from work and their kids.

Of course, he'd promised he'd help out, but really that just meant buying the bike and the hamburgers and hot dogs he planned to barbecue. I had to do everything else—including going to the park at six in the morning to stake out one of the few covered picnic table areas. Because of this, I didn't get to make Yesica pancakes on the morning of her birthday. She was disappointed, but the party seemed to make up for it, and when she went to bed that night, she proclaimed it was the best birthday she'd ever had.

But me being me, I couldn't dismiss the nagging feeling that I'd let her down by not making her pancakes on her birthday. So for birthdays seven through seventeen, that's what she got.

And when I woke up that morning, I was determined to give that to her for birthday number thirty-three.

First, though, I decided to put the pile of sheets and towels I'd seen the day before in the laundry room to wash. Then I began working on getting breakfast ready, since Yesica had mentioned she'd be heading out early to run errands.

I was pleasantly surprised to find eggs, milk, and bacon in the refrigerator. I had expected to see bare shelves. Luckily, I also found flour in the walk-in pantry. But there were no strawberries or whipped cream, so these birthday pancakes would have to be plain.

As the bacon cooked on the stove, I made the pancake batter. Yesica's stove had a cooktop griddle, which made the cooking process a lot easier and quicker. In no time, I had a stack of perfectly rounded pancakes, crispy bacon strips, and a bowl of scrambled eggs set out on the kitchen table. I'd asked my mother not to start eating until Yesica came downstairs so we could sing "Happy Birthday" to her, but seconds dragged into minutes, and there was still no sign of her.

"I need to take my pills," my mother said. "Just go up there and tell her breakfast is getting cold."

"I'll give her five more minutes. Go ahead and eat then."

Mom was on her second pancake when Yesica finally walked into the kitchen. But she didn't look like she'd barely gotten out of bed. She was showered, dressed, wearing some light makeup, and had her hair up in a high ponytail.

She looked ready to head out the door.

"Good morning," I said.

"Good morning," she replied without looking at me. Instead, she pulled a tall metal tumbler from the cupboard and began to fill it with water and ice.

I walked over and gave her a hug. "Happy birthday," I said. Then I pointed to the table. "I made pancakes, bacon, and scrambled eggs."

She barely glanced at the small breakfast buffet I'd set out. "Thank you. But I don't have time to eat, Mom. My alarm didn't go off, and I'm running late." Yesica put the filled cup on the counter. "Have you seen my keys?"

"I think they're over there by the coffee maker," I said, trying to stifle the rising disappointment in my heart. "Are you sure you don't have five minutes to sit down, at least? I made all this food."

Yesica stopped. "Why on earth would you make all this food if you knew I wasn't going to be here? I told you I had an important appointment this morning."

I tried not to let my frustration show. "You didn't tell me that. You just said you had things to do today. I figured whatever you had to do, you could do it after breakfast."

Mama Melda, who was still eating, chimed in: "At least take a pancake and eat it in the car."

"I don't eat in my car. It's a lease. I really have to go."

Then she grabbed her keys and walked out the front door.

"Just put a plate for her in the microwave, Ana," my mother suggested. "Maybe she'll be hungry when she gets back?"

I nodded, but deep down I knew all this food was probably going to go to waste. Moving in with Yesica was proving to be a mistake—just like I had feared.

After I ate and cleaned up the kitchen, I took the sheets out of the washer to put them in the dryer. That's when I noticed it was already full of clothes. I debated about leaving the clothes in a laundry basket and then putting them back in the dryer when the sheets were done, but I knew that would be silly. I wasn't going to fold Yesica's laundry, but at least I could take it up to her room.

I moved the clothes from the dryer to a collapsible hamper I found on a nearby wire shelf rack. Then my phone rang.

I couldn't help but smile.

"Good morning, Mijo," I said as I grabbed the hamper by its two handles. It was my son, Alejandro.

"Good morning, Mom. I was just calling to check in. Are you settling into Yesica's all right?"

Not really, based on our interaction this morning, I thought.

"Yes, yes," I lied. "Me and your grandma are all moved in."

"That's good. I'm glad. I was a little worried."

That was just like Alejandro. He had always been more sensitive—especially when it came to worrying about me.

"Oh. Why?" I asked as I walked out of the laundry room and headed toward the stairs.

"You know your daughter as well as anyone. She's used to doing her own thing. I'm still shocked that she agreed for you to stay with her."

At least I wasn't the only one who thought that.

"Me too," I said with a laugh. "I'm sure Grandma had something to do with it."

"Most likely. Anyway, I also wanted to call and tell you that I have a conference in San Diego in April so I'm going to take a few days off and come visit you and Grandma. Do you think the house will be done by then?"

I reached the top of the stairs and set down the hamper. "Ay, who knows? Everything is pretty much still to be determined. Hopefully the contractor will give me a more definite timeline next week."

He sighed. "What a mess. I'm sorry you have to deal with all this, Mom. Especially since Dad's not here to help."

My throat tightened at the mention of Benny. I didn't want Alejandro to worry about me or the house. He had his own life and career to focus on in Colorado. It made me happy to hear that he would come visit soon. But not if it would only make him feel bad for not being able to help.

I swallowed my emotions and picked up the hamper again. "It's all going to be okay, Mijo. I promise." I was glad he didn't do a video call this time. I didn't want him to see the tears that were now blurring my vision. "I would let you talk to Grandma, but she ate too many pancakes this morning and went to go lay down for a nap."

Alejandro laughed. "Okay, I'll call her tomorrow afternoon. I called Yesica earlier to wish her a happy birthday, but she didn't answer. Tell her I'll try to call her again tonight, okay?"

I stopped in front of my daughter's bedroom and dropped the hamper bag. "I will. Love you, Mijo."

"Love you, Mom."

I stuck my phone in the back pocket of my jeans and wiped my eyes with both hands.

Stop being such a chillona all the time.

I shook my head as if I was shaking off the emotions from this morning. If this living situation was going to work out, I needed to find a way to connect with Yesica. For the billionth time, I wondered where things between us had gone so wrong.

It wasn't that we always ended up in shouting matches or worse. I had friends who disliked their own children—well, who they had grown up to become, anyway. Not me. I loved both of my kids. I was proud of them and everything they had accomplished. And it wasn't like Yesica ever said she hated me or ever said anything bad to me. She called me and her grandma at least once a week to check in and came to visit when she could. Although those visits had gotten less frequent after Jason died. But even before that, there was something prickly between us. Something that made me always feel sad after I talked to her or saw her. Because even though I knew I could ask her for anything, why didn't I feel like I should? Or that she was only doing things out of obligation and not out of love?

After picking up the hamper again, I turned the knob and opened the door to Yesica's bedroom. But I stopped after taking a few steps. This wasn't her bedroom.

My eyes scanned the barren room with its empty beige walls and matching carpet. The white sheer curtains allowed the morning rays to fill the room with natural light, casting an awkward warmth into a room that somehow felt cold.

I realized I'd mistakenly walked into the guest bedroom that was located next to Yesica's. As I turned to leave, though, a flash of red pulled my eyes toward the corner. I took a few steps toward it and saw a small toy train sitting on the top shelf of a built-in bookcase.

My curiosity got the best of me, and I picked it up. Except for a few random lines of silver streaked across one side where the red paint had been long scraped off, the toy seemed to be in good condition. I wondered if it had once been part of a set, and if so, where were the other cars?

Carefully, I set it back on the shelf.

An unexplained feeling of sadness overcame me. Had the train belonged to Jason? It must have. But why was it in this room and not somewhere else in the house?

I took one last look at the toy and walked out of the room.

The train, like my daughter's life, would remain a mystery until she decided to share it with me.

CHAPTER SIX
YESICA

Certain events in your life become a core memory even as they're happening in real time. The day I got the call about my dad dying was definitely one of them.

My first interview with Damien was another.

But me walking into the grief support meeting that Saturday morning was not going to make the list. That's because I already knew I would never be back. I decided right then and there that I would call Damien on Monday and convince him that I could deal with my grief and anger in other ways. I could take a kickboxing class or join the company's softball team.

I would tell him that I would do anything in order for him to let me come back to work.

Well, anything except for group therapy.

Therapy could be a good thing for some people. I accepted that. I believed it. I just knew that I wasn't one of those people.

First of all, I loathed talking about my feelings. Last year, Jason had suggested we go to marriage counseling, and I'd agreed. During our one and only session, I learned that one of his main issues, apparently, was the fact that I never told him how I was feeling when it came to our marriage or relationship in general. I couldn't help the fact that

I'd always been one to keep my feelings close to my chest—or rather, locked up. He already knew this about me, or so I'd thought. Even still, I'd been working on letting him know if something was bothering me. If anything, that one therapy session showed me that he was the one in the marriage keeping his feelings inside. Yet, I was the one who promised to do better because I really did want to save our marriage. And when Jason said we didn't have to go back to counseling, I thought it was because he didn't think we needed it anymore.

I couldn't have been more wrong.

I had been open to the idea of going to therapy because it would be with a professional. And if a professional couldn't help back then, then why would I think a group of strangers would now?

I had even asked Damien if I could just find a therapist in my own time. It was still therapy, but at least I'd have some privacy doing it. It was a very good compromise. Or so I thought. But he was insistent that I needed to come to this specific grief support group. The man who led it—Oscar—was the son of a family friend, and Damien spoke very highly of the guy. Luckily, the group met not that far from where I lived.

"How lucky is that?" he'd said.

Yes, lucky me indeed.

The meeting was being held in the hall of a church off PCH in Malibu. I actually thought I was going to be late, but there were only two people sitting in the chairs that had been arranged in a circle in the middle of the large space. Others were congregated in the corner next to a folding table. I walked over in the hopes of finding a bottle of water, since I'd forgotten to grab my Yeti tumbler in the rush to leave my house that morning.

I tried to dismiss the small pang of guilt still lingering in my gut for what had happened with my mom earlier.

I hadn't meant to sound so frustrated, especially since I knew she'd gone to a lot of trouble. I blamed my irritation on being late and what had happened at the bar last night. I'd barely gotten any sleep because of it. As soon as I'd close my eyes, I'd be back on that dance floor.

Maybe it was the guilt for enjoying being in another man's arms. Not that anything else would have happened with the drummer. I wouldn't have let it get that far.

So why couldn't I shake the feeling that Alice had caught me doing something I shouldn't have been?

It was one of the reasons why I hadn't even taken a piece of bacon from my mom. I didn't trust putting anything in my stomach at that point. And I wasn't about to tell my mom or my grandma I was more nervous than I thought I'd be about attending the support group meeting. Not that I was going to tell them where I was going either.

When I'd said they could stay with me, I hadn't really considered the fact that there would be times when they probably would need to know where I was going or when I'd be back. It had been a long time since anyone even cared about whether I had time to eat breakfast.

The living situation was definitely going to be an adjustment, to say the least.

I spotted an open pack of water bottles on the table and grabbed one. There was also a collection of granola bars and bananas in a large plastic bowl. I was reaching for one of the larger bananas—since now my stomach was angry I'd passed on the chance to eat pancakes—just as another hand was doing the same.

"Oh, sorry," I said, and I snapped my hand back.

"No need to apologize," a familiar voice said. "I can grab a different one."

I looked up and met the dark-brown eyes of the drummer. "You," I said with a gasp.

"Me," he confirmed, handing me the banana I had just tried to grab. I ignored it and instead took another one from the bowl.

"What are you doing here? Oh my God, are you stalking me?" I said loudly.

He motioned for me to follow him toward the back of the room. I hesitated at going anywhere with him—even if there were people standing around.

The drummer must have sensed my apprehension. "I want a chance to explain. Please?"

Despite my better judgment, I nodded.

"I'm Damien's friend's son," he said as soon as we were out of earshot from the others. "I'm Oscar, the group's leader."

My knees buckled a little in shock. "Are you kidding me right now?"

"I swear I didn't know who you were until that woman called you Yesica and brought up the fact that your husband had died. That's when I connected the dots and tried to tell you, but you basically ran away before I could."

I couldn't believe what was happening. No way was I going to bare my soul to the drummer. No matter how nice he'd been to me last night.

"This is too much," I told him. "I can't stay."

"Why? Just because we met last night instead of this morning shouldn't change things."

I ignored the pang of disappointment that stabbed my chest. Our bodies had been pressed together for several minutes. What we had done last night seemed to be a little bit more than just "meeting." But I refused to let him know his choice of words bothered me.

"Aren't these things anonymous? Like, haven't some confidentiality lines been crossed or something?"

I could tell he was trying not to smile, and it only annoyed me more.

"This isn't AA, Yesica. We share as much or as little as we want. And sometimes we even get together outside of meetings to have lunch or celebrate someone's birthday. I'm not a psychologist, or even a counselor. I'm just a guy who helps facilitate a support group for people who have lost someone they loved."

His earnestness affected me more than I'd expected. So did his appearance. Under the hall's bright lights, I could make out more of his facial features. His hair was neat compared to the wild waves of the night before. He wore a black Adidas T-shirt that hugged his biceps and chest, and his matching Adidas track pants fit him just as perfectly.

I realized then that he was waiting for me to respond and that it was probably obvious I had been checking him out. Embarrassment heated my cheeks and the back of my neck. Rather than risk me making a bigger fool of myself, I answered, "Fine. I'll stay." And then went to go find a chair in the circle.

It took another five or so minutes before all the chairs were filled and the chatter had dimmed to hushed whispers scattered here and there. I decided to scroll through Instagram while waiting for someone to officially start the meeting.

I didn't have to wait that long.

"Good morning, folks," Oscar, the drummer, said. "Before we start our discussion for today, I wanted to give our two newest members an opportunity to introduce themselves, and then we'll go around the circle and introduce ourselves to them."

Anxiety zapped my heart rate into high gear as Oscar met my eyes.

A young guy sitting two chairs away from me thankfully went first. "Hello, I'm Eddie."

"Hi, Eddie," the group said in unison.

There were a few seconds of uncomfortable silence before I cleared my throat.

"Hi there. I'm Yesica."

"Hi, Yesica."

The drummer nodded. "Welcome, Eddie and Yesica. We're glad you're here."

Then, one by one, the other people in the chairs announced their names until the introductions had come back to him. "And my name is Oscar," he said, looking first at Eddie and then at me. "I usually like to begin each meeting with a question—kind of a discussion prompt. Then I try to make sure we have at least thirty minutes for anyone who'd like to share something. Participation is voluntary, of course. But I'll say that the more you put into this, the more you'll get out of it."

I nodded, only because Oscar seemed to be focused on me. I wondered how much Damien had shared about why I was there. I also couldn't help but wonder why Oscar was there. If he was the group's leader, then I was pretty sure that meant he must have lost someone too. Who was he grieving? And what had made him want to join a grief support group in the first place?

Oscar sat down, and I relaxed a little now that his attention seemed to be off me. "All right, today's question is this: 'What's the one thing you did this week that was just for you and it made you feel happy?' This is important because sometimes our grief can overwhelm us, and we're so busy just trying to not drown that it's hard to see the buoys or life jackets that the universe is trying to throw our way. We have to grab hold of those moments of happiness, however fleeting they may be, because they help us take a break—sometimes literally take a breath—so we can survive the next wave of grief. All right, who wants to share first?"

Although part of me wanted to roll my eyes at the self-help mumbo jumbo I'd just heard, I did not share my thoughts. Or my doubts.

I once had a boss who would've loved every word Oscar had said. She ate that kind of shit up, and she had the shelves of self-help books to prove it. One night as we were leaving the office, I let her convince me to join her to go listen to some motivational speaker the next day. The guy was motivating all right. So much so that my boss decided to quit her job a few days later to let the universe bring her all the good things she deserved. I heard from an old coworker that the only thing the universe had done for her was force her to move back in with her parents and take an entry-level sales job.

So, yeah, I didn't trust people like that motivational speaker or Oscar the drummer. Their words might inspire in the moment, but they usually had nothing useful to offer when the real world imploded all around you.

Because of that and because of who I was, I obviously had no plans of sharing anything out loud. But as different people began commenting, I tried to think of what would have been my answer. It turned out, I could think of quite a few things.

The other night I had ordered takeout from my favorite sushi restaurant. Miso soup and spicy tuna rolls always made me happy. Then last weekend I splurged on a pair of leather boots I'd been eyeing for a while. New shoes also brought me joy. I'd been feeling pretty proud of myself for having so many happy things to choose from until I started really listening to the others.

The woman next to me said she had visited her daughter's favorite spot on the beach and watched the sun set. A man on the other side of the room said he was able to finish a woodworking project that he hadn't touched since his wife had passed. Someone else said they had booked a vacation to Europe—something she and her partner had always wanted to do but never had the time or the money to do it.

Suddenly, my little happy moments seemed even tinier. Even shallow.

God, I'd only been here for fifteen minutes, and I was already feeling judged. Well, I probably would've been judged had I actually spoken.

"Thank you for sharing," Oscar finally said after the last person had sat down. "I really love how different everyone's answers were. Now, if you're questioning whether or not your happy moments were as big or meaningful as the ones you heard, please don't. Everyone here is on a different grief journey, and that means the things that take us out of our grief are all important, whether they last a few minutes or even an entire day. We cannot compare our grief or even our happiness with anyone else's. We all have our own road to travel, okay?"

Some nodded in response, while others voiced their agreement.

It was as if he'd read my mind. I still wasn't impressed, though. I wasn't on some sort of "grief journey." I was only sitting here because my job and future promotion depended on it.

To be on a grief journey, you had to be missing someone.

And could I grieve for Jason when I still hated him? I thought of my dad. I did miss him. And even the most incompetent therapist in the world could tell I still hadn't come to terms with the fact that my mom had prevented me from saying goodbye.

But I wasn't here because of my dad or even Jason. I was here because it was mandatory.

The meeting ended around 10:30, and my grumbling stomach let me know that a measly banana didn't count as a real breakfast. I was contemplating whether to stop and pick up some bagels or just eat at the brunch café by my house when Oscar stepped in front of me before I reached the exit.

"I hope you got something out of the meeting today, Yesica," he said with a smile.

"Oh. Yeah. Definitely," I lied. Why did it unnerve me to hear him call me by name?

"I promise to bring more bananas next Saturday. Or I might go a little wild and bring some pears or apples too."

He laughed at his attempt at humor, but I didn't join him.

"Sounds . . . fun," I offered. "But I don't think I'll be able to make it next week. I have . . . um . . . I have an appointment."

An appointment to convince Damien to let me off the hook.

If I thought Oscar would be disappointed or even upset that I had other things going on more important than his meeting, I was wrong.

The man simply shrugged. "Well, maybe we'll see you the weekend after that."

"Maybe. I don't know. Honestly, I'm not a group therapy type of gal. I mean it's great that you're here helping these people get through a very difficult time in their lives. I just don't think I need this kind of help. Sorry."

Again, I was wrong about what he would say next.

"No need to apologize. But who knows? Maybe you'll see it differently down the line. Like I said, we all have our own journey to take."

Oscar's kumbaya attitude was beginning to annoy me. It didn't matter that I was here because he knew Damien. It didn't matter that he danced with me and bought me a soda. The man didn't know me or what I was going through. Correction. What I had already gone through. If I had been on some sort of journey, then I was already at the end of it.

I didn't need his help to get over losing Jason.

Because what everyone didn't know was that I had lost him long before that car accident.

"Well, good luck with your journey, Oscar. I think I've got this handled." I moved to go around him and began to walk away.

"Obviously Damien doesn't think so. He's worried about you."

That made me spin back around. I squared my shoulders and took a few steps closer to make sure he was paying full attention to me.

"All right," I said pointedly. "I get that you did Damien a favor by letting me attend your meeting, but coming here today was a mistake that I don't plan to repeat. Goodbye."

He didn't say anything. But his arched eyebrow and clenched jaw told me that I'd struck a nerve. That's when I walked away.

Once I was back in my car, I took out my phone and opened my Notes app. On a brand-new page, I typed, *Things that made me happy this week.* Then below it I added: *Attended my first and last grief support group.*

CHAPTER SEVEN
ANA

Habits can either save you or kill you.

At least that's what my tía Blanca used to say. Well, technically she wasn't my tía, but my mother's second cousin by marriage. And technically her name wasn't really Blanca, but Ernestine. Everyone just called her Blanca because of the one time she decided she wanted to be a cosmetologist and accidently overbleached her eyebrows. The woman had pale-yellow—almost white—eyebrows for only a few months, but the nickname had stuck for years.

But that's neither aquí nor allá. The point is Blanca smoked three packs a day and enjoyed telling people how her daily habit of walking two blocks to her neighborhood convenience store every afternoon at three o'clock to buy cigarettes and a lotto scratcher had made her a millionaire. It didn't matter that the money had eventually run out or that she had to lug around an oxygen tank for the last five years of her life. Blanca still insisted her habit had saved her in more ways than one.

So when I spotted Lucas Padilla standing across the produce section from me smelling a mango, I questioned why I hadn't stuck with my habit of grocery shopping at the market by my house and instead walked into this one about five miles away from Yesica's.

Habits can save you or kill you, indeed.

It had been at least ten years since I'd last seen the man, during the funeral of a mutual friend from high school. His hair had more silver than black now, and the glasses with black square frames on his face were new—well, new to me.

I sneaked one more quick glance and hurriedly pushed my cart away from the produce section and headed toward the carnicería counter to get the meat items on my shopping list. As I waited for my number to be called by one of the butchers, my thoughts drifted back to Lucas—the son of my mother's archnemesis and my former best friend.

I'd known him long before high school. My mom used to work in his mom's bakery, and we both used to hang out there after school and on the weekends. When we were both older, we each spent two summers working the counters of the panadería. Even after Cuca betrayed my mom and we were ordered to stop being friends, we still hung out at school and would meet up secretly on the weekends just to talk. We both loved reading, writing short stories, and going to the movies. There was never anything romantic between us.

Then everything changed our senior year.

"Fifty-six!"

Hearing my number finally called dragged me from my memories, and I waved the little pink ticket up in the air as I walked closer to the counter. "Aquí! Here!" I yelled back.

The young man wearing a black apron over a blue polo asked me in Spanish what he could get me.

I debated answering in Spanish for a second, but decided on English. I had a few things to get, and I didn't feel confident saying all of them in front of the small group of other customers still waiting for their numbers to be called.

"Can I get four chicken breasts and four drumsticks? And I also want two pounds of the ranchera meat," I said.

"Marinado?"

"Yes, marinated, please."

As he worked on grabbing my items from the display case, I couldn't help but smirk at the fact that he'd asked me if I wanted the meat marinated in Spanish, even though I'd spoken to him in English.

I was used to strangers assuming because of my brown skin, dark hair, and dark eyes that I spoke the language as well as them. Honestly, I could carry on a conversation in Spanish if I had to. But I was more comfortable speaking English, since I didn't have an accent and I couldn't roll my r's. What kind of Mexican would they think I was?

Although technically, according to my daughter, we were Chicanas.

"We were born in the United States, but we are of Mexican descent," Yesica had once explained.

My mother, however, said she would never call herself a "Chicana" despite living in Southern California all her life. "When I was young, 'Chicano' and 'Chicana' were bad words. That's what they called us back then because we weren't born in Mexico. And it was worse when we tried to speak Spanish—we were made fun of by the whites and the Mexicans from Mexico. Even our teachers in school wouldn't let us speak Spanish to each other."

"Mama Melda, but that's not the world we live in anymore," Yesica had said.

Maybe it wasn't her world, but I knew there was still some left-over prejudice for people who looked like me and didn't speak perfect Spanish or didn't know how to cook certain Mexican dishes from scratch.

I was in my twenties when I made my first frijoles de la olla, and it was my mother who taught me. I had never been interested in learning to make them before, but Benny, like my mother, insisted on having beans with every meal. So I'd asked my mother to teach me. You would've thought I'd given her a kidney because she was so happy. Yes, my first batch was salty and some beans were burned, but I wasn't intimidated anymore, and I continued to cook them for my family. Eventually, I'd learned how to make them correctly, and that made me want to learn to cook more complicated authentic Mexican dishes like menudo and birria. Of course, whatever I made was never as good as Benny's mom's. But he still cleaned his plate every single time.

Just a few minutes later, the young man handed me my items from across the counter. After placing the paper-wrapped meats in my cart, I checked the list I'd typed into a Notes page on my phone and decided to go search for my mother's favorite instant coffee. I found it two aisles down, but I hesitated before reaching for the container on the shelf. They only had the larger size, and it was more expensive than what I was used to paying. Plus, I knew for a fact we had an unopened one in the pantry back home. I could stop by the house on my lunch break the next day and pick it up. As I stood there debating whether three dollars was worth the inconvenience of making an extra trip, I heard my name as a question.

Instinctively, I turned in the direction of the deep voice and immediately regretted it.

Lucas Padilla and his shopping cart were now standing next to me.

His eyes widened as soon as they met mine. "It is you," he said with a grin.

My cheeks burned as the anxiety of seeing him again came roaring back. "It's me," I said sheepishly as I pushed my dark-red-rimmed glasses along my nose. "Hi, Lucas."

"Um, wow. It's been a while. What are you doing in this neighborhood? I thought you still lived over in Bell Gardens?"

How did he know I still lived there?

I almost asked him but realized it probably wasn't appropriate. I also wasn't sure I wanted to know the answer.

"My daughter lives in Santa Monica. Me and Mom are staying with her for a few weeks while my house is, um, being remodeled."

"Oh," he said. "And how is Doña Imelda?"

"Good. Good. Um, how's your mom?"

I gripped the handle of my shopping cart, hoping to steady my balance.

"She's good too. She moved to Vegas last year."

"Wow. Vegas? I can see that actually," I said, and I couldn't help but chuckle. I remembered Cuca always enjoyed visiting the local casinos whenever she could.

He nodded and smiled, but then his expression seemed to turn more serious. Lucas cleared his throat and then said, "Uh, I was sorry to hear about Benny."

My chest tightened with unexpected emotion. After five years, I was used to offers of condolences or looks of pity when people learned I was a widow. But for some reason, it was different coming from Lucas. And my reaction caught me off guard.

"Oh," I rushed. "Yes, thank you."

I don't know why I was surprised that Lucas knew about Benny. Even though we hadn't spoken at our friend's funeral, we still knew a lot of the same people. It would have been more of a surprise if he hadn't heard.

Still, talking about my dead husband to Lucas was the last thing I wanted to do.

"Well, I need to finish my shopping and get back to my daughter's house and start dinner," I said, and I began to push my cart.

"It was nice seeing you again, Ana," Lucas said as I passed him.

I only smiled. After all, I wasn't sure if I could say the same thing about seeing him.

CHAPTER EIGHT
YESICA

I arrived at Damien's house right on time and armed with bribes.

His favorite wine? Check.

A bouquet of wildflowers for Connie? Check.

Chicken empanadas and alfajores from their favorite Argentine bakery? Check.

Me on my best behavior? Check. Check.

Our call on Monday had not gone as planned, so I knew this was basically my last chance to convince him to let me come back to work, or at the very least, convince him I didn't need to go back to the grief support group.

Luckily, he'd mentioned how Connie wanted to make me a belated birthday dinner, and I'd happily called her immediately after to let her know my mother and grandmother were staying with me and "we definitely should all get together so you can finally meet them. Oh, what about tomorrow night?"

Connie, who could never turn down a chance to host a dinner party, gladly invited me and my family to dinner as I'd suggested. I'd hoped to pull Damien to the side while Connie chatted with Mom and Mama Melda. He wouldn't dare make a scene in front of any of those women.

It was the perfect plan.

"Oh wow," my mom said as we pulled into the driveway of Damien and Connie's luxury hillside home located in the upscale Pacific Riviera neighborhood of Pacific Palisades.

"We're eating dinner here?" Mama Melda asked after I'd turned off the ignition.

"Yes, we are," I said. I grabbed my purse and got out of the car.

As the three of us walked toward the front door, my grandma tapped my shoulder.

"Maybe we should go home so I can change into something nicer," she said.

I couldn't help but smile at her shyness—a rare occurrence for sure. "Mama Melda, you're wearing your favorite Sunday dress. You look beautiful."

She really did. My mom had combed her hair and arranged it in a neat bun on the top of her head. My grandma even let her put some lipstick on her too. I told them they didn't have to go to so much trouble because even though Damien was my boss, he was also a friend, and this was a dinner so they could finally meet him and Connie.

"We just want to make a good impression," my mom said.

I had to admit that I did appreciate the effort. I'd been second-guessing bringing them along, since they didn't know the full story about why I was on leave. And I certainly hadn't shared the whole group therapy thing. There was a risk of them finding out, if Damien said anything before I could get him alone and plead my case . . . again.

But it was too late for second guesses now.

After I rang the doorbell, a housekeeper let us in.

"She's wearing red. Heaven help us all," Damien teased when I walked through the door.

Although I'd told Mom and Mama Melda not to get all dressed up, I'd told myself I needed to do the opposite. So I chose my favorite wide-leg jumpsuit. When I wore it, I felt beautiful, confident, and powerful. Although it was more of a spring outfit, I figured it would give me the boost I needed to help me win this war with Damien. Luckily, the late-January temp was cooperating at a bearable fifty degrees, and I'd only needed to top it off with a black shawl.

"Yesica!" Connie yelled as she greeted me with a warm hug and a kiss on the cheek. "You look amazing. I almost feel bad for the poor fellow," she whispered.

Before I could ask her what she meant, Damien also came over and gave me a hug. "It's nice to see you."

"These are for you two," I said, handing the flowers and food to Connie and the wine to Damien.

"You know us so well," Connie said, then looked behind me. "And this must be your mama y abuela?"

"Mucho gusto," my mom said as she stepped forward and held out her hand.

"Mucho gusto, Señora . . . ?" Connie asked.

"Just call me Ana. And this is my mother, Imelda."

After Damien introduced himself, he guided us toward the living room. Connie handed the items I'd brought to the waiting housekeeper.

"You have a beautiful home. Thank you for inviting us," my mom said as she took a seat on the sofa next to my grandma.

"Gracias," Damien said. "We are very blessed."

Connie nodded and put her arm around Damien's waist. "Dinner will be ready soon. And we're still waiting on our other guest to arrive. In the meantime, what can I get you to drink?"

Another dinner guest? I tried to make eye contact with Damien, but he was looking at everyone else but me. My stomach twisted. My perfect plan didn't involve a sixth person being at dinner. Part of me hoped it was one of their sons. They had five of them, and four either worked or lived close enough that it could be a possibility. Although why wouldn't Connie just say their son was joining us?

No, it had to be someone else. I could only pray it wasn't someone from the firm. Then I remembered Connie's comment about feeling sorry for some "fellow."

What on earth was Damien up to?

"Yesica, honey. What do you want to drink?" I heard Connie ask.

"Oh, I'll just take a glass of red. You choose."

"Let me help you," my mom said and then stood up.

Mama Melda also got up and asked to use the bathroom.

Once everyone was out of the room, I walked over to Damien. "I didn't realize someone else was coming tonight. Do I know him?"

"I'll tell you his name, but first I want you to answer a question."

I already didn't like where this conversation was headed. But saying no wasn't really an option. "Go ahead and ask away."

"Did you come here tonight hoping to change my mind about the leave and the grief support group?"

I wanted to protest but knew it was futile. Especially since he'd know I was lying once I brought up those exact two topics.

"I did," I said. "But to be fair, you did owe me a birthday dinner."

"Yesica . . ."

I decided this was the opening I needed. I had to take my shot. "Look, Damien. I agree I needed to be held accountable for what happened. But can't you see how this is a little extreme?"

"No, I don't see. It was the only way I could make sure you got the help and rest you so obviously need. You didn't even give the support group a real chance. I think once you get to know Oscar, you'll see you were wrong about him. He's not one of those con men who are more concerned about making money off people's trauma. He volunteers his time to lead the group."

A sudden realization slammed the breath out of my chest. "Oh my God," I finally said. "Is he the one coming to dinner tonight? Oh my God, Damien. How could you?"

Fury heated my core, and it took everything I had not to explode into a profanity-laced tirade. Had Damien invited Oscar over for some sort of intervention? Were my mom and grandma also in on it? Was everyone going to gang up on me and shame me into going back to the grief support meeting? A sense of betrayal and anxiety wrung my gut into knots.

Damien held up his hand as if he could read my escalating panicked thoughts. "I know what you're thinking," he began. "I respect your privacy, Yesica. I figured you probably didn't tell your family everything that's going on, so I've asked Oscar to not mention the fact that you went to his grief support group on Saturday. I also didn't share that with Connie—if you want to tell her later, then that's your decision. But I had to come up with an excuse to invite Oscar, so I might have mentioned that perhaps you two might hit it off."

I put my hands on my hips. "Hold on. Connie thinks you're setting us up?" I couldn't believe how bad this night was turning out.

"No, not setting up. I just said I wanted to introduce you two because I thought you might be friends."

I wanted to tell him how mad I was, but Mama Melda came back from the bathroom, and then my mom and Connie were also walking into the room with drinks in hand.

Then the doorbell rang.

"I'll get it," Damien shouted and then nearly ran to the foyer. I was sure then that he knew how angry I was.

Connie handed me a glass of wine. I heard Oscar's voice in the distance and downed my drink in a few gulps.

If my perfect plan was going to unravel right before my eyes, then I definitely deserved to be buzzed for it.

Less than fifteen minutes later, we were all seated in the dining room. It took one more glass of wine and a tasty salad in my stomach before I began to feel more calm and relaxed.

As promised by Damien, Oscar acted as if he was meeting me for the first time that night and seemed to be charming the socks off my mother and Mama Melda. Connie was being a very gracious hostess, and Damien was obviously trying to make amends by telling everyone how good I was at my job and that I'd be running the firm in a few years.

"Yesica is the only reason why I let Connie talk me into finally retiring," he said.

"It's true," Connie added. "Before Yesica joined the firm, I hardly saw my husband. He was always working—even when he was supposed to be on vacation. But now he's home by five o'clock every night, and we've taken three trips since November already!"

"All right, all right," I said, finally speaking up. "We can tone down the Yesica fan club testimonials. My mom is going to think I paid you both to say all those things."

"No, I wouldn't," my mom said, oblivious to the joke. "I know you work hard and that you're good at your job. You should feel proud when others tell you that they value what you do. I know you prefer to think otherwise, but I'm proud of you too."

Embarrassment wouldn't let me say anything. An awkward silence filled the room.

"Well, who's ready for some arroz con pollo?" Connie asked before heading to the kitchen.

A few minutes later, we were all oohing and aahing over the food, and the air of discomfort had dissipated, along with my third glass of wine.

"My Manuel loved arroz con pollo," I heard Mama Melda say. "I tried to make it at least once a week for him. But after he passed, I never really had any desire to cook it. Maybe it's time I tried again. I'll need to get your recipe, Señora Rojas."

Connie's face beamed brightly. "Of course. And please call me Connie."

"You might find that cooking your husband's favorite meal can be a source of comfort," Oscar said out of nowhere. He'd been so quiet for the past several minutes that I'd almost forgotten he was at the table. The wine also helped, of course.

"It's true," my mom added. "Benny loved caldo de res. So I do feel like I'm honoring him in some way when I make it because he's the one who taught me."

The mention of my father added another layer to the defensiveness I'd been feeling ever since I learned Oscar was joining the dinner. Maybe it was because I didn't want him to read anything into the fact that I'd lost both my husband and my father. I was already feeling so vulnerable and exposed. I hated not being in control of what personal information about me and my life was being shared with him.

So I did what I always did when I felt vulnerable—I challenged.

"Dad didn't like caldo de res. His favorite was chicken caldo," I argued.

"He loved both, Yesica," my mom said quietly.

"You can't have two favorites, Mom."

She smiled tightly and slowly nodded. "You're right. You can't. My mistake."

I should've been more satisfied that she'd agreed with me. But even with three glasses of wine in me, I could tell her demeanor had changed. She looked sad. Almost like she was going to cry. Guilt burned my cheeks. I hadn't meant to sound so accusatory. God, why was I acting like this?

Oscar cleared his throat. "Wait. So all three of you are widows?"

"That's right," I said, shaking off whatever it was my mom's expression was doing to me. "All three of us have dead husbands. Kind of a cruel joke for the universe to play on us, isn't it, Oscar?"

It was as if my mouth had a mind of its own. I knew I sounded awful, but I couldn't stop. And I couldn't take it back.

The reference to his little grief spiel wasn't lost on the man. But he took it in stride and had the nerve to agree with me. "It was, it is, a cruel joke. And I'm very sorry all three of you had to go through that."

The look in Oscar's eyes unnerved me. It wasn't pity and it wasn't fake—not the kind of look I was used to getting from people who didn't know me. Even worse, if they weren't feeling sorry for me, then they were uncomfortable and acted as if it was my fault for making them feel like that. As if my husband dying was an inconvenience to them, and they were unsure of how to relate to me, or even have a conversation.

Oscar was different. I could see real sincerity in his gaze. I could even feel it emanate off him. And I didn't know how to handle it.

"Excuse me," I said quickly, and I jumped out of my chair to head for the bathroom.

After dabbing my face with a cool, wet washcloth, I fixed my makeup and hair and walked out. I could hear some lively chatting coming from the dining room, but I wasn't ready to join in so I decided to go hide out in the kitchen for a few minutes.

I hadn't expected to see Connie in there, so I turned to walk back.

"Yesica, could you help and put the cookies you brought on this platter for me? I'm going to start the coffee."

I spun around with a smile on my face. "Sure."

Using the tongs she'd already placed on the tray, I began taking the cookies out of the box.

After about a minute of us working in silence, she said, "You should probably drink some water, dear. Maybe that will help you clear your head a little?"

Embarrassment and shame heated my face. I set down the tongs and faced her. "I'm sorry if I've been acting off tonight. This is not how I wanted the dinner to go . . . at all."

She walked over to me and placed her hand on my arm. "It's okay. I know what's going on, and I'm going to let Damien have it after you all leave."

I froze. "You know?"

Connie nodded and gave me a small smile. "It's too soon, isn't it?"

"What do you mean?"

"It's too soon to think about dating someone else. You're still grieving. And I'm sorry for letting Damien push you when you are clearly not ready."

Relief made me sigh. Connie still didn't know about my outburst at work or me going to Oscar's grief support group. "I know he means well. I know both of you do," I told her.

"He says you've decided to take some time off work."

"Um, yeah. It's been rough." It was the truth.

Connie nodded. "I'm glad. You need to take care of yourself, honey."

She wrapped both of her arms around me and gave me a tight hug. When she let me go, I noticed she had some tears. "You know, we both care about you so much. We hate seeing you all alone."

The roar of emotions in my gut didn't let me reply. Tears gathered in the corners of my eyes and began to spill over one by one. The last thing I'd wanted to happen tonight was to upset Connie. She'd made this wonderful dinner to celebrate my birthday, and I'd gone and acted like a brat for most of it. I knew she and Damien only wanted what was best for me. Deep down, I knew that was why Damien was forcing me to take a leave and get some help for my grief and anger issues. As always, he was only trying to help me.

What on earth would I do without him or Connie in my life? I didn't deserve their kindness or friendship because I hadn't been a good friend to them for months now. Connie had been asking me out to lunch for weeks, but I always had an excuse not to go. Whenever Damien prodded with nonwork questions during our one-on-one meetings, I kept my answers curt and vague.

I had a bad habit of shutting people out when I didn't feel like baring my soul—or being judged about what my soul would expose about me.

But Damien and Connie weren't just people. And when Damien did retire, I would regret pushing them away. A combination of guilt and sadness only pushed out more tears.

"What is it, Yesica?" Connie said as she grabbed my hands.

I shrugged. "I've been so focused on taking over when Damien retires that I forgot I'm only getting this opportunity because he's leaving. What am I going to do without him in the office every day?"

Connie smiled. "Remember what he said to you on your first day?"

I couldn't hide my surprise if I'd tried. "He told you?"

"Of course he did. Do you remember?"

I nodded. How could I forget? Damien had invited me to lunch at his favorite Italian restaurant and then, over their fried ravioli appetizers, explained that he'd decided he was going to be my mentor. "Because, Mijita, people like us need to stick together."

"You mean, because we're both Latinos?" I'd asked innocently. He'd proudly declared his Argentine heritage during my first interview.

Damien had laughed so hard he almost spit his mineral water out of his nose. "No, not that. It's because we both know how to make things happen. And yes, I guess, because we are both Latinos."

I smiled at the memory. It was the first time in my professional career that I felt like my heritage would be seen as a positive rather than a negative. I'd dealt with my fair share of backhanded compliments from colleagues and bosses. Comments like how "well spoken" and "educated" I was or remarks about my work ethic. I was used to having to prove to them and myself that I deserved every success and promotion.

With Damien, though, I wasn't trying to prove I was better than any preconceived stereotype. He saw me for who I truly was and what I could do. Now I just had to not make him regret handpicking me to succeed him.

"You're going to be fine," Connie told me while gripping my hand. "Besides, he's just retiring. We'll still see each other. We're like family now, right?"

A little pang of guilt needled my conscious. My mother was my family too. Deep down I knew she only wanted what was best for me—just like Damien and Connie. Why did I forget that sometimes? I shrugged it off in an effort to regain my composure. "Yes, we are family," I told her.

A big smile lit up her face, and we nodded together knowingly.

I blinked back my own tears. "I'm going to be okay, Connie. I promise."

Connie grabbed a nearby napkin and dabbed at her eyes. Then she handed me one so I could do the same. Once we'd both composed ourselves, her somber expression morphed into a sly smile. "Yesica, you're a smart and beautiful woman. When you're ready, I know you will find someone. Who knows? Maybe even a Rojas?"

I couldn't help but laugh. "I already told you, Connie. If and when I'm ready to date, it will never, ever be one of your sons." Then I thought about it. Of the five Rojas boys, two were married, one was engaged, one was gay, and one had a girlfriend. None should even be an option. "Wait. Did something happen?"

Connie nodded. "Christian and that girl broke up. I'm surprised Damien didn't tell you. He wanted to throw a party he was so happy."

I laughed out loud. Damien had never hidden the fact that he didn't care for his son's latest companion. To be honest, I always thought Christian could do better. Better like Evie. I made a mental note to tell her the news.

The coffee maker beeped, and Connie walked back to start filling cups she'd already lined up on the counter. "Yesica, I know you're not ready to date, but it still might be nice to get to know Oscar. He actually leads a grief support group, and I hear it's pretty popular."

I nearly dropped the platter of cookies I'd just picked up. I set it back down when my hands began to shake. "Really?" I said, trying to sound surprised. "That doesn't sound like an easy thing to do. How . . . how did he get into doing something like that?"

Connie grabbed bottles of different-flavored creamers from the fridge and placed them next to the now-filled coffee cups on saucers. "He started going to the group after his sister died. Then when the group leader decided she couldn't do it anymore, he volunteered to take it over last year."

I stilled. "His sister died?"

"Yes. Que descanse en paz," Connie said, making the sign of the cross. "Pobrecita, she was only nineteen. Leukemia."

My heart broke for the girl I never even knew. And for Oscar. "Oh no. That's so sad."

"It was," Connie said, heaving a long sigh after. "They were so close. It really messed him up. We were really worried about him. I think finding that group saved his life."

I wanted to ask Connie more questions, but the housekeeper walked into the kitchen at that moment.

"All right, Irma will help me take the coffee and creamers to the table. Can you bring the cookies?"

I nodded and grabbed the tray I'd left on the counter. I wasn't sure if I was ready to go back in there, but it wasn't like I could take my cookies and go home. Especially since I was my mom's and grandma's ride.

Luckily, the next thirty minutes went smoothly—even pleasantly. My mouth and attitude were reined in, and I had switched from wine to coffee and water. So when Connie offered to take my mom and Mama Melda on a tour of the house, I felt comfortable enough to join Oscar and Damien back in the living room. But my comfort was short lived after Damien conveniently mentioned he had to return a phone call to one of the firm's partners.

"He's never really been the subtle type, has he?" Oscar said once it was just the two of us in the room.

"Nope," I replied, and I shifted my position on the couch.

Oscar, who had been sitting across from me on an armchair, stood up and walked over to me. Then, to my surprise, he sat down.

"I owe you an apology," he began. "I never should've agreed to come tonight. I'm sure you felt ambushed, and that's not my style."

I raised my eyebrow. "It's not? Then what is?"

He gave me a smirk, and I hated that I thought it was cute. "I prefer the long game, honestly. I understand that it takes some time to build trust. I also should've tried harder to tell you who I was that night at the bar. I'd thought we could start over tonight. But I realize now that you can't trust someone who shows up out of the blue just to convince you to come back to the group and give it one more shot."

I carefully considered how to word what I was going to say next. "Well, I can only trust people who are honest with me. What did Damien tell you about . . . my situation?"

"He told me your husband passed away a few months ago, and he thought maybe I . . . the group could help you cope with the loss."

My soul seemed to unclench. Damien was telling the truth about keeping what had happened only between us. I almost felt guilty for doubting him. Damien was a man who always kept his promises.

I owed it to him to keep mine.

I let out a long sigh. Damien, without even being a part of this conversation, had convinced me to give the group one more try. "Fine," I said. "I'll be there on Saturday."

Oscar's face brightened, and he even let out a little chuckle. "See you Saturday then."

I ignored the flutter in my chest.

As I drove us home, I couldn't help but grin at how the night had turned out so differently from what I had imagined. I was still feeling pretty good when we walked into my house. So I was a little surprised when my mom walked up the stairs to her room without saying good night.

I looked at Mama Melda and motioned to the upstairs. "What's her problem?"

She sighed and took a step closer. "Thank you for inviting me to dinner tonight, Mija. I'll see you in the morning."

Mama Melda took a few steps, but I called out after her. "I know I drank too much wine. Is that why she's mad?"

My grandma slowly turned around. The look on her face gave me the chills.

"I know you and your mama have some issues. But there are things you don't know—things she has suffered in silence in order to protect you."

I froze. "What do you mean?"

"It's not for me to say."

Since when, I thought. But I knew now was not the time for sarcasm. Whatever my grandmother was and wasn't telling me, it was serious.

"Mama Melda, I . . ."

She held up her hand to quiet me. "There are many reasons why you make me proud, Mija. But the way you acted tonight was not one of them. And it had nothing to do with how much you drank. You may have a successful job and a beautiful home and many people who respect you. That doesn't mean you have the right to treat your mother the way you treated her. She is still your mother and deserves more than you will ever know. So think of that the next time you disrespect her in front of strangers."

And then Mama Melda disappeared into her room and quietly closed the door.

CHAPTER NINE
ANA

"What's your Gmail password, and please don't tell me it's your birthday?"

I looked over at Yesica from across the dining room table. "It's not," I said defiantly. "Anymore."

She shook her head. "Seriously?"

"What? That laptop is almost six years old. I wasn't as tech savvy back then as I am now."

My daughter rolled her eyes. "If you're so tech savvy, then why do you have ten thousand emails in your inbox?"

Technically, it was around six thousand, but I didn't bother correcting her since she was doing me a favor. Yesica had offered to take a look at my laptop after I'd complained that it was running slow. She had already apologized for her behavior at dinner the other night, and I figured this was her way of making up for it.

Although I'd insisted I wasn't upset about what had happened, I was taken aback by her reaction to what I'd said about Benny. It was strange how two people could have so many different memories about the past. To Yesica, Benny was her hero. She once told me it seemed like she was the only one who cared that he was gone. It wasn't true, of course. Alejandro was also devastated when Benny died. And I missed him too—in my own way.

I looked over at her from across the table and thought it was nice to finally do something together—even if it was just fixing my laptop. It was almost ten, and Mama was already in bed for the night.

"I really wish you'd let me make you some caldo de pollo," I said as I watched her slurp up noodles from a foam cup container. Yesica had said earlier that she felt like she was coming down with a cold. I'd made meat loaf and mashed potatoes for dinner, but I offered to make her some chicken soup to help soothe her throat. She'd insisted that she wasn't hungry. But before she started looking at my laptop, she'd heated water in the electric kettle and then made herself a cup of ramen mixed with lemon and Tapatío.

"This is fine, Mom," she said.

I didn't think it was, but I knew better than to try to argue with her while she was doing me a favor.

"Jesus, Mom," she said after a minute or so. "You probably have a virus from one of these junk emails. I hope you didn't click on something you weren't supposed to."

"I know better than that. That's why I have so many unopened emails."

"You don't have to open them to delete them," she explained. "A lot of these are notifications from Facebook. Are you really still on there? I closed my account two years ago."

I shrugged and put down the book I'd been trying to read. "Not really. I just check it every once in a while, just to see the pictures from mis primas. My cousin Donna likes to post a lot about her grandbabies."

"Who's Lucas Padilla?"

Shock rippled through my body, and I almost forgot how to breathe. Why on earth was my daughter asking about that man?

"Who?" I asked after I'd cleared the panic from my throat.

"You have a Facebook friend request notification from someone named Lucas Padilla. I just thought you'd want to know before I deleted it. Who is he?"

"Oh," I said, trying to sound nonchalant. "He's just someone I went to high school with. Go ahead and delete it."

"Looks like he messaged you too," Yesica said.

"Messaged? On my email?"

"No, he sent the message to you through Facebook. You have to log in to your account in order to see it."

"What if . . . what if I don't want to see it? Can you just delete it too?"

Yesica closed the laptop to look directly at me. "No, I can only delete the email notification. You'll have to log in to your account to delete the actual message. Why would you want to delete it, Mom? Who is this guy?"

I shrugged and tried not to let on that Lucas messaging me was a bigger deal than it was.

"I already told you. He's just someone I went to school with."

It didn't work. After a few seconds, Yesica's eyes widened, and I knew she had made the connection.

"Oh my God," she said. "Is he related to the infamous Cuca Padilla?"

There was no use trying to come up with an alternative. My daughter could be as stubborn as her grandmother in digging for information. "Yes. He's her son."

She pointed to the hallway. "Why does she hate that woman so much? I don't think I've ever heard the full story."

"Because of the panadería," I answered. "Well, not really the panadería, but because of the stolen recipes."

"Mama Melda stole that woman's recipes?" she yelled.

I shushed her and turned my head, waiting to see if my mother's door opened. After I was sure she wasn't coming out, I whispered, "No.

Señora Padilla stole your grandma's recipes, and that's how the feud between the families began."

Of course, it hadn't always been like that between my mother and Cuca Padilla. In fact, there was a time when my mother truly believed that Cuca had saved our family.

"After your grandfather was killed, we struggled," I began. "Your grandmother had to find a job, but she also had us kids to take care of. I was barely eight, and your uncle and aunt were only seven and five years old," I explained. "So it was hard. She'd get a job but only keep it for a few months, because one of us would get sick so she'd have to stay home. There was always something. But, as you know, your grandmother is a very talented baker. When she needed money, she'd bake all weekend and then sell what she'd made outside the market or any store that wouldn't chase her away. And that's how she met Cuca. She owned a panadería near the church and offered her a job as a baker after she'd tasted your grandmother's breads and pastries."

Yesica sat back in her chair and folded her arms across her chest. "I don't understand. How did she steal Mama Melda's recipes if Grandma worked there?"

"After a few years, Cuca decided that running the panadería was too much, and she wanted to sell it. Grandma was disappointed, but she understood and was able to find a new job working at the church. Then one day, there was some type of event, and Grandma needed to go to the panadería to get some bread. Cuca had sold it to this man who owned other bakeries around LA. Grandma didn't really like those bakeries, but she had no choice because the panadería was close and she was in a rush. Well, she was surprised when she walked into the panadería and saw a lot of the same items she used to make for Cuca—including these particular almond-shaped pastries that she knew the man's other bakeries never carried. She bought some, and when she got back to the church, she tasted them. While they weren't exactly like the ones she used to make with her mother, they were very close. Later that day, she called Cuca to tell her, and Cuca admitted that the man hadn't just wanted to buy the panadería; he'd made it a requirement that the deal include all the recipes too."

"Oh no," Yesica said, glancing over to the hallway again.

My heart hurt as I thought of the day she'd told me what Cuca had done. My mother had said she didn't care as much about the recipes for the rolls or pan dulce. But it was the fact that Cuca had sold her mother's recipe for the cookies that cut the deepest. My mother said she had told Cuca how the recipe had been handed down for generations and that when her family had been kicked out of their home back in the fifties with just an hour's notice, that cookie recipe had been one of the few things she'd been able to take with her. "I can't tell you how much the recipe means to me, Mija. And Cuca sold it behind my back," she'd wailed.

After she'd finally stopped crying, my mother made me swear to never talk to Lucas again. To his credit, he came over and tried to apologize to both me and my mother. But the wound was still fresh, and she refused to see even him. He said he understood if I couldn't be his friend anymore. And I tried not to be.

But after a few weeks, I caved and told him we just had to keep our friendship a secret from both of our families.

"Anyway, that's why she hates Cuca Padilla and anyone related to her," I explained, leaving out the part about Lucas being my best friend.

"Why do you think her son is messaging you then?"

"I have no idea," I lied.

"If he's a creep, then you also need to block him before you delete the message. Do you want me to do it for you?"

I held up my hand to stop her. "No, it's okay. I can do it. I should probably go on there anyway and see if there are any other messages."

Yesica's scrunched-up expression let me know she wasn't fully buying my story. "Fine. But I am going to delete all these notifications and emails about Viagra, okay?"

It took her another half an hour to clean up my inbox. She told me she was going to install some sort of security software, and that would help my laptop.

"Thank you for doing this," I told her when she handed it over to me.

"You're welcome," she said, and she met my eyes. "And I'm sorry again about how I acted the other night at Damien's. I don't know what got into me."

I wasn't sure either. But I took comfort in the fact that she regretted her behavior—even if it had taken my mother to point it out.

"Your boss and his wife seem very nice, and I could tell they care about you. I'm glad you have people like that in your life . . . especially now."

I hadn't meant to bring Jason into the conversation. Because just like with Benny, Yesica didn't seem to think I had the right to bring him up. I'd tried talking to her about it after he died. All it did was make her retreat further behind the walls she'd already put up between us. Regret made me nervously look down at my laptop.

"Me too."

When I looked up again, Yesica was gone.

CHAPTER TEN
YESICA

I wasn't hangry the second time I walked into the grief support group meeting.

With a blueberry muffin and an iced latte in my belly, I didn't feel as irritated as I did the first time. And whatever yuckiness I was feeling earlier in the week had disappeared. Although I did promise Damien and Oscar that I'd try the meeting again, I was absolutely noncommitted to the thought of returning a third time.

There seemed to be a few more people than last week, based on the number of cars I'd spotted in the parking lot. And my guess was confirmed when I saw that the circle of chairs definitely seemed bigger. In fact, most were already taken.

Since I'd remembered my water bottle this time, I didn't need to stop at the snack table and headed straight to the center of the room to find a seat. That's when I saw Oscar walking toward me with a huge grin on his face.

"You came," he said as he reached me.

"I did," I replied. And because his expression seemed to be more smug than genuine, I added, "When you report back to Damien, make sure to let him know I was even five minutes early this time."

Oscar shrugged off my cattiness. "What happens in group, stays in group. If you want to tell Damien you showed up, then that's your decision. I'm not your babysitter, Yesica."

I hadn't meant to sound so bitchy. I tried to smooth it over by asking, "Did you guys play last night?"

That seemed to surprise him. "No, next Friday. You're always welcome to come watch the show. It would be nice if you did."

I didn't know how to respond to his last comment, so I just smiled and walked toward one of the empty chairs and sat next to a woman wearing a yellow Cancún baseball hat.

Oscar officially started the meeting about ten minutes after nine.

"Good morning, everyone. I'm so glad to see so many of you here today. Looks like we have a few new faces, so let's do things a little differently today. Let's go around the circle and introduce ourselves and say one word that describes how you're feeling at this exact moment. No need to explain or defend. Just say the word. I'll start. My name is Oscar and I'm feeling hopeful."

He motioned to the man sitting to his right to go next. In the minute or two it took to get to me, I debated which words to share. Should I be fake and say something like "good" or "inspired"? Maybe I go with being purposefully obtuse and say "indifferent" or "doubtful." But the more I thought about it, the more it also made me think of the reason I was here in the first place. And it was all Jason's fault.

So when it was finally my turn, I blurted out, "I'm Yesica and I'm feeling betrayed."

The rest of the meeting went about the same as the first. Oscar offered a topic for discussion that took up a good portion of the hour and then opened it up to free sharing. I had to admit I caught myself getting choked up at some of the stories. But whether it was the mom who'd lost her son in a car accident or the elderly man who'd lost his wife of sixty years, it was enlightening to see all the different stages of grief on display. Those who had lost loved ones recently were clearly still in denial or anger, while others seemed to be on the path toward acceptance. It was no surprise that I identified the most with the people who talked about how mad they were at the person who had died.

Of course, I didn't say that out loud. It was part of my secret. From the minute I learned Jason had died in that car accident, I had been playing the role of his grieving widow. It was what was expected, and I always did what was expected of me. It was usually easier that way. If people really knew the truth, then my life would go from expected to complicated. And I hated complicated. So, yes, I had a very good reason for being angry at Jason for making me a widow at the age of thirty-two.

But I wasn't just furious because he'd died. I was furious that right before he died, he'd practically blown up the life we'd built together. And then, conveniently, he was gone, and I was left behind to clean up the mess.

When the sharing was done, Oscar stood up.

"Thank you all. Before we leave, I'd like you to think about the word you shared at the beginning. Who would like to share the word they're feeling now?"

I listened as the woman with the yellow Cancún baseball hat raised her hand and said her word from earlier had changed from "alone" to "better." The elderly widow said his word was the exact same: "lost."

Maybe it was a coincidence or a challenge, but that's when Oscar's eyes met mine. My original word hadn't changed either. Still, I had to admit that the meeting had made me feel one other emotion, and, for some reason, I wanted him to know what it was.

Keeping my gaze directed toward him, I raised my hand. His right eyebrow arched in surprise, and he gave me a nod. "Yesica?"

"I'm feeling . . . justified."

No response from Oscar, at least not one betrayed by any sort of expression.

"All right, everyone. Thanks again, and see you next week," he said after one more person had shared.

A low murmur and the sounds of chairs scraping the floor filled the room as people began to get up and leave. I stood, grabbed my purse from the back of the chair, and checked my phone for any new texts.

"So, what's the verdict?" I heard Oscar say from behind me. "Will you be back next week?"

"Unknown," I replied, deciding to stick with the one-word theme.

I turned around, only to see his small smile falter for a second. "Not the answer I had hoped for, but at least it's not a full no. So I guess I remain hopeful."

"Clever."

"I will take that as a compliment. Even if you didn't mean it to be one."

That made me chuckle. I had to give the guy credit. He could turn on the charm and the self-effacing humor just at the right time. But I knew what he was up to.

"Just because I'm not sprinting for the exit doesn't mean I've changed my mind about whether this whole group thing is for me," I said.

He shrugged. "I know. But it did seem like something today did resonate. Am I wrong?"

"You're not wrong. For a drummer in an eighties cover band, you're more perceptive than I thought you would be." I didn't mind admitting that to him. "And, no, that's not a compliment."

Oscar laughed and raised his hands. "Got it." I noticed a few people standing nearby, and it became obvious with their glances they were waiting for him.

"I think you're wanted over there," I said with a nod in that direction.

He looked over at the small group and waved. "Looks like it. But before you leave, can I just ask for a favor?"

The request surprised me. "Go ahead and ask."

Oscar took a step closer. "Before you make any decision about returning next Saturday, can you at least take the week to think over the words you shared today?"

"Why?"

"Think about the words and ask yourself if those emotions are getting in your way. If you decide that maybe they're holding you back from really moving on, then I want you to consider that coming to group can help you find some new words—new emotions."

I hated to admit it, but I was intrigued. It had become clear that something was going on with me. "Why?"

"Not everyone who comes to these meetings is here because they know someone who's just died. Most of the time, they show up after something has happened that made them realize they want to transform their grief into something else. I don't know the details behind what brought you here specifically, but it had to have been something major. I can see you're not a woman who is used to asking for help. And I can tell you are someone who likes to be in control of her life, and grief is something you can't control. Talking about that with others who are going through something similar gives you back some of that control. Even if it's just for an hour once a week. Because, I've learned, eventually, the more you talk about it, the more that control grows. So, if that's what you need, what you're looking for, then I'll see you next Saturday."

CHAPTER ELEVEN
ANA

"What are you doing?"

My mother's voice startled me, and I nearly jumped out of my chanclas. My face burned with embarrassment at having been caught snooping, and I felt as if I was eight years old again and had been discovered searching for hidden Christmas presents.

But I ignored the shame. I hadn't done anything wrong.

It was Tuesday afternoon, and I'd just come home from work and running errands. It had been a slow day, and my boss had let me go two hours early. Usually, I was grateful for a short shift since it gave me time to run errands or even take a nap before starting dinner. But this was the third shift in a row where my hours had been cut from eight to six. January was already a slow time at the nursery. But the past few weeks had been even quieter than usual. My coworker Phil had told me the other day that he was going to start looking for another job because he couldn't afford the cut in hours.

"I wouldn't be surprised if they sold the place or closed it down permanently," he'd said.

I refused to let my mind think of such things. I needed this job, especially now, with all the house repairs. Even though the insurance was going to cover the majority of the costs—thank God—the contractor had warned me that there might be some things that they wouldn't. But he couldn't know for sure for a few more weeks.

Besides the money, I really enjoyed my job. I'd always had a green thumb—one of the things I'd happily inherited from my mother. Before I even started working there, I would be at the nursery at least once a week picking up supplies for my own plants and garden, or some days I'd just stop by to look around, even when I didn't need a thing.

So after Benny decided he didn't really care anymore what I did with my time, the nursery was the first and only place I'd applied to. I'd worked at the nursery for almost six years now. I couldn't imagine working anywhere else.

I was still thinking about what Phil had said when I walked into my mother's bedroom at Yesica's to put away the dress I'd picked up from the dry cleaner's that was in the same shopping center as the nursery. That's probably why I was distracted and hit my thigh on the edge of the nightstand next to the closet. After yelping in pain, I'd realized I had also knocked the small pouch that held her rosary beads off the table.

I'd bent down to find the pouch and had also discovered a plastic bag. Normally, I would've just left it, but I recognized the similar floral pattern of the dress I'd just brought home sticking out of it. So I picked it up and put the bag on the bed. I was just about to go through it when my mother came inside.

"I picked up your dry cleaning, and after I put your clothes in the closet, I accidentally bumped the nightstand," I explained. "Your rosary fell between the bed and the wall, and when I reached for it, I found the bag. What is all this?"

She stomped into the room and took the bag from me. "What does it look like? They are my things."

"I see that. But why are you keeping them in a grocery bag?"

"Because I ran out of room in my suitcase. Which, by the way, I need another suitcase."

I was so confused. "You have a dresser and a closet. Why are you still keeping things in a suitcase?"

"These are my extra things. Just in case."

"Just in case what?"

She opened her mouth as if to explain, but then shut it. Instead, she put the bag in the closet and walked out of the room.

Usually, that meant she was done talking. It was her way of physically leaving the conversation. But not this time.

I grabbed the bag from the closet and followed her into the kitchen. "Mama. What is the bag for?"

"I already told you," she said as she pulled a mug out of the cupboard.

"Actually, you didn't."

"I don't want to talk about this anymore, Ana."

"Too bad."

I pulled the dress out of the bag and placed it on the counter. "You told me you got a stain on this dress last month, and that's why I bought you another one—the one I just had dry-cleaned." I grabbed the jar of face cream and showed it to her. "You told me last week to buy you two jars of this because you wanted to make sure you didn't run out again. I know you keep one on your nightstand, but why is the second one in here?"

She waved her hand at me as if to dismiss my questions away. "Why are you getting so loca about this? What does it matter?"

My mother was right. In the grand scheme of things, it was silly of me to interrogate her about a bag full of her own things. But I had my reasons.

"It matters because this isn't the first time I've found a bag like this, Mama. I found one months ago in the garage, I found one a while back stuffed inside a box in your bedroom closet, and I found others when I was a kid. I just want to know why you're hiding things from me?"

"I'm not hiding them from you, Ana." The look in her eyes was genuine. I knew when my mother was lying. And this time she wasn't. My confusion only grew.

"Then why keep things in bags all over the house?"

"Just in case we have to leave—in case someone comes to the door in the middle of the night and makes us leave again!"

And then she did something she hadn't done in years. She covered her face and burst into tears.

My heart broke all over again for what she'd gone through as a little girl. She and her family were one of the last to be evicted from Chavez Ravine—the Los Angeles neighborhood razed in order to build a low-income housing project, but then it became the new home to Dodger Stadium in the 1960s instead. Although she never told me exactly how or what had happened, I knew that she, my tíos and tías, and my abuelita had to leave their house with basically the clothes on their backs. That made me immediately understand the bags. I went to her and grabbed her by her arms. "Mama, no one is going to make you leave your home again."

Her eyes still brimmed with tears. "Do you promise?"

"I do."

I held her as she cried, and then I cried with her. I felt guilty for not realizing how hard it must have been for her to leave our house after the flooding, even if she knew it was only going to be temporary. She'd lived there almost as long as I had—moving in with me and Benny right after my brother joined the army. Benny had actually been the one to insist on it. Back then I'd thought it was because he didn't want my mother living alone. I realized later it was just another way of making me look bad for not suggesting it in the first place.

My house may not have been as big and as modern as Yesica's. But I'd worked hard to make it feel like a home for my mother.

And I was going to do whatever it took to keep it that way.

Later, after my mom had gone to her room to lie down and rest, I couldn't help but wonder how hard it must have been for her to constantly be afraid of the past repeating itself. I'd always considered her to be a strong woman. Even after my father died, she showed a brave face to us kids. Yes, she was devastated. But it was as if she knew she had to put her grief aside in order for our family to survive without him.

It killed me to see her so broken and afraid over something that had happened so many years ago.

It made me think of Lucas and his message on Facebook. I hadn't opened it, but I also hadn't deleted it. I was both afraid to read it and curious.

I grabbed my laptop from the kitchen table and took it up to my bedroom. Nerves twisted my stomach into knots, and it took me a few minutes to remember my account log-in information. When I finally did, his message appeared right away. I took a deep breath and clicked on it:

> Hi Ana,
>
> I hope it's OK that I'm messaging you like this. After I ran into you at the market, I couldn't stop kicking myself for not asking for your email or phone number. I was glad to find you on Facebook. Anyway, I would love to meet you for coffee so we can catch up. I know it's been a long time, but I'm hoping it's been enough time. Does that make sense? LOL. And if it's not and you'd rather I never contact you again, I will understand. I hope you're well. Take care, Lucas.

I reread his message three more times. Had enough time passed to put what had happened all those years ago behind us? Or was I going to be like my mother and hold on to things just on the off chance history repeated itself?

CHAPTER TWELVE
YESICA

When a spouse dies, most people wonder if they'll come back to visit them as a ghost.

I would bet, however, that most people don't expect the ghosts to be the people who are still living.

That was my thought as I called my mother-in-law yet again that Saturday morning. It had been over a month since the last time she'd answered one of my calls. Not that she was the one who I really wanted to talk to anyway. But my father-in-law had been on my mind, and I couldn't shake the feeling that I needed to go for a visit to see Henry.

After the fourth ring, I was just about to hang up when I heard her answer.

"Hello, Yesica," she said. Her tone indifferent, almost bored sounding.

"Oh, hello, Celeste. I'm so glad I caught you. How are you? How is Henry?"

"We're fine, thank you. How can I help you?"

I bristled at her question. She was acting as if I was a stranger who'd asked to see the store manager. Not the woman her son had been married to for almost eight years.

"Well, I figured it's about time I came for a visit. How about tomorrow?"

"Oh no, that won't work. We're going to a brunch with some friends after church."

"Okay, I could come Monday then. Is morning or afternoon better?"

"Monday? Won't you be working?"

No way was I going to tell her about my leave. "I have the day off. So let's do Monday."

She sighed. "We can't do Monday either. I have some appointments I must get to. How about this? How about I call you next week, and we can go through our calendars?"

"That's what you said last month." I tried to rein in my irritation. Profanity might make me feel better, but it wouldn't get me closer to seeing Henry.

"Did I?" she said; the fake innocence in her tone was one I was familiar with. As usual, it raked down my back like a set of cat claws and made me actually wince. "I can't help it if we're busy people, dear."

I counted to five before responding. "Of course you can't."

And I can't help it if you're a miserable old woman I've grown to hate over the years.

The first time I'd met Celeste, I knew immediately she didn't like me. Jason, who also grew up in California, had invited me to spend his birthday weekend with him at his parents' house in Calabasas. By then we'd been dating for six months, and I knew our relationship was getting serious. To his credit, he'd warned me about his mother in advance.

"She can seem a bit standoffish, but she's like that with new people, so don't take it personally," he'd said.

It turned out "standoffish" was just code for "rude."

After barely acknowledging my presence once we'd arrived, she turned to me to ask where my parents were from. I told her they were from Bell Gardens.

"Where is that? I've never even heard of it," she said.

"It's just outside Los Angeles," I said. It didn't matter that my answer was vague; I could tell from her nonexpression that she couldn't have cared less.

Later, when we all sat down for dinner, she said, "I'm sorry we don't have salsa for you, Yesica. I know you people like your food spicy."

And that's when I knew she wasn't just rude; she was racist too.

And the only reason I didn't walk out the door right then and there was because of Henry. He'd welcomed me into their home with open arms—literally.

"Can I give you a hug? I'm a hugger," he'd said after Jason introduced me. From that moment on, Henry went out of his way to be warm and kind. After that very uncomfortable first dinner, it was Henry who pulled me into his library to show me his collection of trains and confessed that if he could do it over again, he'd become a conductor instead of a lawyer. In return, I'd shared how I'd once dreamed of being a lifeguard so I could spend my days hanging out at the beach. That had made him laugh.

Then, out of the blue, he told me, "I like you, Yesica. I hope you'll be around for a long time."

That was the reason why I'd told Henry and not Celeste when Jason died. She had answered the phone, and I asked to speak to my father-in-law. That wasn't unusual. I called to chat with him almost as much as Jason did. And since she didn't like talking to me anyway, she'd gladly yelled for him to come to the phone. It broke my heart to tell him the bad news. But I wanted him to hear it from me first. Celeste took the phone away once Henry had started crying and demanded to know what I'd said to him. And that's when I'd told her that her only child was gone.

Of course, our relationship only became more strained after that. Celeste hated the fact that since I had been his wife, I was in control of what happened after. She questioned every decision I made for Jason's funeral. Although she'd offered to help pay for the service, I declined because I knew what accepting her money would mean. Jason and I had actually talked about what our final wishes would be, and he was adamant that he didn't want a Catholic funeral. It wasn't that we were atheists. We just weren't religious.

At first, Celeste was horrified when I told her I was only going to plan a simple service at the mortuary. On the day of the funeral, she and Henry showed up and sat next to me, and she behaved. I was relieved and a little bit impressed. But all of that went away when I learned from one of Jason's cousins that Celeste had held her own funeral Mass at her church in Calabasas for Jason the week before—just for her friends and close relatives. When people asked why I wasn't in attendance, she'd told everyone that I was not emotionally stable enough to go through two funerals.

I'd wanted to confront her right there and then, but Evie had talked me out of it. She reminded me it wouldn't change anything. And while it might have made me feel better for a few seconds, I probably would've ended up regretting it immediately after.

So, I kept my mouth shut and swore I'd never talk to her again unless I absolutely had to.

I'd heard from that same cousin a few months ago that Henry had been having more episodes of confusion. Doctors first thought it was an infection, but when tests didn't back it up, they told Celeste he was just grieving. Then he had a seizure that landed him in the hospital, and that's when the cousin had called me. She said Celeste had told the family not to visit and that she would update them herself. But I didn't listen. I showed up the next day and had a nice conversation with him until she came into the room and demanded I leave.

I had promised Henry I would see him again. And I was determined to keep that promise.

Even if that meant calling Celeste every day for the rest of my life.

I hung up after agreeing to call next week—knowing full well she wouldn't answer for another few more weeks.

My anger was seething and burning me from the inside out. I jumped out of bed, looking for something to punch or throw.

Stay away from the windows, Yesica.

Desperate for an outlet for this fury, I considered going for a run or to my gym. Then I checked the time on my phone. I still had time. I honestly hadn't planned on showing up to the grief support meeting. I'd woken up feeling lazy and only wanted to stay in bed for another hour. I'd even decided already that I'd tell Damien I had a migraine if it somehow got back to him that I hadn't shown up. But then my thoughts had drifted to Henry, and that's what had made me call Celeste.

Of course a conversation with her would drive me to seek therapy for the day.

Thirty minutes later, I arrived at the church hall. I was a little late, and there were still a few empty chairs in the circle. Introductions had already been made, and it seemed like the group was discussing journaling.

As I sat down, I couldn't help but look at Oscar. He acknowledged my arrival with a quick nod and then went back to listening to the person who was talking about what she'd written that morning.

After the discussion portion of the meeting ended, Oscar opened it up to individual sharing.

I was the first one to raise my hand.

"Yesica?" he questioned.

"Something happened today that brought up these feelings I've been having about how to deal with the fact that there are people who no longer want to be in your life because someone else died. And I'm not talking about the ones who are just uncomfortable because they don't know what to say or do around you anymore. I'm talking about the people who have decided that their relationship or friendship with you was only tied to the life of your significant other. What kind of shit is that?"

Soft murmurs floated around the circle. I wasn't sure if the others were agreeing with me, but it still gave me the push to continue. "For example, ever since my husband passed away, it's as if I've become invisible to not just certain people in his family, but also to friends that I thought were my friends too. I mean, sure, we did couple things together, but I really thought they were my friends just as much as they were my husband's. And, yes, I already knew my mother-in-law wasn't my biggest fan, but it's still like she's decided that my marriage never existed. I know I should just cut these people off and walk away. But at the same time, part of me wants to ask them why. It's not my fucking fault my husband died. So why am I the one who's constantly being punished?"

"Exactly!" a woman two chairs down from me shouted.

The rest of the room was silent for a few seconds. I hadn't meant to raise my voice or be so candid. I guess the call with Celeste had affected me more than I thought. My face burned with embarrassment, and I contemplated running out without saying another word.

But then Oscar stood up.

"When my sister died, a mutual friend stopped coming around to the house. And when I'd reach out to invite him to things, he always had an excuse. One day I ran into him and kind of joked that it seemed he was purposefully trying to avoid me. I was shocked when he admitted that he felt as if he was betraying my sister by continuing to be my friend, since he was hers first. I didn't understand it, but for my own grieving process, I had to accept it. Just like we don't want other people dictating how we grieve, I think we need to do the same for them. It could be as simple as the relationship you had with them wasn't at all what you thought it was. And it sucks, but it won't do any good to hold on to them. For your own sake."

What Oscar said made sense. I knew that. But it still bothered me. At least I wasn't fuming anymore.

Oh God. Had talking about my feelings with strangers actually helped?

The meeting ended about forty-five minutes later. Rather than try to race toward the exit this time, though, I lingered and watched as Oscar chatted with a couple of people. I told myself I'd only wait ten minutes. But the longer I waited, the less urgent it seemed for me to talk to him. So after only five minutes, I stood up, grabbed my purse, and decided to go home.

"Yesica, wait."

I turned and saw Oscar hold up his hand toward me. I nodded and sat back down. He joined me about five more minutes later.

"Thanks for waiting," he said, taking a seat. I nodded, suddenly not sure why I had.

Oscar continued: "I just wanted to say how much I appreciate you sharing today. I hope it helped?"

"A little," I admitted with a shrug. "But I didn't mean to sound so . . ."

"Angry?"

"Bitchy."

He laughed. "You didn't. And for what it's worth, I saw a lot of others nodding when you were talking, so what you said definitely resonated for some of them. You don't have to apologize for expressing your emotions here. That's kind of the point."

"What do you mean?"

"Well, it's like I mentioned earlier. Sometimes it seems like there's this belief that if we don't talk about our grief in public, then we must be doing okay. And eventually that's exactly what we want others to think, so we start to censor ourselves and not express every emotion."

It's what I had been doing at the office. I had been so concerned about portraying myself as being in control and nonemotional that I hadn't really allowed myself to deal with everything. I threw myself into work because the alternative was facing what I'd been trying to hide about Jason's death.

"And then you explode," I offered.

Oscar nodded. "And then you explode. Did Damien ever tell you how I ended up going to these meetings after my sister died?"

"No, he didn't."

He waved at a couple walking past us before continuing. "Melissa— my sister—was my best friend. She was much younger than me, but we did everything together. She had the best sense of humor and could always make me laugh, even when I was determined not to. So when she was gone, I kind of spiraled. It was almost as if I had all this emotional pain trapped inside me, and the only way I knew how to get it out was to hurt myself physically. I got into fights, I hit walls, and then one day I got in my car and decided I was going to go as fast as I could and see what happened. I don't think I really wanted to die—I just wanted to be in so much pain on the outside that it would make me forget about the pain inside."

I winced at his admission. My heart broke for Oscar and his family. "I'm so sorry."

"Well, I got what I wanted it. But that was enough to scare the people around me, and after I got out of the hospital, they sat me down and begged me to get help. And I was exactly like you—I told them I didn't need therapy, and I didn't need to talk about my feelings. But I agreed only because of my mom. She told me she couldn't bear to bury another child, and she knew that if I continued down the destructive path I was on, I would probably be dead within the year."

The gravity of his words struck me. Throwing my phone had landed me here—but I couldn't imagine being so destructive that it scared your family. It was true how grief affected people differently. It made me want to know more about Oscar's path.

"So you really think this group saved your life?"

He shrugged. "It helped. I also did some other things, like quitting an office job I hated and going to work for my dad at his construction company. Hitting things with a hammer really helped with my anger issues."

I thought about the second of relief I'd felt after chucking my phone. "I can see that. Maybe I need to buy myself a hammer and start a home improvement project or something," I said jokingly. "Seriously, though, I can see now how talking about what you're feeling instead of

When We Were Widows

holding it in can help. The fact that no one here knows me did make it easier to share."

He nodded, and then it was as if a thought came to him. "What are you doing this Thursday? If you're free, I know a place that offers a different kind of therapy. You don't even have to talk."

I hesitated before answering. Was he asking me out on a date? No, he said "therapy." Of course it wasn't going to be a date.

"I'm not sure what kind of place this could be, but I admit I'm curious. Let's go."

As I drove back home, I wondered if I'd made a mistake by agreeing to spend time with Oscar outside of group. Maybe if we hadn't met the way we did, I would've felt differently. It was hard to set up boundaries after you'd kind of crossed them already.

Before I could continue my second-guessing, though, a call came through my car's speaker. It was my brother, Alejandro.

"Hey there," I said after accepting the call.

"Hey there," he said. "Are you in your car?"

I laughed. "Why do you always ask me that when you call?"

"Because you tend to always answer my calls when you're in the car. You've always been a good multitasker."

"Thanks, I guess?" I replied, making sure to exaggerate my sarcasm. Alejandro might have been younger than me by three years, but he liked to act like he was the oldest—which included pretending to give me a hard time. As much as I sometimes got annoyed, I missed his teasing and the joking. I missed him. Maybe it was time to finally go visit him in Colorado.

He laughed. "You're welcome. Anyway, I'm calling you instead of replying to the text you sent last night about the repairs for the house. What is it that you're worried about exactly?"

The conversation with my mom the night before about the status of the repairs had me concerned. "I'm worried that Mom might be over her head with all of this. I ask her questions about costs and deadlines, and she just tells me not to worry about it."

In fact, the reason I'd texted my brother in the first place was because I'd offered to go with her the next time she met with the contractor, and she'd accused me of treating her like a child.

"If she's saying not to worry, then why are you worrying?" he asked.

I rolled my eyes as I turned onto my street. Of course Alejandro would take my mother's side. He always did.

"Why aren't you more worried about it? How do we know this contractor isn't trying to cheat her, or maybe she's not understanding everything he's saying. I just don't want her thinking everything is fine and then get hit with having to spend more money or have to deal with delays."

Alejandro said, "Ah, now I understand. You're worried she and Mama Melda are going to have to stay with you longer than you'd planned."

I had just pulled into my driveway and stopped the car but didn't open the garage. I didn't want to chance my mother overhearing the conversation—especially after what my brother had just accused me of.

"That's not true," I said defensively. "And it's also not fair. I've always said they're both welcome to stay as long as they need or want to. This has nothing to do with me wanting to kick them out. God, give me some credit at least."

My brother's assumption had hit a nerve. Maybe I hadn't been overly excited about my mother and grandmother living with me—but that didn't mean I was trying to find a way to make them leave.

"Fine. But why can't you give Mom some credit too?"

"What do you mean?"

"She's not helpless, Yesica. Despite what you and Dad used to think, she's pretty capable of taking care of herself. Hell, I'd say she's done a pretty great job of taking care of all of us."

Alejandro's words surprised me. I didn't understand where they were coming from. "What on earth are you talking about? And what does Dad have to do with this?"

I heard a long sigh on the other end of the line. "Look, I didn't mean for it to come out the way it sounded. And I really don't want to turn this into a fight. It's just that you're doing what he always did—he always assumed she wasn't capable of understanding even the smallest of tasks. Remember that time the dishwasher broke, and he didn't believe her that Gene said it couldn't be fixed? He had to go over to Gene's house after dinner and hear it for himself. Or that time she took you to open your own savings account at the bank, but then you wouldn't turn in the paperwork until Dad read it and told you it was okay to sign?"

I remembered. But it wasn't because I didn't think my mom didn't know how to open a bank account. The truth was my Dad was supposed to have been the one to take me that day, but he ended up having to work. It was silly, but I just had it in my head that I wanted him to still help me do it.

But I didn't tell Alejandro that. "So?" I asked instead. "I was just being cautious. Just like I'm being cautious now."

"All I'm saying is that, instead of automatically assuming she doesn't know what she's doing, how about you trust that she has it handled?"

"Okay," I told my brother, although I still wasn't convinced my concerns weren't valid. But I didn't feel like going back and forth with him. "And I gotta go. I just got home."

"Fine, I'll let you go," he said. "Don't be mad at me for the rest of the day, though, okay?"

I had to laugh. He really did know me so well.

"No promises," I replied. "Love you. Bye."

I opened the garage door and drove my car inside. But I didn't get out right away. Instead, I sat there thinking about what my brother had said about my dad. It was true that he'd definitely ruled our household. But wasn't that how it was in most Latino families? Of course, I knew now it was an old-school way of thinking. When Jason and I got engaged, I made it clear that we needed to be equal partners in our marriage. I was never going to give up my career or my independence.

In other words, I was never going to be the kind of wife my mother had been. And he agreed.

I had always assumed those things weren't as important to my mom. And she always seemed perfectly fine with letting my dad take charge. I just figured it was because he knew better.

So, why did my brother think that was a bad thing?

Alejandro's phone call, combined with my conversation with Celeste earlier, had taken its toll on my emotional stamina. I leaned back in my seat and closed my eyes. I had definitely hit my limit with peopling for the day.

And now I was supposed to go do more by attending my cousin's baby shower in a couple of hours?

The anxiety about having to go had been building for days—and it had nothing to do with how my morning had gone. And the more I thought about having to put on a happy face and make small talk with relatives I barely knew, the more my gut twisted.

I exhaled and inhaled and then did it again before my anxiety spun out of control. No, I wasn't going to go to the baby shower. My mom was going to be livid, but I couldn't think of that.

I'd just have to trust that she was capable of going to the party without me.

CHAPTER THIRTEEN
ANA

Babies were blessings.

I'd always believed that. For me, babies were a sign of hope and new beginnings. And I always welcomed the chance to celebrate the arrival of a new one.

Especially when it was going to be a new member of my family.

My niece Monse was expecting her first baby later this month, and we'd been invited to her baby shower at her house that afternoon. I was sitting in Yesica's den, happily wrapping the unisex clothes and other baby items I'd bought as a gift, when she walked into the kitchen from the garage door.

She'd left before nine to go wherever it was she went on Saturday mornings, so I was pleased she'd made it home on time.

"You might want to jump in the shower now," I called over to her. "I think we should probably leave here by twelve thirty. I can't believe street traffic in LA is now just as bad as freeway traffic. We're only going to Hollywood, but it just takes so long to get there. Plus, you know there's never ever any parking on Monse's street. If anything, you're probably going to have to drop me and Grandma off first and then go park in that Smart & Final lot around the corner."

"Um, I don't think I'm going to go after all. Just take my card for her with you," she said from the kitchen.

Normally, I wouldn't have tried changing her mind. I had accepted years ago not to expect Yesica to attend every family party. But not this time.

I stopped wrapping. "Why?" I asked. "Yesterday, you said you were going and offered to drive us."

"I know. But I guess I just don't feel like it today. It's not a big deal. I'll call Monse next week or go see her after the baby is born."

It bothered me that she didn't think the baby shower was a big deal. I stood up from the couch and walked over to her. She had just pulled a yogurt out of the fridge.

"You RSVP'd. Monse is expecting you to be there."

"It's just a silly party, Mom," she said with her mouth full of yogurt. "I'm sorry I'm not in the mood to play games like guessing how big around Monse's stomach is with sheets of toilet paper."

Familiar irritation knotted my stomach. Truth was, I had been looking forward to spending the day with her. Ever since we'd moved in, we hadn't done anything together outside the house, other than that dinner at her boss's home.

"Are you not feeling well?" I asked. My maternal instinct told me there had to be something else going on with her.

"No, I'm fine. I just don't feel like going anywhere today."

"You went somewhere this morning," I argued, my frustration growing at the fact that whatever it was she did earlier seemed to be more important than spending time with her family.

"I mean, I don't feel like going to the baby shower. Okay?"

It wasn't okay. Not by a long shot. This was one argument Yesica wasn't going to win. Although I hated it, I knew I had to bring out the big guns if I wanted to convince her to go to the baby shower.

"This baby is going to be Mama Melda's first great-grandchild," I said as sternly as I could. "It's important to her and to my sister that the family be all together today to celebrate. So if you have a better reason as to why you're not going besides you don't *feel like it*, then go tell your grandmother what that reason is right now."

Yesica's eyes grew big and dark with emotion. Almost as if I'd struck her. For a second, I thought she would either scream at me or burst into tears. That's when it occurred to me—the reason why she didn't want to go.

Most of our family was going to be at the baby shower. My sister Claudia—Monse's mother—had driven down from Fresno just for the occasion. The last time I'd seen her—the last time I'd seen most of the relatives who were going—was at Jason's funeral.

Of course it would be hard for my daughter to face everyone again.

Guilt sank my heart, and I immediately took a step closer to pull her into my arms. But as quickly as it had appeared, the pain I'd seen on her face moments earlier was gone.

"Fine," she said, squaring her shoulders. "I'll go." Then she threw her spoon in the sink, tossed the yogurt container in the trash, and walked out of the kitchen.

CHAPTER FOURTEEN
YESICA

As I expected, the baby shower was cuteness overload.

Every decoration was either a pale or bright yellow to match the "You are our sunshine" theme. Blegh.

It wasn't that I hated babies or baby showers. I just had had limited exposure to both. And I had very good reasons for not wanting to be at this shower in particular. Reasons I wasn't ready to tell my mom or my grandma or the rest of my relatives.

So I'd shut my mouth and showed up to welcome the newest member of our family.

Even in my grumpiness, though, I had to admit my cousin Monse looked absolutely beautiful in her yellow dress with white polka dots and perfectly rounded belly.

"I'm so glad you came," she squealed after seeing me walk through her backyard gate.

"Of course. I wouldn't miss it for the world," I told her as I gave her a hug. Unexpected emotion choked me, and I swallowed it down before she could see it on my face. But then I noticed she looked like she was holding back tears too.

"Stop it, chillona," I told her. "This is your baby shower. You're supposed to be disgustingly happy."

Monse smiled and nodded. She rubbed her eyes with the back of her hands. "Don't mind me. It's the hormones. It seems like I'm crying about something all the time now."

"Well, get used to it. I hear motherhood is no joke." I had meant it as a tease, but it had come out more bitter than I had intended. Luckily, my tone seemed to go over Monse's head, and she turned to give my mom and grandma their welcome hugs next.

I was happy for my cousin. I really was. Her dream was coming true.

When we were little girls and playing with our dolls, Monse would say she couldn't wait to be a mom for real because she loved babies so much.

"Well then, if I ever have kids, I'll bring them to your house to babysit them so I can go to work," I used to tell her. Even back then, it was hard for me to imagine having children of my own. Maybe it was God's way of preparing me.

"Mija, I think you're having a boy," Mama Melda said now and patted the top part of Monse's belly. "You're carrying him very high."

"She's having a girl," my mother insisted. "Claudia told me this morning over the phone that she'd swung her ring over Monse's stomach, and it went back and forth, not side to side. That means it's a girl."

I rolled my eyes. "The ring thing is an old wives' tale, Mom. It doesn't prove anything."

Monse laughed. "The only thing I know for sure about this baby is that he or she is going to have lots of hair, because my heartburn has been out of control."

Another old wives' tale? I thought my cousin didn't believe in such things. I shook my head at her in disappointment.

"By the way, where *is* your mom?" my mom asked.

"Oh, she's inside helping my dad and Mathew get the trays of fruit and vegetables ready to bring outside. I'll tell her to come out and see you. In the meantime, help yourself to drinks over there in the ice chests by the barbecue area—there's bottles of water, sodas, Coronas, and Modelos. We'll be serving the food soon. Sit wherever you want."

We handed her our gifts, and then she disappeared inside her house, and we were left to make the rounds and say hello to everyone.

Just then, a trumpet blared from just beyond the gate, and an ensemble of seven mariachi musicians strolled into the backyard playing a song I recognized.

Mama Melda let out a grito. Then yelped in delight, "Mariachis!"

I couldn't help but laugh. "Is this a baby shower or a wedding reception?" I asked my mom as my attention turned from the musical group to the rest of the party setup.

A huge white tent took up most of the grass area. Inside, alternating panels of yellow and white fabric draped across the ceiling and sides. Round tables covered in yellow-checkered tablecloths and surrounded by white chairs had been set up under the tent. I estimated at least ten tables of eight in all. And each was adorned with a lovely arrangement of sunflowers and white daisies inside a white watering can.

A photo backdrop sat off to the side. There were two white wooden arched panels next to a six-foot wall covered in plastic greenery and a neon-yellow sign that read YOU ARE OUR SUNSHINE.

In a way, it was true. Monse had lucked out that the gray skies from this morning had cleared. And even though the temperature was probably still in the high sixties, the sun shone big and bright just in time for her party.

"Claudia said Monse and Mathew went all out for this shower," my mom shared.

"They sure did," I mumbled.

It took us about fifteen minutes to go around the tent and say hello to our relatives. Then my tía Claudia found us and led us to a table toward the front of the tent so we could sit with her and Tío Ricky.

Mama Melda asked me for a pen after pulling out a random piece of paper from her purse as soon as she sat down.

"What are you writing down?" I said as I gave her one of the ones already scattered in the middle of the table.

"The songs I want the mariachis to play," she explained.

"Mama, remember we're paying *them* to sing, not you," Tía Claudia said.

Mama Melda rolled her eyes at her daughter and then went back to her list. My mom and I looked at each other and laughed because we both knew Tía Claudia's warning wasn't going to deter my grandma. Mama Melda had never met a mariachi band she didn't want to perform with. It usually started with handing them a list of her favorite songs; then she'd sing along from her seat. Eventually, one of the singers would be so entertained that they'd invite her to sing a song all on her own.

"What are we eating?" Mama Melda asked a minute or two later. "Please don't tell me it's one of those long sandwiches. The pieces get too soggy."

Tía Claudia put her hands on her hips. "Mama, that was one time and like seven years ago. You'll be happy to know there's a taco man."

"Tienen al pastor?" she asked.

"Carne asada, pollo, and, yes, al pastor."

Mama Melda clapped with joy. Pork marinated in spices, chiles, onions, and pineapple slices and freshly sliced off a hot rotating trompo was one of her most favorite foods in the world. She asked me when she'd first moved in with me if I knew of food trucks nearby that sold al pastor tacos. Luckily, we'd found one the other day in Venice, and she'd already been asking me to take her back. Hopefully, this would satiate her craving for now.

Besides the tacos and the usual toppings of cilantro, chopped onions, marinated carrots, and salsas, Tía Claudia said the taco man was also providing rice, beans, and aguas frescas like Jamaica and horchata.

"And I made my potato salad and macaroni salad. Monse's suegra made a green salad," she said. Then she bent down between me and Mama Melda and said in a hushed voice, "The poor woman can't cook to save her life."

Since I knew my tía Claudia, it was more likely that Monse's mother-in-law did in fact know how to cook, but my tía didn't like her cooking. Still, I nodded as if I believed her.

My phone dinged with a text, and I couldn't help but smile at seeing Oscar's name.

How about five on Thursday?

Sounds good, I texted back.

I'll send you the address later this week.

No hints then?

Nope.

I don't like surprises.

I think you'll like this.

Confident much?

Always.

That made me laugh.

"What's so funny?" my mom asked, craning her neck to look at my screen.

I turned over my phone. "Inside joke," I said, not offering that it was Oscar who had made me laugh. I wasn't about to answer a million questions about why the man from dinner at Damien's was texting me. Especially since I still hadn't told her about my Saturday grief support meetings. Part of it was the fear of her or Mama Melda sharing with other relatives and then my having to worry about facing them at the next family function. Not everyone believed in therapy—I knew for a fact there were some tíos, tías, and even cousins who believed there was no such thing as depression or rolled their eyes at the subject of mental health. Going to therapy—to them—was a sign of weakness. Even though I was starting to see how the group was helping me, I wasn't ready to advertise just how messed up Jason's death had made me. Luckily, my mom didn't question where I had gone earlier. But I had a feeling that wasn't always going to be the case.

Wait. Did that mean I had already subconsciously decided to keep going to the meetings?

Before I could answer my own question, Tía Claudia let us know the food was ready. As we got in line to serve ourselves, the aromas of the cooked meats and corn tortillas warming on the portable cooktop had me salivating. I hadn't realized how hungry I was. I filled up my plate with everything and grabbed a Modelo beer from one of the numerous ice chests. The mariachis continued to play as the crowd's conversation grew more lively and animated.

I had to admit it was turning out to be a nice afternoon.

Until it was time for the games.

First it was a quiz of sorts, with different baby-related words jumbled, and the goal was to decipher as many of the words as you could. I didn't want to play, so I told Mama Melda I'd help her with her sheet, but even she grew tired of it after just solving four of the twelve.

The next game was the toilet paper game, and I enjoyed glaring at my mother as I pulled my sheets from the roll being passed around. She just shrugged and smiled.

I almost considered participating in the contest where you had to drink beer from a baby bottle. But since I was driving, I thought better of it. Plus, I hadn't chugged a beer since college, and I didn't have a desperate urge to do it again in front of my grandma, mother, and other relatives.

The last game turned out not to be a game at all.

We all received a yellow index card and were told to use our pens from the first game.

My cousin and her husband stood up and walked to the front of the tent. "Before we cut the cake and open the dessert bar, Mathew and I just wanted to thank all of you for coming today. It means so much to see all of the people we love and now who get to love our baby. It may be corny, but I really do believe the saying that it takes a village to raise a child. You are our village. So, we know we're going to have to lean on you at times for support and advice as we navigate being new parents. We ask that each of you write down a piece of advice for us on those cards. Even if you aren't parents, share something your own mom or dad did that you think is important for us to know. When you're done, place the cards in the white basket we've set up by the gift table. No rush. Take your time. And we promise to read every single one once the baby is born. Thank you again. We love you all. Now let's eat some cake!"

I stared at the blank card for several minutes, unsure of what I was supposed to do with it, even though Monse had just told us what to do with it. I wasn't a mom and, most likely, would never be a mom. What qualified me to be giving her advice?

"I need to go to the bathroom," I mumbled and got up from the table.

Once inside, I made my way to Monse's guest bathroom on the first floor. But there were two women I didn't know waiting outside the closed door. Rather than stand there with them and make awkward eye contact or small talk, I decided to go upstairs and use another one. But that door was locked and closed too.

Just then Tía Claudia walked out of Monse and Mathew's bedroom and told me I could use the Jack and Jill bathroom in there. A few minutes later, I'd washed my hands and checked my makeup. I thought about hiding out upstairs until the end of the shower but knew I'd have to show my face soon. And leaving early was out of the question. My mom and Mama Melda had already said they wanted to stay to see Monse open her gifts. And judging by the multiple towers of presents

I'd seen, there was a good chance we weren't going to be leaving for another couple of hours.

Deciding it was time to head back, I reached for the doorknob and heard voices I didn't recognize right away.

"Which box did she say it was?" one woman asked.

"She said it was next to the nightstand," another voice said.

"I know, but there's like three here. Oh wait, I think it's this one."

"Yeah, that's it. Monse said it was the one with the tissue paper. There should be a smaller box inside that she wants to give to her abuelita."

I decided to open the door at that point, but I paused when one of the women said, "Did you see Monse's cousin came with her abuelita? I'm honestly surprised she showed up."

"Which cousin? I don't know all of Monse's family that well."

"Trust me, you know this cousin," the woman scoffed. "She's the rich, stuck-up one."

I rolled my eyes at the petty description of me and figured out who the voice belonged to. The woman had to be Monse's sister-in-law, Flora. She'd always acted standoffish with me, and it had gotten to the point where I'd stopped even acknowledging her when we were both in the same room. I'd tried hard to be friendly with her when we met for the first time at Monse's bridal shower a few years ago, but I gave up once it became clear she didn't like me. I'd even asked Monse if I'd done something to her unknowingly, but my cousin said Flora was a sweetheart, and maybe I'd misunderstood. I knew better, though. After working in the cutthroat corporate world for more than a decade, I'd developed a pretty good radar for detecting women who hated me or had it out for me. And Flora had set off every alarm. I put my hand on the doorknob again and prepared to walk out. I couldn't wait to see her expression when she realized I'd heard her talking about me.

But I froze when I heard the other voice ask, "Oh. Isn't she the one whose husband died?"

"That's her," Flora said.

"How sad. She's so young too. I can't even imagine. Does she have kids?"

"Nope. Monse always told me Yesica was one of those 'my career is my life' kind of women and never even talked about wanting to be a mother. Guess that turned out to be a good thing—at least for her anyway."

Suddenly, all the oxygen deflated from my lungs, as if someone had popped them with a sharp, painful pin. I grabbed the edge of the bathroom's counter in an attempt to steady my wobbly legs. I didn't know what was worse. The fact that Flora thought that me being a childless widow was somehow a positive or learning that my own cousin thought I only cared about my career.

As Flora and the other woman continued chatting about other people they'd seen at the party, I composed myself and found my breath again. But there was no way I was walking out there now. Luckily, the bathroom's other door was unlocked, and I sneaked out on the other side into the adjoining room.

I immediately knew the bedroom I'd walked into was the baby's nursery.

"Monse, you little liar, you," I whispered, kind of proud my cousin had been able to keep this big of a secret for so long.

The walls of the nursery were a blush pink, and a matching sheer canopy hung over the white wooden crib. The rest of the all-white furniture included a four-drawer dresser, a changing table, and a rocker with pink cushions. Above the dresser, in white wooden cursive letters, was the name *Isabella*.

It was a nursery worthy of a princess. It was perfect.

All the emotions I'd been fighting with since the minute I'd woken up that morning broke through, and I couldn't stop the torrent of sobs as they finally escaped. I sat in the rocker and held my face in my hands and just cried.

The emotional and physical pain I'd endured during my two-year journey with struggling to conceive came roaring back. The surgery, the fertility drug injections, the daily ultrasounds, and two rounds of in vitro fertilization had nearly broken me. And some days, like today, my mind failed to protect me from the visceral memories of one of the most traumatic times of my life.

Ever the overachiever, I still couldn't quite wrap my head around how I could have failed at achieving this one very important goal.

After all, there was one thing all the women in my family seemed to do well. And that was have babies. After I got married, it was always the topic of conversation whenever I'd see a female relative. Everyone always wanted to know when I was going to get pregnant. And as the years went by, I noticed that what had started out as playful curiosity turned into serious interrogation. Although no one ever said it out loud, I felt as if they thought I was somehow a bad daughter for taking so long to give my parents a grandchild.

It was the main reason why I never told anyone when Jason and I started trying.

When I didn't get pregnant right away, I was a little surprised. I naively figured that when I'd had my IUD removed, it would only be a matter of weeks before I'd see two little pink lines on a pregnancy test. But weeks turned into months, and still nothing. So I did what I always did. I researched and then researched some more. I tracked every cycle, regularly checked my basal body temperature, and invested in a bulk supply of ovulation strips in order to make it happen. Six months later, my womb remained empty. I walked into my gynecologist's office completely perplexed.

"I don't understand," I'd told her. "I eat healthy, I exercise, I only drink occasionally, and I've never done any drugs. So why can't I get pregnant?"

Dr. Asher agreed to refer me to a fertility specialist, who ended up running all sorts of tests on me and Jason. The answer to our inability to conceive was that there was no real answer. We were diagnosed with unexplained infertility. The good news was we had lots of treatment options to try—meaning we had hope. But it didn't last. That's when we decided to try IVF.

To say IVF was a nightmare was an understatement. It was excruciatingly tedious. Between the ultrasounds and multiple injections, my life was no longer my own. Every spare minute of every day was dictated by what I could or couldn't do because of the IVF. I became obsessed with trying whatever I could to boost my chances to make sure the treatment was successful. Teas, supplements, acupuncture—even cupping. If I heard or read about something that had worked for someone else, I did it.

The egg-retrieval process was probably the worst part of it all. I was constantly anxious and stressed while waiting to find out if any eggs had successfully fertilized.

It was ironic that Jason and I had decided to have a baby in order to save our marriage. Yet, the journey itself threatened to kill it for good.

After two years of trying and one successful embryo transfer, we finally got pregnant. I couldn't describe the euphoria I'd felt at seeing that positive pregnancy test for the first time. I ended up taking three more just to be sure. Jason was just as thrilled as I was, of course.

Although we both knew it was way too soon to share the news, we allowed ourselves one small act of celebrating. We cleaned out the room we'd been using as a shared office and agreed it would be the nursery. I refused to decorate it or move in any furniture, though. I told Jason we had to leave it empty until my last trimester.

He agreed except for one thing—the beloved red vintage Lionel caboose his dad had given him as a little boy.

Six weeks after he'd placed the caboose on one of the room's built-in shelves, I miscarried.

It was horrible. Mainly because no one knew what we were going through. We hadn't told anyone about our struggles to conceive. I didn't even tell Damien when I was going through IVF. All he knew was that I was getting treatments for a female-specific issue. But one morning after Jason couldn't calm my sobs, he begged me to let him call my mom.

For the first time in a long time, seeing my mom was exactly what I had needed. So he called and lied and said I'd had an ovarian cyst rupture and was in a lot of pain. She was at my bedside within two hours with an entire arsenal of herbs, teas, medications, and a big tube of Vitacilina: her go-to cure-all for every physical ailment out there. She stayed with me while Jason went to the office, nursing me back to health with her homemade albóndigas soup and comforting presence. My mom left sometime later that night after Jason came home and I'd finally fallen asleep. She'd called to check on me the next day and never asked me for any details about what had happened. And I never told her.

Weeks went by, and my mind and body began to heal. But I wasn't ready to start the process all over again. I wasn't sure if I could take another long, expensive ride on the emotional roller coaster of infertility. When Jason told me he wasn't sure he wanted to keep trying, either, part of me was devastated.

Somehow, deep down, I knew that us taking a break really meant that we were giving up. And we did. We gave up on trying to have a baby and, in some ways, gave up on our marriage too.

So I sat in the rocker in the perfect pink nursery and continued to cry for the both of us.

CHAPTER FIFTEEN
ANA

I was never good at sneaking around.

My Catholic guilt and fear of my mother made me sick to my stomach whenever I lied about where I was going or who I was meeting. Because it would be my bad luck that I'd get in an accident or murdered, and that's how my mother would find out I had lied to her. If I survived such trauma, then she would certainly use it against me for the rest of her life or mine.

So I'd tossed and turned all night, trying to decide what I was going to tell my mother instead of telling her the truth. Which was that I was going to meet Lucas Padilla for coffee.

The irony wasn't lost on me that I was basically sneaking out to go meet him just like I had when I was a teenager.

It turned out my sleepless night was for nothing. I had forgotten that Yesica had promised to take my mom to her hairstylist, and they planned on being gone all morning. I decided I'd stop at some of the shops near the café just so I could say I'd been shopping if either of them asked me what I'd done while they were out.

But I knew that still wouldn't cleanse me of all my guilt. After all, I was still voluntarily meeting with the son of Cuca Padilla.

It took me three tries before I finally worked up the courage to go inside the coffee shop. I'd already told myself I would only wait five minutes for him before leaving.

But as I walked toward the counter to order myself a cappuccino, I heard my name called.

It was Lucas, and he was already seated at a table in the back of the café. It was too late to turn around and run back to my car.

"Hey," I said with a small wave. Then I pointed at the counter to let him know I was going to order my drink.

I stayed near the counter as I waited for my name to be called. I needed the extra minutes to calm my nerves and ignore the feeling that I was about to open a door I should've left locked.

I was eighteen when I told him I didn't want to be his friend anymore. I used our mothers as the excuse, even though that hadn't stopped me from sneaking out to spend time with him before then. The truth was he'd broken my heart without even knowing it.

Because at some point in our friendship, I'd begun to see him as more than a friend.

He was absolutely clueless and seemed content to keep our relationship the same. That all changed when it was time to buy tickets for our senior prom. Lucas had mentioned us going as friends, which made me panic. A night out with him at a dance with both of us dressed up? I was afraid I wouldn't be able to control my emotions, and he'd see how desperately in love with him I'd fallen. So I did what I always did—I pretended not to care about the dance and told him I didn't want to go. I told him that if he really wanted to go, then he should take someone else.

A week later, he told me he was taking Lucy Fremont from his biology class. That wasn't the worst of it, though. He confessed that he'd actually been dating Lucy for a month but had been afraid to tell me. That, in fact, he was relieved when I'd turned him down because he really wanted to take Lucy.

"I only asked you because I didn't think anyone else was going to."

That sentence not only ripped out my heart, but it destroyed whatever feelings I'd had for Lucas Padilla. And to get him back, I asked my friend's brother to go with me to the dance, just to prove to Lucas that I wasn't as pitiful as he'd thought.

The friend's brother was Benny. And Yesica was conceived on the night of my senior prom.

Of course I never regretted having my children. But I have to admit there were moments over the years where I wondered how different my life would have been if I'd confessed my feelings to Lucas or had just gone with him to prom.

It didn't matter, though. Too much time had passed. I wasn't the same shy teenager who used to write love poems about him in my diary. Whatever power he'd held over me back then was long gone. And I was grown enough to have one cup of coffee with him.

Wasn't I?

Carrying my cappuccino and new confidence, I joined Lucas at the table a few minutes later.

"Sorry I'm late," I said as I sat down.

He shrugged. "You're not late. I was early. I was worried if I made you wait even a minute, you'd leave."

I laughed. Maybe he still did know me just a little.

"Well, if I'm being honest, I thought about canceling a few times," I admitted.

Lucas nodded. "I was kind of surprised you didn't. It's been a long time, and I wasn't sure if you still felt the same way."

"What way?" I said carefully. My chest tightened with a building embarrassment. Was Lucas about to confess that he knew all along that I'd been in love with him back then?

"You know. The thing between our moms, and you not wanting to have anything to do with me because of it?"

Relief relaxed my shoulders. "Oh, that," I said with a laugh. "Well, my mother can hold on to a grudge like a raccoon with a cupcake. But I believe being angry takes up too much energy. Besides, I was a dumb teenager back then. What did I know? I like to think that I've grown wiser and more forgiving in my old age."

"You're not old. *We're* not old," he replied. "But it's still nice to hear. And I'm really glad I ran into you that day. I've often wondered about what you were up to these days. Are you still writing?"

My eyes widened in surprise. "You remember?"

"Of course. I used to love reading your short stories. Especially the ones about the girl who used to solve mysteries in her neighborhood. Those were really good."

My face couldn't help but transform into a smile as I remembered the collection of stories I'd written about junior detective Carlita Zapata. Lucas was the only person who'd ever read them. And the only reason I'd even let him was because he wrote short stories, too, and let me read his. His stories, though, were much better than mine. He'd even won some contests and had one story published in a magazine.

"Gosh, I haven't thought about those stories in years," I said after taking a sip of my coffee. "Anyway, it was just something fun to do back when I was a kid. I haven't written anything in a long time. Not like you, though, Mr. Author. I heard you had a book published?"

Truth was I hadn't really heard so much as actually saw it recommended to me on Amazon and bought it and read it in a day. But I decided he didn't need to know all that.

Lucas smiled, and the color of his cheeks deepened. Was he blushing?

"Yeah," he said with a nod. "I'm actually in the middle of writing my second one."

I couldn't help but be impressed. "Wow. That's great. Good for you. So when is the movie coming out?"

He laughed, and I think his face turned even more red. "Maybe one day. In the meantime, I'm just writing my next book and teaching others how to write."

"Really? You teach writing? Where?"

"At East LA City College mostly. I also do some online courses, and I'm about to start a creative writing class at the Learning Lab over here on Olympic. I was there for a meeting on the day I ran into you at the store. It's kind of funny. I almost didn't stop there because there's another Mexican market closer to my house. But something just told me to check it out. What are the odds that we were both in the same neighborhood on the same day after all these years?"

Someone else—probably my daughter—would've called it fate. I called it a coincidence.

"That is funny," I told him, even though I didn't think it was. "So it sounds like you're doing exactly what you always wanted to do. What about your family? Are you married, have kids?"

I was a little surprised by how much I really wanted to know.

"Uh, divorced. Two kids and one grandbaby."

"You're an abuelo?" I exclaimed in delight and awe. I would never have imagined teenage Lucas as a dad, let alone a grandparent.

He proudly pulled out his phone and showed me a photo of the chunkiest baby I'd ever seen. "His name is Noah, and he's almost seven months old now. My daughter and her husband live out in Temecula so I try to visit most weekends. He's growing up so fast. I don't want to miss any second."

Warmth spread across my chest, and I knew I was probably grinning from ear to ear. I was happy for Lucas. I really was.

"He's adorable. Congratulations."

Lucas put his phone away. "What about you? What have you been up to all these years?"

I shrugged. "Not much, really. I have two kids. Alejandro lives in Colorado and works as a physical therapist. Yesica, my daughter, lives here in Santa Monica, and she works for a firm that handles corporate mergers . . . I think?" I said with a laugh. "Every time she tells me what she does, it kind of goes over my head. But I'm proud of both of my kids."

"You should be proud of yourself, too, for raising them to be so successful," he said.

"I don't know about that."

We continued chatting and catching up on the friends we were still in contact with. Before I knew it, almost two hours had passed.

"Oh wow," I said after checking my watch. "I can't believe we've been here so long. I need to get going." Mom and Yesica would probably be done at the hair salon soon.

Maybe I was mistaken, but Lucas looked disappointed. "Of course. I didn't mean to take up so much of your morning," he said.

"Don't be silly. This was nice."

We both stood up at the same time. "Is it okay, uh, if we keep in touch?" he asked. "Maybe even grab lunch or dinner sometime?"

I stilled. I hadn't expected that Lucas would want to see me again. "Sure," I said, already telling myself I wasn't committing to anything.

"Great. I have your number and you have mine, so we don't have to do that whole Facebook Messenger thing again. I really hate Facebook."

That put me at ease. "Me too."

"Ana, I really enjoyed seeing you. I hope this means we can be friends again."

I didn't know what to say, so I just smiled and grabbed my purse, which had been hanging on my chair.

The thought that I'd just opened a door to something bigger than I'd planned for chased me out of the café as fast as my legs would take me.

I should've known then that you can't always outrun your past.

CHAPTER SIXTEEN
YESICA

I met Oscar the following Thursday evening at an industrial park off Jefferson Boulevard in Culver City. He didn't tell me exactly what we were doing. Instead, he'd only instructed me to wear long sleeves, pants, long socks, and closed-toe shoes for it.

"Should I be afraid?" I asked as he walked me toward one of the nondescript buildings next to the parking lot.

"You don't trust me?" he asked as if he was offended.

I wanted to tell him I didn't know him, so the jury was still out. Instead, I said, "It's just that you're being very mysterious about this, and I'm the type of person who needs details and plans."

"That must get tiring, trying to be in control of everything all the time. Now I'm absolutely sure this is going to be exactly what you need."

Maybe I didn't know him, but it sounded like he knew me. I was all about having control.

Oscar pointed to the door we were now standing in front of. My eyes grew big as I read the sign above it: **RAGE AND SMASH**.

I looked at him and noticed the huge smile on his face. "What is this place?"

"They have these private rooms, and you pay to go to town on pieces of junk like broken or outdated household items with a smash tool of your choice. Think of it as a grown-up way to throw a tantrum. It's a safe space to unleash your anger and destroy things without being judged or worrying about consequences."

I had heard about these rage rooms popping up all over Los Angeles, but I'd never visited one before. "You're serious?" I asked.

"I am. But this place does have other options, if you're not quite ready for the rage room. They also have an axe-throwing area or a splatter room, where you can throw paint on walls. Which one do—"

"I want to break things." I was surprised by my sudden urge to destroy. Oscar laughed and held open the door for me. "I knew you would."

A young guy sitting behind a counter greeted us as we walked inside the small nondescript lobby area. "Welcome to Rage and Smash. Do you have an appointment?"

"We do," Oscar answered as he walked up to the counter. "Ramos for two at five o'clock."

The employee typed up something on his laptop and confirmed the appointment. Then he handed Oscar two clipboards with pens. "Please fill out these safety waiver forms, and then we'll get you started."

A few minutes later, we both were done, and the guy led us to a back room and instructed us to put on the required safety gear, which included coverall jumpsuits as well as industrial gloves, goggles, face shields, and hard hats. I couldn't help but laugh at the sight of us.

"Are we going to go unleash some pent-up anger or clean up a hazmat spill?" I joked.

The employee handed us each a large crate and pointed at a tower of metal shelves stacked with various glassware and ceramic dishes, computer keyboards, rotary and flip phones, figurines, old appliances, Christmas ornaments, and even a couple of computer monitors. He told us to choose our unlucky targets.

Oscar, who said the experience was his treat, had paid for something called the "Anger Management" package, which bought us $150 worth of things to break, and we had thirty minutes to smash it all.

After filling our crates, we followed the young man into a windowless gray room with metal walls and a cement floor. It reminded me of some secret underground room where a serial killer might keep his victims.

"You can use anything on those shelves," the employee said, pointing to a wall of more metal shelves containing a variety of blunt-force weapons, such as metal and wooden bats, golf clubs, crowbars, and sledgehammers. "There's also a Bluetooth speaker inside that wire cabinet, and you're welcome to connect to your phone if you have a specific playlist you'd like to use."

"Wait. People actually make playlists to break things to?" I asked incredulously.

"All the time," he said with a shrug. Then he told us to have fun and said the timer started as soon as he closed the door.

Oscar took out his phone and walked over to the speaker. "How about some Metallica?" he asked.

"Perfect," I said as I walked toward the shelves to pick out my weapon of choice.

Head-banging music began to blare as I debated between the metal bat or a crowbar. I chose the bat, while Oscar picked up a sledgehammer.

"Nice," I said approvingly.

"I thought so," Oscar said. "All righty then. Shall we?"

"We shall," I said.

I grabbed a mug from my crate and set it up on one of the tables. As if I had the faintest idea of what it meant to hit a baseball, I positioned myself just a foot away from my target and raised the bat over my left shoulder. Of course, I missed the cup entirely on my first swing. My aim was as terrible as ever.

"Here," Oscar said, coming up behind me. He maneuvered my bat into position. "You want to stand with your feet a little bit apart. Then do a practice swing or two to make sure you know exactly where to hit. And make sure to use your whole body to swing, and follow through with your arms."

His proximity to me made my stomach flip. I hadn't been this close to him since the night we danced. Although his hands weren't on me,

I could feel the warmth of his body. I was sure my face must have been turning red as my heart rate sped up. It took everything I had to focus on the mug in front of me and not on the man behind me.

"Ready?" he whispered.

I nodded, clenched my jaw, inhaled, and swung.

Crack!

Shards of white flew in all directions as my bat made contact with the target.

I'm not normally a violent person. But the exhilaration coursing through my body in that moment the mug exploded was indescribable. I wanted to feel it again.

Oscar laughed and then went to the other side of the room to wreak havoc on an old computer keyboard. I picked a green glass vase for my next hit.

I got into the same position as he'd shown me. Then I closed my eyes and thought of the day Jason had died and what he'd confessed to me right before.

Dark pain erupted from deep within my gut, and my mouth filled with a sour taste that nearly made me nauseous. I let out a guttural yell as I swung the bat full throttle. Remnants of green glass sprayed against the wall like hail.

Next, I destroyed a small TV with all the force I could muster and jumped up and down in glee after obliterating a chipped black-and-white cow cookie jar.

I was definitely drunk on adrenaline.

Thirty minutes later, both of our crates were empty. Oscar had been kind enough to give me his last two items, and I happily obliterated them as well. When we finally walked out of Rage and Smash, I was sweaty and out of breath and feeling very satisfied. I hadn't smashed away all of my fury. But I came pretty damn close.

"That was amazing," I said as we arrived at my car.

"You were really into it," he said with a laugh. "I wouldn't be surprised if your arms are sore tomorrow."

"Oh, I am absolutely sure I will be sore tomorrow. But it will be worth it. I can't wait to come back."

In fact, I was already thinking of making an appointment for next week. Breaking things had just become my most favorite form of therapy.

"If you want, you could even bring in your own items," Oscar shared. "Sometimes they even have junk cars out in the back for people to hit."

"I don't know about bringing in my stuff, but trashing a car does sound like fun. I should bring my mom with me next time. She definitely has some tightly wound emotions she needs to get out of her system."

Something was definitely going on with her. She seemed more quiet than usual. I wasn't sure if she was hiding something or just mad. Either way, she hadn't been acting like herself. I had even asked Mama Melda if she'd noticed anything. But all she said was if my mother wanted us to know something, then we'd have to wait for her to tell us.

"Since when?" I'd said. "No one in this family shares anything unless someone else figures it out first or makes them say it. We're Latinas. We don't voluntarily talk about our feelings. Instead we hold it inside and carry grudges until we die."

Mama Melda just said she didn't know what I was talking about and went back to her knitting.

I made a mental note to figure out how to bring my mom here soon.

"How about a beer?"

Oscar's voice pulled me out of my thoughts. His question, though, made new ones run through my head. When I'd agreed to meet him tonight, I hadn't thought of it as a date. Now I was worried he had.

"Um, I don't . . ."

He held up his hand. "It's just a beer. Nothing else. I was going to get one anyway, and I just thought you might want one too."

His explanation did calm my rising anxiety. It was just a beer. It couldn't hurt to have one, right?

We ended up at a place a few blocks away. Although it was giving more lounge-type vibes than bar vibes. Besides small tables, there were couches and armchairs set up around the small space. The dim lights and low jazz music evoked a cozy, intimate ambience, which was a nice change from the brightness and high-charged setting at Rage and Smash.

Oscar asked where I wanted to sit, and I pointed to an empty love seat toward the back. He told me he'd get our drinks and would meet me there.

By the time he took a seat next to me, I was feeling relaxed. And grateful.

"Thank you for tonight," I told him. "I really needed it."

He tipped his beer in my direction. "You're welcome. I'm glad. I was a little worried I'd made the wrong call, and you'd be offended that I thought you needed to break things for fun."

"You definitely made the right call. Although now I'm wondering if I should be offended? Do I give off scary, angry vibes all the time?"

"Not all the time."

I laughed and softly kicked his leg. "Thanks for lying."

"Seriously, you don't. But being angry is just a part of the grieving process."

"I guess. But how many people throw their cell phone and break a window at work?" I said it without thinking. My initial embarrassment only lasted a few seconds, though, because Oscar didn't even blink.

"We all react to grief in different ways," he said with a shrug. "Some people throw things; others deliberately crash their car."

"Or become a drummer with an eighties cover band," I teased. When I mentioned the band, a little tinge of guilt pressed my heart. I hadn't gone back to see him perform again, even though he'd invited me. I dismissed it, though, since Oscar seemed intent on keeping the conversation serious.

"At some point we realize that the satisfaction we feel from destroying things is fleeting. In order to get rid of the anger altogether, we have to stop running from it and deal with it head on."

The more I thought about Oscar's words, the more I realized I'd been running away from the truth about Jason and the day he died because I didn't want to face it. And that's why I hadn't told anyone—not even Evie—the full story.

A thundering anxiety rolled across my chest. Part of me wanted to free it by telling Oscar. Maybe it was because he never knew Jason? Maybe it was because he didn't know me when I was with him? But suddenly, I felt as if I could trust him with the secret that had been eating me up for months.

I downed my beer and set the bottle down on the small table in front of us. Then I took a long breath. "Sometimes I lie awake at night just stewing in anger," I admitted.

"I already told you that's normal, Yesica."

"You don't understand." I shook my head. "The day that Jason—my husband—died was the day he told me he had gone to see a divorce lawyer."

It was the first time I had ever said those words to anyone. It was a relief to finally share my secret. But I wasn't done confessing.

"I'm sorry," he said softly.

"That's not the worst of it." I could've stopped then and there. But like a champagne bottle that had been shaken too much, the story bubbled up to the top and shot out of me.

"He wanted a divorce because the woman he'd been sleeping with was pregnant, and he wanted to go be with her and their baby," I began. "He told me he was leaving that night. He packed a bag, told me he'd call me to discuss things later, and then walked out of our home. I think he must have realized that he forgot his cell phone when he was about a mile away and stupidly tried to make a U-turn in the middle of the street. The main street to our house is narrow and curvy. Police said he must have lost control of his car, went off the road, and hit a tree. He died on impact."

The darkness I'd felt that day returned, and my body trembled in response.

Oscar scooted closer to me on the couch. I didn't realize I'd clenched my hands together until he was covering them with his own.

"I can't even imagine how traumatic that day must have been for you. I really am sorry that you had to go through all that. You've kept this to yourself all this time, haven't you?"

I nodded through tear-filled eyes. "At first, I told myself it was to protect him and his reputation as a good guy. Plus, how would it look for me to say all these things about someone who wasn't here to defend himself? Then, the longer I kept quiet, the more I realized it was also to protect me. I was embarrassed, honestly. I was ashamed that Jason's last words to me were that he didn't love me anymore. And I'm so angry that I can't hate him for his betrayal. What kind of widow is pissed off that her husband isn't here so she can hate him?"

Oscar nodded and squeezed my hand. "You have every right to be angry at him for leaving you to deal with the repercussions of what he did."

Truth be told, I wasn't just hurt that Jason had had an affair. I was more devastated that he was going to have a baby without me. Even as he was destroying our life together, I could see how excited he was about starting a new one.

And that was what made me wish for the most awful thing in the world—for him to die or at least hurt as much as he had hurt me.

The fact that my rage-filled thought had actually come true was my biggest shame of all.

"What about the girlfriend?" he asked.

That was the million-dollar question and the one I'd been dreading. I'd done some Olympic-worthy mental gymnastics to not think about "the girlfriend" for months. Because just the thought of her somewhere out in the world carrying Jason's baby was almost too much to bear. I removed my hands from his grasp.

"I don't know what happened to the girlfriend because I never met her or talked to her. All he told me was that she was a barista at some coffee shop near his office. I don't even know if she knows that he died. I don't even know her name."

In other words, I didn't want to know it. Ever.

"Oh."

I stiffened at his response. Was he judging me? "I know. I know. But in my defense, there are about five different coffee shops within a ten-block radius of his building. And maybe I'm a terrible human, but I honestly didn't feel like walking into every one and asking if there was someone who worked there who was having an affair with a married man and got knocked up!"

Oscar grabbed my hands again. "You're not a terrible human. And I doubt anyone, least of all me, would expect you to try to find your husband's mistress."

A small sense of relief washed over me. There was at least one person in this world who didn't think I was some kind of wicked witch. Despite his assurance, though, I could tell he wanted to say more. "But?"

He let out a breath. "But . . . maybe that's something that you need resolved in order to move on."

My blood ran cold. Oscar had voiced one of my fears—one of the reasons I had never wanted to talk about the whole situation. "Are you seriously suggesting that if I don't confront my husband's mistress, I'm never going to get over Jason's death?"

"All I'm suggesting is that it might be something to consider."

I bowed my head in silence for a few seconds and then looked at him again. "Fine. I considered it, and I decided that I'd rather lay down on a hill of fire ants."

CHAPTER SEVENTEEN
ANA

"The church burned down!"

I looked up to see my mother walking into Yesica's den. I closed my laptop so she wouldn't see the email from Lucas I'd been reading in case she looked over my shoulder. Although it was still highly unlikely she'd be able to make out anything on the screen. The woman needed a magnifying glass to read her Bible. Still, I wasn't going to take any chances. Not just because of who the email was from, but because it included a registration link for the creative writing class Lucas was going to start teaching next week.

He was still trying to convince me to join. I wasn't ready to explain him or the class to my mother.

"What do you mean it burned down?" I asked.

Yesica came running in from the kitchen about the same time. "St. Patrick's?" she asked.

My mother plopped onto the couch. "Pues, not the church. The church's hall. There's nothing left. No roof, no doors. Nada."

"How? When?" Yesica asked.

"Was anyone hurt?" I added.

"Sometime this morning, I guess. They think it was something electrical in the hall's utility closet. Luckily, someone driving by saw the flames and called the fire department. They put it out before it could damage the rectory or the classrooms. Nobody was hurt, gracias a Dios."

Relief swept over me. I also thanked God that it wasn't worse. Although the hall burning down was still pretty awful. Not only did the church use the hall for all its Bible study classes and fundraisers, but it had also been the hub of our little neighborhood. Residents could rent it for wedding receptions, birthday parties, and other events. Our community was definitely going to feel the loss.

Why were so many things going wrong today? I wondered.

First, it was the flat on the 110 freeway. I'd stupidly volunteered to pick up some supplies for the nursery over in South Pasadena before my shift started. With its narrow lanes and basically nonexistent merging distance at each entrance, the 110 was the scariest freeway in all of Los Angeles. Rather than risk my life by pulling off to the side, I'd driven to the next exit—cringing with every wobbly bump as my broken car limped off the freeway to a residential street.

Luckily, my car insurance included roadside service and flat tire repairs. Still, I was over an hour late to work, which put me behind for the rest of the day. A fact my coworker Lorraine made sure to remind me of several times. That woman hated me and was always trying to make me look bad. Today, though, I'd given her the ammunition. It didn't matter that I was late because I was doing a favor for our bosses— all Lorraine cared about was that my being late meant she'd had to start on some of my duties.

A computer system malfunction after lunch made sure my day continued to go downhill. I'd been trying to convince the Brewsters for three months to upgrade their system. But like with everything else in her life and her business, Fran Brewster saw no need to change things, and her husband, Al, agreed. With no way to charge customers, we had to resort to handwritten invoices and cash only. Everything took three times as long and we lost customers who either didn't want to wait or didn't have the money on hand.

Then, after work, I stopped at my house to meet with the contractor. He had found more mold in my bedroom, which meant all the flooring and drywall would have to be replaced, just as we'd feared.

I hadn't tried to hide my disappointment or frustration. He must have felt bad for making me so upset, since he tried to make it seem like it was a good thing. "It's an excuse to get rid of that carpet and get a fresh coat of paint in there. It's like you can come back to a whole new bedroom!"

I appreciated the effort, but it didn't help.

And if that weren't enough, now there was the fire. Because that meant our upcoming women's club tea and scholarship fundraiser was now without a location.

"I can't believe it," I told Mom. "What are we going to do about the tea? It's only three weeks away!"

A deep breath answered me first. "Maybe we cancel."

"Absolutely not," I said right away. "This is too important. We already promised Father Nelson that we were going to be able to fund this school year's scholarships again. They've already started accepting applications."

Yesica sat down next to my mom. "You could look for another venue?" she offered.

"We could. But this is a fundraiser. The whole point of having it at the church hall was because it was free. Now if we have to rent a place, then that just takes away from our budget and could affect any money we raise. Plus, where are we going to find a new location on such short notice?"

"What about having it at someone's house then?" Yesica said. "Maybe someone who's on the committee?"

I shrugged. "I guess. I'll start making some calls and see if someone has a backyard that's big enough to hold a hundred people, plus have room for the silent auction tables."

Just as I stood up to grab my phone from the table where I'd left it charging, my mother clapped her hands. "I know the perfect backyard," she said, pointing to Yesica's sliding glass door.

A small pang of uneasiness wrung my gut like a wet towel. What was my mother thinking?

"Mama, we are not going to have the tea in Yesica's backyard," I said with a nervous laugh. I met Yesica's eyes, and I didn't miss the panic reflected in them. "I'll call Doña Paulina, and I'm sure we'll find a new event location by the end of the day."

It was as if I hadn't said a word. My mother turned to Yesica and grabbed her hands. "Your home is so beautiful, Mija. We could charge a little more this year for tickets just because it will be in Santa Monica. I know the planning committee would love changing things up. I'm very upset about what happened to the hall, but maybe we can turn this into a good thing. An opportunity to raise even more money! What do you say, Yesica?"

I tried one more time to save my daughter. "Mama, don't you think Santa Monica is a little too far for people from the neighborhood to drive for something like this? We've been selling tickets for weeks. What if some people get upset? I don't want to risk not matching the money we raised last year. We already committed to ten scholarships. It would be embarrassing to have to go back to Father and tell him we can only do eight or five. Or even worse, give those students less money. I think it's better if we just find a place close to the church."

She let go of Yesica's hands and sighed. "Maybe. I don't know."

"How about this, Mama Melda?" Yesica said. "Why don't you talk it over with the rest of the committee, and if you can't find a place in the neighborhood, then you can have your tea here, okay?"

My mother yelped. Actually yelped. "Oh, thank you, thank you." She hugged Yesica and kissed her forehead. Then she got up. "I'm going to call Paulina right now to set up an emergency committee meeting for tomorrow here so we can make a decision. That way they can come see the house, and if they think it's too far, then we can have it somewhere else."

After I heard her bedroom door close, I shook my head at Yesica. "I tried to give you an out, but you didn't take it. I don't think you realize what you've just offered. It looks like your house is her first choice, not the backup option."

She tucked her legs underneath her and leaned sideways against the couch's back cushion. "You know I can never say no to her. And don't even say anything, because you're the same way."

She had me there. A realization hit at that moment. If the tea was going to be at Yesica's house, then there was a very good chance a lot of the planning and coordination was going to end up on my lap. Yesica wasn't a member of the women's club or the committee. That meant I would probably have to coordinate almost everything.

Yesica might have agreed to let them use her home, but she'd also basically volunteered me to run the event.

Not exactly what I needed. Work and dealing with the house repairs were already overwhelming me. I didn't know how I was going to add one more thing to my plate. It was one of the reasons why I was still deciding on taking Lucas's class. Now, the decision seemed to have been made for me. Unexpected disappointment made my heart sink.

"You okay, Mom?"

Yesica's voice brought me out of my near panic attack. "Um, yeah. Why?"

"Because you look like you're gonna cry. Did something happen today?"

I was about to tell her that I was fine. I hated bothering her with my problems, especially when it sometimes felt like I was doing exactly that—being a bother. But there was something in her voice that made me decide to share. At least one thing. She didn't need to know about Lucas or his class.

"It's just that I talked to the contractor today, and they're going to have to do more work in my bedroom. He wants me to pick out flooring and a paint color, and part of me just wants to have my old bedroom back."

"Why? This is your chance to change things up."

I laughed. "That's what he said. I guess I'm not a fan of change. I like keeping things the same."

"Oh, I know," she said. "You're almost as bad as Mama Melda."

"What does that mean?" I said, curious about her tone.

Yesica sighed. "It's just that you still do things like you've always done. You've barely changed anything since Dad died."

A familiar pang of tension squeezed my chest. I was surprised by the mention of Benny. "Maybe that's just because it's what I'm used to."

"I know. But don't you ever want to do something that maybe you couldn't when he was here?"

"Like what?"

"Like not making spaghetti on Monday nights. You don't even like spaghetti that much, yet that's exactly what you cooked us for dinner last week."

"I thought you liked my spaghetti?" It was silly, but I couldn't help but get defensive.

"I do. But that's not the point. I'm just trying to say that when it's time to pick out your new paint and floor, pick what you like. Not what's cheapest or what you're used to. That's all."

Yesica gave me an unexpected smile before telling me she was going to go watch TV up in her room.

I sat there for a few more minutes, thinking about what she'd said. I began to think of all the things in my life I still did as if Benny was still alive. Some were silly, stupid things like drinking regular milk, even though I wanted to try almond milk to see if it was easier on my stomach. Others were bigger and had more of an impact, like not going to visit Alejandro. Benny was the one who hated to fly. So why hadn't I booked a trip yet to see my son?

Had I been with Benny for so long that I'd forgotten how to be someone other than his wife?

And why did it scare me to find out?

I opened up my laptop and read the email from Lucas for the third time.

I'd given up so many things in order to be there for Benny, my kids, and even my mother. And what had it gotten me? What did I have in this world that was just for me?

Yesica was right. It was time to stop doing things the way I'd always done them. It was time for a change.

And before I could talk myself out of it, I clicked the link and registered for my first ever creative writing class.

CHAPTER EIGHTEEN
YESICA

The members of the planning committee of the St. Patrick's Women's Club were expected to arrive in less than an hour. But the way my mother was running around, you would've thought a certain royal couple now living in California was planning to make an appearance.

"Mom, I think that's enough food," I said, pointing to the large tower of finger sandwiches filled with egg salad and sliced cucumber she was still arranging. "I thought you said there were only six women on the committee."

"There's seven, and plus us three, that's ten people. I figured each person will probably eat like four sandwiches, so I need forty," she said.

"First of all, finger sandwiches are not supposed to fill up anyone's stomach. Second of all, I highly doubt Mama Melda is going to be eating anything."

My grandmother had in fact wanted to cancel the meeting at my house altogether because she was convinced we were going to have to take her to the hospital instead.

I knew very well that no emergency visit would be required. Mama Melda was just feeling the consequences of her own stubbornness by eating the pint of butter pecan ice cream last night that I'd just bought for a movie night with Evie later this week. The woman refused to accept the fact that she was lactose intolerant.

"I've been drinking leche my entire life. How can I be allergic to it all of a sudden?" she'd told me after my mom had scolded her for eating the ice cream.

Now karma had landed her in the bathroom all morning and, most likely, all afternoon.

"Did you need me to do anything while you're preparing the food for the small army of señoras about to descend upon my house?"

She looked up with her eyes wide. "Why did you say it like that? Are you having second thoughts about them coming today to look at the backyard? Are you regretting saying yes to us having the scholarship tea here?"

"Whoa, Mom. It was just a joke. Why are you so . . . stressed?"

"I'm not stressed," she insisted.

All I had to do was raise one eyebrow in doubt.

"Okay, okay, I'm a little stressed. It's just this women's club is really your grandmother's thing. They're her friends. I only joined because I was her ride to the meetings and was going to be there anyway. And then she volunteered us to cochair this year's scholarship tea. It's been a lot more work than I thought it would be."

I sympathized. After all, I knew how persuasive Mama Melda could be, and my mother seemed to always be the one doing her bidding.

"Can I ask you something?"

"Only if you ask while you open that jar of salsa and pour it over the cream cheese on that plate over there," she said, pointing to all the items she'd mentioned. "Then find me a bowl for the tortilla chips, please."

I nodded and began doing everything she'd instructed.

"Has Mama Melda ever said that she'd like to go stay with Tío David or Tía Claudia? Not forever, but maybe for a few months with one and then a few months with the other?"

"No," she said. "Why? Did she say something to you?"

"No. But I just thought, they're her kids too. It just seems like you do a lot for her, and maybe they should help out more."

It wasn't lost on me that my brother also came to mind.

"It's come up. But Grandma doesn't like change. You know that."

"Oh, I know. I think I buy her a new wallet every other Christmas, but I see she's still carrying the same one she's had for twenty years because she says it has the exact number of card slots she needs. Not one more, not one less."

My mom laughed as she pulled out a tray of vegetables from the fridge. "Your grandmother is definitely set in her ways."

"So you're just going to take care of her all by yourself? Forever?"

She looked up at me from across the island counter. "I am, because that's what I promised to do when she came to live with us. You have to understand that Grandma is very . . . sensitive about things like this because of what happened to her as a little girl. So I would never ever force her to leave the home she's had for over thirty years."

I didn't know all the details because Mama Melda refused to share most of them. All I knew was what my own mother had shared years ago. My grandmother's family was one of the many who were evicted in the fifties from the Los Angeles neighborhood known as Chavez Ravine. The city had used eminent domain to buy up the houses and other properties. Mama Melda's parents were part of a group of owners who refused to sell and tried to fight to keep their property. In the end, the remaining families were evicted from their homes and forced to leave. Some left with only the clothes on their backs or a few mementos.

Eventually, the city sold the land to the Brooklyn Dodgers to build a new stadium.

And so that became the origin story of Mama Melda's hatred for "los pinche Doyers."

I guess being forced to leave your childhood home would imprint some lasting emotional scars. My mom had told me the other day about the bag she'd found in Mama Melda's room. It all made sense now.

I felt terrible for even bringing up the conversation. Especially since I could admit that maybe I had wondered a few times if my mom had ever thought about moving to Colorado to go live near my brother.

"I'm sorry, Mom. I didn't mean to—"

"What are you sorry about?"

We both turned to see Mama Melda walking into the kitchen.

"Um, I was just telling Mom I was sorry that I didn't get the tray of cheese and crackers she wanted," I lied.

"Feeling better, Mama?" my mother asked.

Mama Melda sat down at the kitchen table. "I think so. I took some Mylanta, and I'll make me some yerba buena tea. That should do the trick. Don't worry, Ana. I'll be fine by the time everyone gets here."

Everyone showed up exactly at eleven thirty on the dot.

As promised, Mama Melda seemed to have made a complete recovery and had put on her cochair hat by greeting each woman at the door and then introducing me.

"My nieta, Yesica. She's the one who owns this beautiful house," Mama Melda said proudly.

"Oh, thank you so much for allowing us to have our tea here," said a small dark-haired woman named Paulina.

"Yes, we're all so excited about having it somewhere new this year," added another woman named Geneva.

I put on my brightest smile. "Of course. I'm happy to open up my home to such a worthy cause. Why don't we go to the backyard so you can see where everything will be set up that day."

My mom joined us as I took the group outside to the back. As they walked around, I realized it had been a while since I'd spent time there. My biweekly gardener was responsible for the lush grass and nicely trimmed hedges. But I noticed a grouping of potted plants on the patio that seemed new. For a minute, I wondered if the gardener had added them as part of a seasonal landscaping project. Then I thought of a more likely reason.

"Mom," I said as she walked past me. "Are these your plants?"

She looked over at the pots I'd pointed to. "No, they're yours. I brought them from the nursery the other day. Is that okay?"

I shrugged. "It's fine, but you know I don't know how to take care of living things. They'll just die after you go back home."

"I already talked to Guzman, and he assured me that he'll take care of them."

"You talked to my gardener? When?"

"I asked him before I brought them over. I wanted to make sure they would survive. But if you don't want him taking care of them, I can take them to my house. Or I could teach you?"

Before I could answer, Mama Melda called us over to the gazebo in the corner of the yard because Geneva had a question.

I looked back at the plants.

Six months ago, I was the only living thing I had to worry about in this house. Now I had my mother, my grandmother, a committee of elderly church women, and a group of plants sharing my space.

How on earth had I let this happen?

CHAPTER NINETEEN
ANA

If anyone had told me I'd go back to school in my fifties, I would've laughed and then told them there was a better chance of me becoming a millionaire.

Not because I didn't like school. I'd actually loved it. I was always an excellent student and especially loved English classes. They gave me an excuse to read books and write stories about people and places that only existed in my imagination.

My grades were so good that I'd won scholarships to help pay for tuition at Cal State Los Angeles. I had planned to get a degree in English or communications and even join the school newspaper. But a month before I was going to graduate high school, I found out I was pregnant.

School had to take a back seat to me being a wife, then a mom, by the time I was nineteen. I'd accepted that my dream of becoming a writer would remain just that—a dream.

Yet here I was about to take a creative writing class. It didn't matter that it wasn't at a college or other kind of official school; it still felt good to be a student again.

That didn't mean I wasn't nervous. Or that those nerves had more to do with who was going to be my teacher.

Especially after the conversation I'd had with Evie and Yesica the night before my first class.

While I hadn't told my mother that Lucas was the instructor, I did end up confessing it to the girls—even the part of us being best friends. Although I'd left out the tiny embarrassing detail of me being in love with him back then. Yesica expressed her reservations about why Lucas would invite me to take his class. Evie, on the other hand, was more excited than I thought she should be.

"He's her invisible string person!" Evie had shouted, and she hit my daughter on her shoulder over and over again.

"My what?" I asked, directing my question to Yesica.

My mother was already in bed watching her telenovelas, which was the only reason I didn't mind the conversation continuing.

She didn't explain and instead rolled her eyes. "You and your invisible string theory," she told her friend. Then she got off the couch, picked up our plates from the coffee table, and headed toward the kitchen.

Evie just shook her head and yelled after her, "It's not a theory. It's been proven. And your mom and this guy are just another example in a long line of examples that it's true."

Still lost, I asked, "Evie, what are you talking about?"

This time my daughter's friend met my eyes. "Some people believe—like me—that we're connected to certain people because they're meant to be in our lives, meaning you're destined to have some sort of experience with them," Evie explained. "Sometimes we meet these people before we're supposed to. Kind of like a 'wrong time, wrong place' sort of thing. So we drift apart, only to be pulled back together again by an invisible string when the universe decides you're both ready to be in each other's lives again."

Her explanation didn't make it that much clearer to me. "I . . . I still don't think I understand."

"Because it's silly."

I turned to see Yesica coming back into the den with a bottle of wine and three glasses.

"It's not silly. How do you explain us then?" Evie asked.

My daughter opened the wine and shrugged her shoulders. "Easy. My husband died. I needed my friend, and I finally got over myself and texted you."

Evie opened her arms. "And I texted back! If the universe didn't want us to be friends again, then you wouldn't have texted, or I wouldn't have seen the text, or I would've said 'F you' and deleted your text. But I didn't. Why? Because the invisible string pulled us back together."

I thought about Evie's theory but wasn't sure if me attending one class that Lucas was teaching had anything to do with it.

"I don't think it's the same," I said. "It's not like we're going to be friends again. He's just my teacher."

"Well, it's not *not* like you could be friends again. Never say never."

My daughter shook her head. "Maybe we should just not overthink it. Sometimes coincidences are just coincidences."

"Why are you always such a cynic?" Evie said. "It wouldn't kill you to believe that there are forces out there that can't be explained."

"Like fate?" I asked. "I don't really believe in fate."

"Or UFOs," Yesica said with a laugh.

Evie wasn't going to be deterred. "Funny. I don't care what you say, Yesica. I stand by what I believe."

"Good for you, Evie," I added. "Even though I may not be totally sold on the universe pulling us by strings, it's good that you believe it and stand by it. You know it's like that saying, 'If you stand for nothing, you fall for everything.'"

"Who said that?" Yesica asked. "Abraham Lincoln?"

"I think it was Alexander Hamilton," I answered.

"Really?" Evie added. "I thought it was Katy Perry."

We all had a good laugh that night, and my nerves about the class had waned a little. That is, until I actually walked into the classroom.

Lucas, who'd been seated at the desk at the front of the room, got up to greet me.

"You made it," he said after giving me a small wave.

"I did. I wasn't sure where to park, so I had to walk around the building before I found the classroom. I was worried I was going to be late, even though I'd given myself a lot of time for traffic." My rambling was a definite sign of my increasing nerves.

He nodded and gave me a wink. "You're going to do great. I know it."

I had no business believing a word Lucas said. After all, this was only the second time I'd seen him in person since our first meeting at the coffee shop several weeks ago. Although we had become frequent texters once I told him I'd signed up for his class. He'd even sent one this morning saying he was looking forward to seeing me tonight.

"Thanks," I replied to his encouraging words. "I'm sure you're going to do great too."

More people began to arrive, so I told Lucas I was going to go find a seat.

I took out the notebook I'd bought at Target and opened it up to the first blank page.

Just like that, the nerves began to dissipate.

I couldn't wait to fill that page.

CHAPTER TWENTY
YESICA

I met Damien for Sunday champagne brunch at our favorite Spanish restaurant.

He said over the phone that Connie had plans with her friends and he was craving paella. I welcomed the invitation but also knew we weren't just going to be gossiping over tapas. This was my check-in. Damien wanted to gauge if I was ready to come back to work.

If he'd asked me five weeks ago, the answer would've been a resounding yes. Now I wasn't so sure.

"God, I love this place," he said after taking the first sip of his mimosa.

"Me too. When was the last time we were here?"

"After we signed the Baxter contract?"

"That's right. Seems like forever ago, but it's only been like two months."

That contract was pre-incident. I was so proud that day. It was one of the first contracts I'd started working on just after Jason died. I killed myself making sure every detail was perfect. I thought I was the shit. But in reality, I was a complete mess, both mentally and emotionally.

We spent the next half hour talking about Connie and their sons and how they were planning a trip to Argentina in a few months. Then the conversation turned to my family.

"My mom thinks her house will be ready in a few more weeks. There was more damage than they originally thought, but thankfully it's not going to delay the timeline by that much."

"That's good," he said. "I'm sure she and your abuela miss their home. And what about you? Are you going to miss having them around?"

I thought about that for a few seconds. "I think so. It's been nice not being in that big house all by myself. Plus my mom cooks almost every night, and even though I tell her not to, she also cleans. My poor housekeeper asked me the other day if I was going to fire her because the house is pretty much spotless every time she comes over."

Damien laughed. "No matter how old we get, we all need our mothers to take care of us again at some point. I would give anything to have my mama still with me. She made the best alfajores."

Damien's mom had died when he was only a teenager. Then he'd lost his father just before graduating from college. And even though he'd now lived more years without them than with them, he still missed both terribly.

I waited a few seconds before continuing our conversation. "I have to admit, though, I miss my freedom," I joked. "I'm looking forward to not having to report in. I'm surprised she hasn't given me a curfew."

"She just worries about you, Mija."

A small pang of guilt needled at me. "I know. But we haven't always had the best relationship. We tend to argue a lot, even about the tiniest things. It's exhausting sometimes."

Damien nodded in sympathy. "I will never understand the relationships between mothers and daughters because they're so complex. Even Connie once said she wished we'd tried one more time for a daughter, but I told her she had five mama's boys, and that was more than enough."

We finished our main dishes and started on our desserts. We brought back an assortment of pastries, cookies, and churros from the buffet so we could share. After we'd tasted almost everything on the plate, Damien finally got down to the real reason he'd invited me to brunch.

"You know Oscar hasn't said anything to me about whether you're still going to the meetings, but I can tell that you are. Either that or you're a very good actress."

I put down my churro to meet his eyes. "What do you mean?"

He waved his hand in a circle. "You have a different aura around you. It's lighter. Not so bottled up. Plus you haven't mentioned coming back to the office once. Something is definitely better with you."

In other words, I didn't seem so bitchy. I should've been offended. I wasn't, though, because it was the truth. "I think I'm better too. And, yes, for your information, I have been going to the meetings every week. I admit it took me a while to warm up to the idea of group therapy, but I have found it beneficial."

I was surprised by my own admission. I knew that I was trying to be more open about the meetings, and I was now on a first-name basis with most of the regulars. And even though I had yet to share more than just a few sentences out loud, my respect had grown for those who had the courage to stand up and bare their souls. I couldn't explain it. But I had been feeling lighter recently. Cell phones were safe around me again. I also knew stepping away from the hectic pace I was keeping at work had also helped.

I cleared my throat. "What would you say if I extended my leave for two more weeks? My mom and grandma will be moved out or close to moving out by then, and it just seems like it would be a good time to go back."

He leaned back in his chair and folded his arms across his chest. "Well, I was not expecting that."

My gut twisted. I had expected a different reaction—from me. I was disappointed he didn't immediately agree.

"Believe me, Damien. I do miss the work. It's just I feel like once I go back, it will kind of distract me from what I've started when it comes to dealing with these unresolved feelings of grief. I don't want to risk going back to where I was five weeks ago. Like you said, it was affecting my performance. And I don't want to do anything to ruin my reputation or yours."

Damien was quiet for a few seconds. "All right. Let's agree that your leave will be two months. But Mija, I don't think I can extend it any more than that. The partners are eager to get you back. They actually wanted me to try to convince you to come back earlier."

That didn't surprise me. Although Damien was a proponent of work-life balance, the partners were only concerned with work and making themselves more money.

I reached out to grab his hand. "Thank you for always having my back. I won't make you regret it . . . again."

CHAPTER TWENTY-ONE
ANA

My mother always told me the secret to a good meal was that you couldn't be angry or sad when you were preparing it.

It was a superstition she believed in wholeheartedly, just like never putting your purse on the ground because you'd lose your money, or if you ate twelve grapes at midnight on New Year's, then you'd have good luck for the next twelve months. I figured she'd also watched the movie *Like Water for Chocolate* a few too many times, so I never really gave it much credence. That is, until the last few years of my marriage, when Benny had started complaining about my cooking.

"You're doing something different," he'd say after only eating a few forkfuls of my meat loaf or pot roast. "They're too salty," he'd insist about my ground beef tacos or the meatballs in the albóndigas soup. I hadn't consciously changed anything about the ingredients or the way I prepared his meals. But even I had to admit that I no longer found joy in making my husband food.

By then it was getting harder and harder for me to pretend I still loved him. Or think about whether I had ever loved him in the first place. Not that it would've mattered to him anyway. We had been basically roommates for years but putting on a show that we were still a happy couple whenever the kids were around. Cooking was my love language—it was how I showed people how much I cared about them. So, why on earth would I voluntarily waste any more of my time making something for a man who didn't appreciate it or me?

Even still, I stayed. I told myself back then it was to keep my family together—just like my mother had. If she could make sacrifices for us, then I could do the same for my children. I'd grown up without a father, and so had my mother. I told myself I would put an end to that generational curse. It didn't matter that I was basically a single married mom. All that mattered was that my children's father was still in their lives. Then, once Yesica and Alejandro were out of the house, I used my mother as an excuse. If I left Benny, then where would she go? I didn't even have a job back then to get us a house or even an apartment of our own. Sure, she could've gone to live with one of my siblings. But as the oldest, I was responsible for her. At least, that's what I told myself back then.

Truth was, I was afraid of blowing up the nice, comfortable life I'd built in Bell Gardens. If putting up with a husband who seemed to be growing increasingly annoyed by my presence was the price, then so be it.

In the months leading up to his death, Benny was eating outside the house for most of his meals anyway. Or when he was home by dinnertime, he'd say he wasn't hungry, leaving me and my mother to eat by ourselves. And for a woman who liked to criticize as if it was a sport to practice for, she never said a bad word when it was my turn to cook.

My point was, if my mother was to be believed, our dinner tonight was going to be delicious.

The menu: entomatadas with homemade corn tortillas, frijoles charros, and rice.

The chefs: me, my mom, my daughter, and her best friend, Evie.

When Yesica mentioned earlier that day that Evie wanted to come over to visit with us, I immediately offered to make everyone dinner. To my surprise, Yesica had agreed and even asked if my mother could make entomatadas, since she hadn't had them in years. It was my mother who said she would make the beans and rice, but I would make the main course.

I was already happy to be cooking for everyone, but then Evie arrived early and asked if she could help. Which meant Yesica also had to help.

After everyone had put up their hair, washed their hands, and put on the extra aprons I'd brought from home, I gave the marching orders.

Yesica was in charge of pressing the balls of tortilla dough my mother had already prepared into the metal tortilladora (also brought from home) and then cooking each one on the cast-iron comal heating on the stove. I asked Evie to help my mother cut up onions, tomatoes, bacon, and hot dog wieners for the frijoles charros.

In the meantime, I prepared the fresh tomato salsa for my entomatadas.

"What's the difference between entomatadas and enchiladas again? Aren't they both just rolled-up tortillas with stuff inside?" Evie asked from her seat at the kitchen island.

"For enchiladas, the tortillas are coated in a red chile sauce. And entomatadas use a tomato-based sauce. But, yes, the fillings can be similar," I explained as I filled a blender with the tomatoes, jalapeños, and onions I'd already boiled. Then I added some of the boiled water, along with cloves of garlic and about half a tablespoon of chicken bouillon.

"What are we filling these with?" Evie asked.

"Pollo y queso fresco," Mama answered. "I already boiled and shredded the chicken. But we can make some with only queso if you're one of those vegetarian people."

Yesica and Evie both laughed. "Don't worry, Mama Melda," my daughter replied. "Evie is definitely a meat eater. I've seen her chow down on a twenty-ounce rib eye steak and a rack of ribs before."

"Qué bueno," my mother said, sounding both impressed and proud for some reason.

As everyone went back to quietly working, I pulsed the blender until everything inside had become a smooth puree. Once I was satisfied with the consistency, I tasted the sauce and added a little more salt. Then I poured it all into a pan on the stove, where I'd heated up a tablespoon of oil.

I slowly stirred the sauce, making sure it didn't burn while also watching Yesica as she carefully pressed each ball of dough into a flat disk between two sheets of parchment paper. My heart warmed with the memory of this exact scene taking place when she was about nine or ten.

"You know that comal is older than you," I said.

She smiled as she transported the newly formed tortilla and placed it on the pancake-shaped pan heating on the stove next to my sauce.

"I know, Mom. I wouldn't be surprised if it was older than you too. Mama Melda doesn't get rid of anything."

"While that is definitely true, that comal is not your grandma's. It's the one she bought me when I was pregnant with you."

"From TJ, Mama Melda?" Yesica asked. It was a family truth that my mother insisted on buying all her cooking utensils in Tijuana.

"Pues, of course. They don't make them here like they do over there."

I looked at my daughter, and we both rolled our eyes and laughed. It felt good to share a moment with her that was just between us. I was so happy that I didn't even try to stop her when she used a pair of tongs instead of her fingers to flip the tortilla.

After I decided the sauce was heated enough, I pushed the pan to the back burner.

"Okay, do you want to fry or fill?" I asked Yesica.

She shrugged as she wrapped a tea towel around the tortillas she'd just finished making to keep them warm. "Um, I'll fry. I never know how much stuff to put inside."

"Mama, are you two done chopping? I think we need to start cooking everything for the beans now before we start making the entomatadas."

"We were just waiting for you to move out of the way," she said.

Yesica and I did what my mother wanted and stepped aside so she and Evie could take our places at the stove. We both sat at the counter and sipped the wine we'd poured just before we'd started cooking.

"Evie, I hope you're taking notes because I'm going to expect frijoles charros at least once a month from you now," Yesica teased.

Her friend pointed to my mother. "If I ever bring this to you, it will only be because she made them and I drove all the way to Bell Gardens to pick up a pot."

"You just call me, Mija. I'll make a pot for you and a pot for Yesica," my mother said. Like me, she never turned down a request to cook for someone.

From our seats at the island, Yesica and I watched for the next few minutes as my mother cooked the bacon until it was browned, but not crispy. To that she added the diced wieners and then the chorizo. After she was sure each of the separate ingredients had now become one aromatic and sizzling concoction, she dropped in the diced tomatoes and jalapeños. The combination of everything cooking together made my mouth water.

"And this is what you add to the beans?" Evie asked. She, too, must have been salivating, since she lowered her head closer to the pan and inhaled. "God, that smells so good."

"It's about to get even better," my mother said with a nod. She then poured the chorizo mixture into a pot of pinto beans that had been cooking with onions and garlic for almost two hours. "In fifteen minutes, van a estar listos."

I turned to Yesica and told her it was our turn at the stove again. It took us about ten minutes to fry the tortillas and then fill them with the chicken and cheese. I arranged the entomatadas in a rectangular baking pan and then poured the tomato sauce over each one. After sprinkling crumbles of queso fresco on top, I put the pan in the oven and set the timer.

Less than fifteen minutes later, the four of us were seated in Yesica's dining room enjoying the delicious fruits of our combined labor.

"These are amazing, Ana," Evie said. Her groans and moans while chewing had already hinted at how much she was enjoying the food.

Yesica, who was sitting across the table from me, met my eyes. "These are really good, Mom. Even better than I remember."

I tried not to look surprised at the compliment. I couldn't remember the last time she'd said she liked something I'd made. "Thank you," I said. I caught the quick smile on my mother's face out of the corner of my eye.

We continued eating and chatting about different things in between. My mother was especially interested in hearing about the students at Evie's school and their celebrity parents.

"Speaking of students, how's your writing class going?" Evie asked me.

The change in conversation made me nearly cough up a frijole.

"Um, good, I guess," I said after taking a long drink of my water.

"You guess? Come on, Mom. Spill it," Yesica said.

I didn't know what I was more surprised about. The fact that my daughter was interested in my class at the Learning Lab on Wednesday nights or that she was obviously trying to prod me into talking about Lucas.

"Fine," I said. "I like it. A lot. In fact, I'm thinking about going back to school to get my associate of arts degree."

"Really?" Yesica asked.

"De veras?" my mother repeated.

My stare moved from one to the other. "Why do you both seem surprised?"

My daughter shrugged as she lifted up her glass of wine. "I don't know. I guess I never thought you were interested in going back to school."

I didn't know whether I should be offended. "Why?"

"No real reason," she said.

Evie, on the other hand, seemed more impressed than my blood relatives. "So what have you written so far in your class? Short stories? Articles? A novel?"

"Definitely not a novel," I said with a laugh. "It's just a beginners' class, and we haven't written anything yet. Right now, we're just reading a book about writing. But based on the syllabus, we'll probably mainly be working on short stories."

I'd only been to a total of two classes, so the truth was I still wasn't quite sure what to expect. Lucas, it turned out, was a very engaging instructor. He spent most of the first class talking about his road to getting published. The boy I had known as a shy but passionate writer had grown up into a dynamic and passionate speaker. Despite my reservations about signing up for Lucas's class, I had yet to regret my decision.

"That's very cool." Evie's compliment brought me back to the conversation at the table.

"It's not, really. But thank you anyway," I said, suddenly feeling embarrassed by the attention.

"I guess it makes sense," my mother said. "You always liked to write."

"She did?" Yesica asked her, yet she was looking directly at me.

I didn't say anything as my cheeks grew hotter. Maybe I shouldn't have had that second glass of wine. Alcohol seemed to be a trigger for my hot flashes.

"Oh yes. She was always scribbling these little stories in her notebook. And then when she'd fill one up, she'd ask me for a dollar so she could go to the store with that Lucas Padilla and buy another one. The two of them could spend an entire afternoon on our porch just writing and reading and then laughing about whatever it was they'd written."

Yesica's eyes narrowed, and her mouth turned upward in a sly grin. "Lucas Padilla? Why does that name sound familiar?"

"I don't know why it would," I said through tight lips. I stared at my daughter and tried to tell her with my eyes not to mention the fact that Lucas was my instructor.

"He wrote that big thriller novel a few years ago, remember?" Evie said. "All the moms in our school were reading it for their book club. I think they even got him to visit one of their meetings. I guess he lives in the area somewhere."

Evie, bless her heart, had gotten the hint.

I watched in growing panic as Yesica continued to smirk. I could tell she was still waiting for me to spill the beans.

"Lucas Padilla wrote a book? A book people can buy?" my mother asked Evie.

"Yep. Although I don't think he's written one recently."

Yesica met my eyes. "Maybe he's teaching writing now instead?"

Before she could say anything more, I jumped out of my chair. "Who wants dessert? We have ice cream."

CHAPTER TWENTY-TWO
YESICA

"So, do you have any blood left?" I asked as Mama Melda stepped inside my car.

She shook her head. "No. They took it all."

I laughed at Mama Melda's reply and watched as she buckled her seat belt. I was her ride to an early-morning appointment for regular lab work.

"Well, I guess that means we need to get some pancakes so your body can start replenishing all that blood you lost."

"I'm going to need bacon too," she said.

"Of course you will."

We arrived at the pancake house a few minutes later and were seated right away. I'd expected a wait, since we were here in the middle of what would be the usual breakfast rush. But it was a Tuesday. I had always wondered who had time to go to a restaurant for breakfast during the week. Now I knew. Millennials on a forced leave from their work and senior citizens who wanted to eat after getting their blood drawn.

Mama Melda ordered her pancakes and bacon, along with two eggs over medium and hash browns. I opted for an avocado omelet and a side of fruit. And we both got coffees.

"So what do they look for when they take all that blood?" I asked after the waiter had walked away.

My grandmother shrugged. "Who knows? Maybe they just need a reason to give me more pills to take."

I wanted to tell her that she should be taking her health more seriously. But the woman knew more than me about most things. Who was I to tell her anything?

I decided I'd ask my mom my questions later. The thought of my mom, though, brought up some new questions I'd been wondering.

"Hey, Mama Melda. Is it really true that Mom used to write a lot when she was younger?"

"Yes. Like I told you the other night, she always had a notebook with her. Who knows? Maybe if she'd gone to college like you, she'd be a famous writer like that Lucas Padilla boy."

I tried not to smirk at the mention of Mom's old friend and very new writing instructor. I'd finally confronted her after our dinner, and she'd begged me not to tell my grandma because of her long-standing grudge against Lucas's mom. I had agreed only because I think I was still kind of surprised that she'd decided to take a class in the first place.

"Why do you think Mom never went back to school. I mean, she could've, once me and Alejandro were older, right?"

Mama Melda added more cream to her coffee and seemed more focused on her mug than looking at me. I could tell she was trying very hard to keep her mouth shut.

"What?" I asked.

"It's just that I don't think your mom, no, I mean, I don't think your dad would have liked it very much if she went back to school. Remember, he didn't even want her to work—even when you kids were out of the house?"

I squeezed my brows together in confusion. "What? I don't remember that. He told me it was his idea for her to get a part-time job at the nursery because she seemed sad after Alejandro moved to Colorado."

This time she frowned and stirred her coffee again. "Well, what do I know? My memory isn't the best anymore. Anyway, she probably decided now was a good time to do it. Sometimes we have to do things we've never done in order to grow. Because when you stop growing, you die."

The waiter showed up with our food, and we ate in silence for a few minutes. It gave me time to think about what Mama Melda had said about my dad. Despite her claim about having a bad memory, my grandmother often remembered the most random things. Like the time when Alejandro was eleven and he thought it would be funny to hide all her right shoes. He told me that the day before he left for college, all his left shoes had disappeared. She shipped them to his dorm a few weeks later.

Needless to say, if Mama Melda could remember that, she should've remembered the real reason why my mom had gone to work for the first time in my life.

"Did you ever do anything to shake up your life, Mama Melda? Maybe after Grandpa died?" Even though I'd never met my mother's father, we still called him Grandpa. And I felt as if I had known him thanks to my grandmother's stories and the photos she always kept in her room. My mom, on the other hand, rarely spoke about him. Because she'd been so young when he was killed, she said she barely had any memories of her own.

"Oh sure," she said with a chuckle. "But mostly it was life itself doing the shaking. I guess you grow that way too."

"You sure do," I added. Becoming a widow in my thirties was all the life shaking I needed for a while. That's when the realization hit me. "Mama Melda, were you my age when Grandpa died?"

She furrowed her brow in thought. Then her eyes opened wide. "I . . . I was thirty-two."

"I was also thirty-two."

We sat there for a few minutes just staring at each other. How had we never realized that we'd become widows at the exact same age?

She was the first to break our trance by reaching out and grabbing my hands. "I'm so sorry, Mija."

"For what?" I was surprised by how thick and deep her voice sounded.

"For not doing more to help you in those first few days and weeks. I know how hard it is to be so young and to lose the love of your life. I know that pain, and I should've helped you get through it."

Unexpected tears made her face blurry, but I knew she was there because of the grip of her hands on mine. "You have nothing to apologize for, Mama Melda. Besides, what I went through doesn't even come close to what you suffered."

"What do you mean?"

I almost told her. Just so I could lessen whatever guilt she was feeling now. Yes, Jason had been my husband, but I hadn't loved him the way she had loved—still loved—my grandpa. But this wasn't the time or the place to get into my sordid life-shaking moment. So instead I said, "You had to raise three kids all on your own. I don't even have a dog."

That made her laugh, and she let go of my hands in order to grab a napkin and dab the corner of her eye. I did the same.

"Okay, it's my turn to ask you a question," she said after a few seconds.

I froze. Had she figured out what had happened with Jason anyway?

"Okay," I said slowly.

"Why don't you do this with your mom?"

"What? Take her to get blood work done?" I asked, not quite sure what my grandmother meant.

"No, I mean this." She pointed to herself and then to me. "You two never do something on your own. When was the last time you took her to breakfast or to go shopping? I bet she would love to go to the hair salon you took me to—you know, like a mother-daughter day."

"We do things together," I insisted.

"Like what? And I'm not talking about the nights after I go to bed and you stay in the den watching your shows and she's there, too, on her phone or laptop."

I opened my mouth to protest again until I realized Mama Melda was right. I couldn't remember the last time my mom and I had hung out, just the two of us. The truth was, we really hadn't even hung out that much even before she moved into my house. The more I thought about it, the more I remembered that, for the most part, anything I did with my mom usually included my grandma.

"I guess I never really thought about it that way. I mean, ever since I was little, wherever Mom went, then you went too. You're kind of like a package deal."

"I'm no deal," she scoffed. "I'll have you know that I have my own life without your mother."

Now it was my turn to scoff. "Yeah, right. You don't drive, and you barely learned how to text. You need Mom and she needs you. She is la hija de su madre, and you are la madre de su hija."

She raised her eyebrows and pointed a finger at me. "Just because you say it in Spanish doesn't mean it makes it less insulting."

"Oh, Mama Melda. It's not an insult or anything bad. It just means you two are just like each other, that's all."

"Well, I could say the same thing about the both of you."

"Ha! Mom and I are nothing alike."

"Ha! You are more alike than you realize. In fact, I think that's the reason why you don't always get along."

That made me pause. "We get along fine," I insisted.

"Mija, my blood must be back and rushing to my head or I'm drunk on pancakes, because I'm about to tell you something I probably shouldn't."

"And what's that?"

"Maybe you are right about me and your mom always being together. But there's going to come a day when I will be gone. And I worry about your mother being alone. I know Alejandro will do what he can to help her; maybe he would even move back. But the thought that keeps me awake some nights is that I have no idea what will become of you and her."

My throat tightened with emotion at the thought of Mama Melda not being here one day. Obviously, I knew she couldn't live forever. It didn't mean that I preferred to think that she'd do it anyway. I wasn't expecting the stab of pain that the rest of her words gave me.

"I love Mom. We've had our differences. But that doesn't mean I wouldn't do anything for her if she needed it."

My grandma nodded. "That's good to hear. Just don't wait until I'm dead, though, okay?"

CHAPTER TWENTY-THREE
ANA

"Are you hungry?"

I turned around to find Lucas standing behind me. Our third class together had just ended, and I was deep in thought about our first assignment. He wanted us to draft a first-person fictional account of a real event in history. I'd been trying to come up with an idea, which was why I didn't hear him walk up to me.

"Hungry?" I asked, still not sure what he'd said.

He nodded. "I didn't eat lunch, so I'm starving. I think that burger stand on the corner is open twenty-four hours, and I was going to walk over. Did you want to join me?"

As if it knew what Lucas was asking, my stomach rumbled. At least it didn't roar. A burger did sound amazing. I'd cooked dinner for my mother before I'd left for class but hadn't had time to eat myself. And leftovers didn't sound appetizing.

"Sure. That sounds good. Let me put my backpack in the car. I can meet you in the front after."

Five minutes later, I found him waiting for me, and I couldn't help but notice he'd taken off his tie altogether and unbuttoned the top two buttons of his dress shirt. He looked relaxed for the first time that evening.

And why that made me want to smile, I had no idea. But analyzing the thought would give me something to do later.

As we walked the few feet to the corner restaurant, I noticed his steps were light. He'd even swung his jacket over his right shoulder—a carefree gesture I hated to admit made him more attractive.

"You can talk, too, you know. I don't think you've said one word since we left the building," he said.

It was true. Although I'd been very chatty in my head, I'd kept quiet during our walk.

"Sorry. I'm thinking about the assignment. I have no clue what I'm going to write about."

He laughed. "Of course you're thinking about an assignment that isn't due for weeks. Classic Ana."

I stopped. "What do you mean?"

He stopped just a few feet away from me. Even in the shadows, I could see his eyes light up. "It's a compliment, I swear. You were always so determined to do everything exactly right. That's what made you an A student in high school. I was a little jealous."

"You were?"

"Yep. And you made me want to try harder too. I mean I couldn't let you win all the awards, could I?"

I laughed. "Thanks," I told him before he turned around and started walking again. I wanted to tell him more. I wanted to tell him that I was already learning a lot from him as well. He was way more creative than I'd remembered. He was also super smart. I could tell the others in the class were impressed with what he knew about the writing craft and how he'd had success putting that knowledge to work.

Fine. I was impressed too.

Before I could tell him anything, though, we'd arrived at the restaurant. More of a diner than a burger stand. I was surprised to find most of the place's red vinyl booths filled with customers. And even more walked in behind us.

"There's an open one over there in the corner. We better get it before someone else does." I inhaled sharply when he grabbed my hand and pulled me toward a booth. His grip was strong, but it didn't crush. Even though his hand was much bigger than mine. And then it was gone.

He slid into one side of the booth while gesturing for me to take the other side.

Suddenly, I became nervous about being with Lucas like this. So familiar. Just like the old days.

"I was thinking I'd probably just take my burger to go," I said after sitting down.

"Why?" His face dropped.

I tried to act nonchalant. "It's late, and I'm a little tired."

"But I thought we could talk?"

"Oh. Okay. Did you want to go over the assignment?"

"No. I meant, I was hoping we could talk about anything but class."

A cute dark-haired waitress bounced over to our table at that point and handed us plastic menus. "Hey, Lucas. How's it going?"

"Hey, Kara. Since when do you work nights?"

"I'm just picking up an extra shift—you know, to help me fix my car."

"That's good," he said with an extra-toothy smile. When his eyes finally moved from the waitress to me, he added, "Oh, this is Ana. She's . . . an old friend."

I tried not to bristle at the word "old."

Kara turned to me and nodded. Then she looked back at Lucas.

"So are you going to have your usual?"

Usual meal or usual flirt-with-the-waitress fun?

"Yep. I'll take the double bacon cheeseburger . . ."

"No onion or tomato and a side of waffle fries," Kara finished for him. "And for you, ma'am?"

Ma'am? Oh, that called for a wince.

177

"I'll have his usual, too, and a Diet Coke. Thanks, sweetie," I said with a wink.

"So do you still want to take it to go?" Lucas asked.

Whether it was the possible flicker of hope I saw reflected in Kara's eyes or suddenly remembering Yesica was home in case my mother needed something, I decided I could eat here.

"No, that's okay. I can stay and talk."

Lucas smiled and nodded, and I couldn't help but feel a sense of satisfaction.

"So you still love the bacon, huh?" I said after Kara had walked away.

"What?" he asked.

I shrugged as I sat back. "You ordered a bacon cheeseburger. That's what you used to order back then, whenever we'd go to Dino's."

"That's right," he said. "I'm surprised you remembered."

"I've been remembering lots of things. You actually haven't changed that much."

"Really? Impress me with your knowledge then," he said with a smile.

"You take your coffee black and your sandwiches dry. You whistle when you're trying to figure out math or directions. And you still like to tell that story about the time you almost drowned in the Pacific Ocean because you thought a Victoria's Secret model was surfing next you."

He laughed hard.

I couldn't help but laugh too. I was glad I hadn't embarrassed him.

"Okay, that was pretty good," he said after catching his breath. "But I'm sure there are things you don't know about me."

"Maybe," I said. "Go ahead and tell me something I don't know."

"Well, let's see. Did you know I once broke both legs during one summer?"

I nodded. "Yep. You were ten, and the first time happened when you jumped out of a tree, and the second time happened when you tried to hit a ball out of that same tree with one of your crutches, and you lost your balance and fell off the ladder."

He laughed again. Over the next hour, Lucas tried to think of things I didn't already know about him. I knew a lot, but I also learned new bits of information. Just like his coffee and love for bacon, this was the Lucas I remembered. He was easy to talk to, he seemed to like to make me laugh, and he listened to every word I said.

And the icy glares Kara kept sending my way only made the whole evening that much more fun. After we'd paid the check and started walking back to our cars, I finally asked Lucas the question I'd wanted to all night.

"So what's up with you and Kara?" I teased.

"The waitress?"

We were walking side by side. Every so often a streetlamp would cast a warm light on his profile, and I had to admit that time had been very good to Lucas.

"Yeah, she seemed to know you pretty well," I said, trying to sound nonchalant.

"I go in there sometimes either before or after class. She went back to school last semester. She's majoring in communications and also likes to write. She likes to hear about the book I'm working on. Why are you asking?"

"No reason. Just curious."

"If I didn't know better, Ana, I'd think you were a little jealous."

I almost tripped over my feet. "Jealous? I don't think so. I told you I was just curious."

"Sure. Whatever you say."

Heat burned my cheeks, and my stomach flip-flopped. I didn't want Lucas thinking I was jealous of Kara or anyone else he might have been interested in. "Wouldn't you be the slightest bit curious if we went somewhere and another man started talking to me like he knew me?"

"Depends. What man?"

"What do you mean, what man? Any man. A strange man."

"Hmm. I guess I'd be curious. But I'd also be concerned. I'd care about his intentions."

His serious tone made me laugh. "His intentions? I'm not a teenager anymore, Lucas. You don't have to protect me."

"Of course I do. I care about you, Ana."

The flip-flops turned into about a million butterflies. I was grateful for the shadows so he couldn't see how much his words were affecting me.

CHAPTER
TWENTY-FOUR
YESICA

I wasn't exactly sure what I was doing here again.

It was the Thursday night before the scholarship tea, and I probably should've stayed at home in case my mom needed any help with preparations. Then Oscar had texted me that a few of the group members were meeting at the Deck because it was the one-year anniversary of the passing of the mother of someone named Casey, and they wanted to help him through it.

I couldn't remember who exactly Casey was, so I'd politely declined.

But Oscar persisted. I promise to behave myself. No dancing.

That made my stomach flutter in a way I hadn't expected. Was he flirting with me via text?

Well, now I'm really not going, I'd texted back.

It had been a few weeks since our extracurricular therapy session at Rage and Smash and my confession of everything about Jason, his mistress, and the baby. To his credit, Oscar hadn't brought it up unless I had. And I'd become more open about talking about it, but only with him. I knew he didn't judge me for not trying to track the woman down, and that made me feel safe around him.

It also made him even more attractive.

So, yeah, my guard was slowly dropping around him. And so text flirting, although a little surprising, didn't scare me. Not yet.

I changed out of my leggings and T-shirt and into a blouse, boots, and a pair of jeans. Then I told my mom and Mama Melda I was meeting a friend for one drink and that I'd be back in time to help with anything they needed.

Now I was walking into the Deck, not quite sure if I should just turn around and head back home. Because as much as I told myself I was there to support a fellow group member, deep down I knew I'd made the trip just to spend time with Oscar in person. And that would mean no hiding these new feelings for him behind a phone screen.

I debated one more time about leaving. Then it was too late.

"You made it," Oscar said with a huge grin. He'd spotted me almost immediately and came over to where I'd stopped by the bar.

He looked so handsome in a long-sleeved black buttoned shirt and dark-blue jeans. His thick wavy hair was neatly combed, and I resisted the urge to reach up and run my hands through it to give it the tousled, wild look he normally wore.

"I did. But I can only stay for one drink. Saturday is that scholarship tea I told you about, and I have to help get some last-minute things ready."

"One drink is good. I'm just glad you came. Come say hi to everyone."

He grabbed my hand and led me to one of the tables near the bar. His touch was warm, and it brought me back to the night we met. A thrill ran from my fingers to my toes and everywhere in between. My heart fluttered with a familiar giddiness. It was as if I was back in high school—the excitement of being near him made me lightheaded.

There were three people sitting around the table, and I recognized all of them from the group. One of the women was named Terri, and she had lost her sister to cancer. The other woman was Monica, and she was a widow like me. The only man was Casey. He was probably one of the youngest in the group. As soon as I saw his face, I remembered him. He'd stood up a few weeks ago and talked about the day his mom had died.

There hadn't been a dry eye in the room. Even I had fought back sobs imagining this twentysomething and the moment he found out his life would be forever changed.

I went to him first and touched his shoulder. "Hey, Casey. I know we don't really know each other that well. But I hope it's okay I'm here."

He nodded enthusiastically. "Of course, Yesica. Thank you for coming. I wasn't sure about going out tonight, but Oscar here is very persuasive."

"That is exactly what he is," I said, looking over at our leader and my onetime dance partner.

"But I'm glad he convinced me and all of you to hang out," Casey added.

I gave him a smile and then said hello to the others. Oscar got my drink order and left for the bar.

"I've never been here before," Terri said. "But it seems like a fun place. The DJ is pretty good."

"You should come back tomorrow night," I said. "They have an eighties cover band that plays every other Friday, and I hear they're pretty good . . . especially the drummer."

Terri and Monica seemed to like that information, and I couldn't help but smile when I thought of them discovering that they already knew the band's drummer.

The four of us made more small talk, and Oscar returned to the table a few minutes later with my beer and one for him. He took the seat next to me, and I definitely noticed when he scooted his chair closer to mine.

"So, Casey, why don't you tell Yesica what else we did today," Oscar said.

The young man nodded and looked at me. "Oscar and I met with the principal of the school where my mom used to teach. I've been debating about doing something in her memory, and Oscar suggested planting a tree at the school. The principal agreed to the idea. I just need to provide the tree and plaque, and he said he'd schedule a special tree-planting ceremony so the teachers and my mom's former students could attend."

My heart warmed at the wonderful gesture. "I love that idea," I said. "And my mom works at a nursery, so let me know if you want any help picking a tree out. She knows all about that kind of stuff. Unlike me."

Everyone laughed, and I felt more at ease. So much so that the time got away from me, and when I finally checked my watch, I was shocked I'd been at the bar for over two hours.

"I can't believe it's so late. I'm sorry, everyone, but I need to take off," I announced as I stood up.

Casey also stood up and asked if he could give me a hug. I agreed.

"Thank you again. You'll never know how much it helped me tonight," he said.

I smiled and then said my goodbyes to the others. Whatever doubts I'd had earlier about coming had disappeared. Maybe these people weren't my family or even friends, but we shared a bond that grew stronger every time we were together. I now understood the power of group healing.

"I'll walk you to your car," Oscar said and then followed me out the door.

"Thanks for inviting me," I told him as we walked through the small parking lot.

He nodded. "You're welcome. And it meant a lot to Casey that you came. So thank you."

"He's such a nice guy. It's easy to see how much his mom's death has affected him. I hope he'll be okay."

"I think he will be. He's got a good head on his shoulders. Plus, he has everyone in group to help him reach the other side."

We'd arrived at my car, but I didn't unlock it just yet. "What's the other side?" I asked as I leaned against the driver's side door.

Oscar stood in front of me. "The other side of the mountain. Casey is still climbing it. His grief is new and raw, and sometimes that can be so overwhelming that you just want to give up and let the avalanche take you down. And while I'll never get over losing my sister, every day without her isn't a struggle anymore."

I considered his words for a few seconds. "I guess I'm still climbing, too, then. Hey, so does that make you like my mountain guide or something?"

"If that's what you need from me right now, then yes," he said. "But . . ."

I eyed him suspiciously. "But what?"

"But if you ever decide you need me for something else, just let me know."

The night air carried a chill with it. Yet, my body instinctively warmed up. He didn't have to explain what his words meant. The way he looked at me told me everything.

And just so there was no misunderstanding, he stepped closer and met my eyes.

"There's something here, Yesica. I know you feel it too."

The raspiness of his voice sent a thrill down my body. The lights of the parking lot illuminated Oscar's fiery eyes and determined expression—an expression that seemed to scream desire. For me.

My heart pounded. I swallowed hard. That look of his did things to me. I told myself to snap out of it and just say good night and get inside my car. But my feet wouldn't move. Even when Oscar took another step closer. Even when he put both of his hands on the car behind me, his arms trapping me in between it and his body.

My breath caught in my throat as my body trembled under his determined gaze. It had been starved way too long for this kind of closeness. Because even before I became a widow, I was a celibate married woman. The months of trying to conceive had turned our sex life into an emotionless act. Eventually, neither of us seemed interested in finding our way back. I had told myself it was just a phase, and I'd needed some time to feel like a woman again rather than just an empty womb. When Jason didn't ask or pressure me for sex, I figured he was going through something similar. Now I knew he was just getting his satisfaction with someone else.

When I didn't speak, Oscar moved one hand to the back of my neck. The touch zapped me into responsiveness. I shook my head.

"I can't. We can't," I whispered.

"Why not?" He searched my eyes, and I feared for what he might find there. Because at that moment, in his grasp, I had no good answer as to why I shouldn't let him kiss me. Let him do more than kiss me.

"Because of Jason?" Oscar asked.

And there was my answer. The sound of his name was enough to free me from whatever spell Oscar was weaving. Even though I felt no loyalty to the man who had betrayed me, he was still the reason why I wasn't ready to be with someone else. Sleeping with Oscar would be an easy fix to my loneliness, but it wouldn't solve the rest of my problems. Truth was, I really liked Oscar. So much so that I wanted to protect him. From me.

What was that saying about hurt people hurting people? I didn't want to be the one to hurt Oscar.

I took his hand and removed it from my neck.

"No, not because of him. Because of me. My life is a complicated mess right now. I need to focus on fixing it. I don't have the energy for anything else."

He nodded. "And I respect that. I just needed you to know how I felt."

I reached up and touched his cheek. "You're a good man, Oscar. You deserve to be with someone who has her shit together."

"How about you let me decide who I deserve to be with?" he said with a shrug.

He moved out of the way so I could open the door. He watched as I put on my seat belt and turned on the ignition. As I was about to shift into drive, he knocked on the window.

I rolled it down and he leaned in. "I meant what I said about letting me know if you ever want something more from me. In the meantime, I'm going to be there by your side every step of the way up the mountain. Got it?"

And with that, he stood up and walked back into the night.

CHAPTER TWENTY-FIVE
ANA

The day of the scholarship tea came before I was ready for it.

I still had several things on my to-do list to cross off by the time I woke up that Saturday morning. Some of those things included one more trip to the market, but I couldn't leave the house because the rental company was supposed to arrive by seven to start setting up the tent and tables.

Luckily, Yesica said she would go to the store after going wherever she always went on Saturday mornings. A few weeks ago, I finally realized that she was still disappearing at the same time every week and returning to the house about two hours later. First, I figured she was going to the gym, but a few times I noticed she was wearing jeans and a sweatshirt, not workout clothes. Then I thought maybe she was just running errands. But that didn't explain being gone during the same two-hour time period.

When she offered to go to the store to pick up the last few supplies, I tried to find out exactly what city or neighborhood she would be around so I could decide if there was a store there that would have the things I needed. But she didn't explain and insisted she could go to whichever store I told her to go to.

Frankly, I was too stressed and too tired to press the issue. I didn't need to trigger an argument and have that added to my list.

As usual, my mother also wasn't helping much. Last night, I'd expected her to help me fold the auction programs and assemble some framed placards. But after dinner, she complained the arthritis in her fingers was flaring up and said she was going to go to bed early and would do them in the morning.

Rather than wait for her or risk it not getting done, I was the one who'd stayed up late to finish those two tasks.

Of course, she was offended after I told her I'd taken care of it.

"I told you I'd do them," my mother said. She'd just finished her coffee and toast and proclaimed she was ready to work.

I was emptying the dishwasher—something I'd thought Yesica had taken care of last night but hadn't—and I tried my best for my words not to betray the growing irritation.

"I know, but sometimes your arthritis flare-ups last more than one day. I had the time, so I did them," I said, lying about having the time. "Don't worry, I have lots more stuff for you to help with."

She got up and brought me her empty coffee cup and plate to rinse. "Okay. But first I have to take my shower. I'll help you after."

"You just said you were ready to help now," I snapped.

"I didn't mean right this minute," she said. "I have to take my shower first. Or do you want me to walk around como una cochina?"

I sighed. "Just go."

"Yesica was right. You are extra moody these days."

"What's that supposed to mean?" I called out after her as she walked toward her room.

It didn't matter, though. I didn't have the time to think about anything extra today.

Luckily for my blood pressure, the rental company arrived on time. I gave them their instructions and then went back to the kitchen to finish up the last of the prep work for the silent auction table. The florists arrived next, and then a few committee members followed.

Before I knew it, two hours had flown by. Yesica still wasn't home, though.

I texted her to ask if she was at the market yet. No reply.

My mother finally emerged and decided she needed to go supervise the setup in the backyard. She barely said a word to me, so I knew she was still annoyed about earlier.

I checked my watch and decided now was the best time for me to get in the shower and get ready too. I let Lupe know that Yesica would be arriving soon with the last two gift cards for the raffle and some other supplies. The caterer was due within the hour.

Satisfied things were under control for the moment, I ran upstairs.

I tried to relax as the hot water hit my face and neck. But I couldn't steam away my anxiety or my frustration. The entire week had gone exactly like my morning. It seemed as if I was the only one in the house worried about the scholarship tea. And whenever I said as much, my mother or Yesica would simply reply, "It's going to be fine. Don't worry so much."

Usually my mom would also add, "That's why you already have wrinkles."

I got out of the shower only after the water had run cold. I checked my phone and noticed Yesica still hadn't texted back.

Where on earth could she be?

After getting dressed, doing my hair, and applying makeup, I headed downstairs and was met with chaos.

Actually, it was Lupe.

"The rental company shorted us two tablecloths and six chairs," she rushed out as soon as I walked into the kitchen. "Plus, the caterer called me and said she was stuck on the freeway, and her GPS was showing she wouldn't get here for at least another thirty minutes. Is that going to be enough time to set up the hors d'oeuvres? And isn't she bringing the containers with the iced tea and lemonade? What if people want something to drink as soon as they arrive?"

I pinched the bridge of my nose and took a long, deep breath.

"I'll call the rental company and tell them to come back with our missing items. They need to give us what we paid for," I began. "The caterer is bringing both cold and hot hors d'oeuvres. If the hot ones need to be warmed up, then we'll just bring them out when they're ready, or we don't. People won't know what's missing. My daughter has bottles of waters in her garage and a nice stand-up cooler. I'll text her to stop and get ice on her way home. We can serve the lemonade and tea during the main course."

Lupe nodded and seemed relieved.

I was not.

I pulled out my phone and texted Yesica:

Please stop and pick up two big bags of ice too. Try to get here as fast as you can.

Three little dots appeared, and I blew out a breath.

Already home. Getting in the shower. Gave the stuff to Mama Melda.

I was disappointed about the ice, but at least she was back with the other things I needed.

Guests began arriving exactly at eleven, and I was pretty proud of myself for having put out the small fires before the first person walked through the door. Bottles of water were chilling in the cooler with every ice cube I could squeeze out of Yesica's freezer, the rental company had come and gone the second time, and the caterer was unloading her van.

Mama and Yesica were also ready right on time.

I walked over to where they were standing to give them their instructions.

"The basket and raffle tickets are on the kitchen table. Here's an envelope with cash and the list of the raffle prizes. Remember each ticket is five dollars."

My mother took the money and gave the clipboard with the list to my daughter. Yesica glanced at the list and then said, "Oh wait. The store didn't have any Visa gift cards, or ones for Amazon. I got four for Whole Foods instead."

I froze and stared at her. Why had she not done what I'd asked, today of all days? "Whole Foods?"

Yesica gave me a confused look. "Yeah. Why? What's wrong with Whole Foods?"

"What's wrong is that there are no Whole Foods locations in Bell Gardens or nearby," I explained tightly—trying to keep a lid on the irritation now bubbling up to the surface. "Why on earth would parishioners of St. Patrick's bid on gift cards to a store that would cost them money just to drive to?"

My mother shrugged. "They might. Or maybe they could give them as gifts to someone they know who likes to shop at those stores?"

My frustration and stress that had been building all week couldn't be contained. "That's not the point, Mom! The point is that I asked Yesica to do something to help me, and she didn't. The point is I've been asking all week for you to help me get ready for today, and you didn't."

"Whoa," Yesica said. "Aren't you kind of blowing this out of proportion? I told you they didn't have the gift cards you wanted, so how is this my fault?"

I balled my fists next to my sides. "Because you didn't ask me what to get instead. You could've called or texted me. You didn't even text me back this morning. You ignored me. Both of you did. Just like always. And I guess I'm just tired of it."

Both of them looked at me with their mouths open. My body was shaking with all the emotion I'd tried desperately to contain. I was tired of being ignored. It was their turn. I didn't care what they had to say next. I needed to get away from the both of them, so I ran upstairs to my room.

I sat down on the edge of the bed and put my head in my hands. I hadn't meant to explode like that. Especially not with a hundred or so people just a few feet away in the backyard.

The door opened, and I heard someone walk in.

I didn't look up. "Just give me a minute, Mom. Don't worry. I'll still do everything I need to for the event."

"Grandma went to go find Lupe so she could deal with the caterer."

I lowered my hands, looked up, and saw Yesica standing near the bed. "Good." I wasn't sure what else to say.

"What was that, Mom?"

"Nothing," I said and then sighed. "I've just been a little stressed about the tea today. I'll be fine."

"I told Mama Melda weeks ago that I thought something was going on with you."

"Weeks ago?" I said, confused. Yes, I had been stressed about today, but I'd really only felt overwhelmed the past week. I'd tried to ignore my worries about my hours at the nursery, the little hiccups with the house renovation, and not knowing what to do for my writing assignment and just focus on the tea. "I don't know what you mean."

"You've just seemed off. Like you're deep in your thoughts or mad about something."

"I'm not mad . . . all the time. I just . . ." I didn't want to say anything more. But she wouldn't let it go.

"You're just what?"

Irritation pricked the back of my neck. After everything, why was I the one who needed to explain herself? I tried not to sound overly emotional as I told her what had been bothering me lately. "I guess I'm just a little disappointed that even though we're living under the same roof again, I still feel like you're a stranger. You disappear every Saturday morning and don't tell me where you're going. And then today, you couldn't even bother to text me back."

Yesica shook her head. "Oh my God, Mom. Again with the text. Fine, I'm sorry that I didn't reply to you. And in case you hadn't noticed, I'm thirty-three, and this is my house. Why do you need to know where I am all the time or when I'll be home?"

I stood up. "Not all the time. And it's more than that. I just thought things would be different between us. I thought living together would help us resolve whatever it is that's broken between us. I thought that we could . . ." I couldn't finish.

She shook her head. "We could what?" she asked, her brows furrowed in confusion. Then her expression changed as if she'd realized something. "Hold on. Did you think we were going to bond over dead husbands or something?"

When I didn't answer, Yesica said, "Oh my God. You did."

I threw up my hands in surrender. "Fine. I was wrong. But forgive me for thinking that you might need me for once in your life."

"Need you? For what? It's not like I was ever going to cry on your shoulder, Mom. I might be a widow like you, but our marriages were nothing alike. You don't know anything about me or my marriage. And I gave up a long time ago trying to understand yours."

"That's enough, Yesica," I said, unable to contain the shakiness of my voice.

"I don't think it is. I'd like to hear how Jason dying was the same as Daddy dying. Jason's death was unexpected, tragic. I had no warning. Oh wait, it was the same as Daddy's. Except, you could've told me what was happening. But because you didn't, I wasn't able to do something."

My chest tightened so hard that I clutched my blouse as if to try to ease the pain that was making my heart thump rapidly. "It was a stroke, Yesica," I said slowly, trying in vain to sound calm, even though I feared where this conversation was going. "And then a heart attack. You couldn't have done anything."

"I could've been there, Mom!" she yelled. "If you had called me when the stroke first happened, I would've jumped on the first flight home. I could've talked to his doctors, got him transferred to a better hospital or something. I don't know. At the very least, I could've said goodbye. You took that away from me."

My heart stopped. Not just because the accusation was so wrong, but because she believed it to be true. And because I hadn't tried to convince her otherwise all those years ago, I had allowed my daughter to think I was a monster.

"She didn't take anything away from you, Yesica. She didn't know your daddy was in the hospital until it was too late."

We both spun around to see my mother standing in the doorway.

My heart was pounding with both anger and fear. This wasn't how I wanted Yesica to find out.

"Mama, go back downstairs," I pleaded as I wiped the tears from my cheeks.

Of course she didn't listen. Instead, she walked inside the bedroom and shut the door behind her. "Tell her, Ana. Tell her what really happened. Or I will."

"No," I said adamantly. "It doesn't matter anyway."

Yesica threw up her hands. "What are you both talking about?"

"Ana?" my mother began. But when I didn't answer right away, she exploded. "For God's sake. Stop being the martyr, Ana! You think you're protecting her, but all you're doing is hurting the both of you. She deserves to know, and you deserve to not be blamed anymore."

I stood up and walked over to the window. I looked down at the small crowd of women laughing and talking as if they didn't have a worry in the world. I realized I could never be one of them—not really. I always had a worry. I could never let my mind rest and just enjoy the moment. Even as a little girl, I always felt like I had to worry about everyone else. Because if I didn't, bad things would happen. Things like my father getting shot.

I was only eight when it happened, but still I thought for the longest time that if I'd come up with an excuse as to why he didn't need to go to the store that night, then he would still be alive. Instead, I'd barely waved when he walked out the door because I was too busy wrapping a present for my best friend for her birthday party the next day.

I knew now that was silly. And sad.

But I couldn't help it. Nor could I help why I'd decided not to tell Yesica the truth about Benny's death. Well, not the whole truth.

A hand grabbed mine and pulled me out of my regrets.

"It's time, Mija. Tell her." My mother squeezed hard and then walked out of the room, closing the door behind her.

After a few seconds, Yesica sighed. "Fine. Keep your secrets like always. I'm going back to the party."

"Two weeks before he died, your father left me for another woman."

The words rushed out before I could stop or censor them. I panicked for a second. Then a small wave of relief filled my chest at finally saying the words I'd held inside for five years.

"What?"

Slowly, I turned around to face my daughter and saw the look of confusion and horror on her face that I'd been dreading ever since that day.

"Well, technically, I guess she really wasn't another woman. She was his girlfriend—the same woman he'd been seeing for the last twenty years of our marriage. Her name is—"

"Stop! Stop lying, Mom." I could tell Yesica was angry. But her voice cracked, and I knew she was also terrified. Deep down, she knew I was telling the truth.

I sat back down on the bed and stared at the floor, knowing I'd never get through my story if I kept looking at her. "I guess her name doesn't matter anyway. They worked together. He thought he was being careful. At least in the beginning. But despite what your father thought about me, I'm not a dumb woman. I figured it out eventually and confronted him. He denied it at first. Then he promised to break it off. Of course he didn't. By the time you were in high school, I guess he was tired of all the sneaking around and told me I had two choices. I could accept it and we could stay married for yours and Alejandro's sakes and just go on like always. Or, if I wanted to be ridiculous about it—that's how he put it—then he'd file for divorce and kick me and your grandma out and keep you kids. The house was in his name, so I believed him."

When she didn't say anything, I forced myself to look up. I shouldn't have.

I had expected to see sadness in her eyes; instead I saw disgust.

"You let him have an affair all those years?"

My back stiffened in both defense and shock at the accusation. "I didn't *let* him, Yesica. But what choice did I have? Really? Who was going to take in your grandma? Not my sister or brother. She was my responsibility, and so were you and your brother. So I stayed. Yes. But don't think for a second that I allowed him to do that. And until you find yourself in the same situation, you can't judge or know for sure what you would have done."

Her face paled, and for a second I thought she wobbled as if she was going to pass out. She dropped onto the opposite side of the bed. "What does this have to do with his death?"

I took a deep breath and attempted to steady myself by bracing my hands on the bed. This part of the story was even more difficult than what I had already shared. I hated that I had to take myself back to that time and relive some of the worst and lowest days of my life.

"The woman must have finally grown tired with their . . . arrangement and gave him an ultimatum. He had to either leave me for good, or she was going to move back east with one of her kids. So he moved out and moved in with her. Your dad told me that our marriage was over, and he was going to get a lawyer. He said that me and Grandma could stay in the house until the divorce was finalized, and then he was going to sell it because he wanted to buy his girlfriend a new one."

My heart broke all over again. I could still feel the pain of his words as if it were yesterday. After everything I'd done for the man. He was still going to leave me without a home.

I choked back my emotions and continued. "Anyway, I hadn't heard from him for a few days, and then one night I got a call from his phone.

But it wasn't him. It was her. She told me he'd had a stroke and was in a coma in the ICU at the hospital by her house. She told me that the doctors said the stroke had damaged his brain and his heart, and if he recovered, he would probably need around-the-clock care. She said she didn't want to be a nursemaid, so he was all mine if I wanted him back. Then she told me that if he ever woke up, to tell him that she was moving and not to go after her."

Yesica gasped and clapped her hand over her mouth.

My throat tightened, and I struggled to get out the next words. "Whatever he'd done to me or how much he had hurt me, he was still my husband and the father of my children. I couldn't leave him in that hospital all alone. So I packed a bag as soon as I hung up the phone and drove to the hospital. I decided to wait until the morning to call you kids. But before I got there, he had a heart attack and the doctors couldn't save him. I don't know. Maybe somehow he knew his girlfriend had abandoned him, and he just decided he didn't want to be here anymore."

Yesica leaped from the bed and began pacing around the room, holding her head. "I . . . I . . . This can't be true. It can't. You must have done something to make him leave, or you kicked him out. He wouldn't do that. He couldn't."

My daughter's tears ran down her cheeks, black mascara marking their path along the way. But as much as it broke my heart to see her upset, other bigger emotions began to swell within my chest and overtook the sadness. Frustration. Anger. Disappointment.

As far as my daughter was concerned, Benny was perfect. And I was the bad guy, like always. I wasn't sure what was different this time. But something inside me flipped a switch. I decided I wasn't going to sit back and let her paint me as the parent who was always in the wrong. Benny was gone. I was still here. I could speak up now.

I got up and grabbed her by her shoulders and waited until she looked at me. Her eyes were wide and full of shock. My go-to instinct as a mother was to continue protecting her from the truth I knew would hurt her. I realized in that moment that keeping Benny's secret had also been a way of protecting myself. Because I had always been afraid of Yesica looking at me the way she was looking at me now.

My daughter hated me.

I bit my lip and ignored the warning bells in my head and heart. I had to do it. I had to tell her everything. "I'm sorry for telling you like this, but it's all true. Every bit of it. You may think your dad was some kind of hero because he brought you ice cream on Fridays or took you to the movies. But what you're not remembering is him not showing up for your honor roll ceremonies or canceling plans with us because he had to work. The truth was, your dad had another life away from us. And at the end, he chose that life. I'm not saying your dad was a villain. But I need you to finally understand that I'm not a villain either. Everything I've ever done in my life was for you, Alejandro, and Grandma. And I would give anything for you to forgive me for whatever pain I've caused you because I let you believe Benny was a good husband and dad."

She was hysterical now, and so was I. After her sobs seemed to be under control, she pulled away. "This is too much. I can't do this right now."

CHAPTER TWENTY-SIX
YESICA

I think I was seven or eight the first time I went to the beach.

It was during the summer, and I remember being so excited about it that I couldn't sleep the night before. My mom had made bologna sandwiches and packed them in a small cooler, along with bags of chips and cookies. Our Capri-Sun juice pouches and bottles of water were stored in another cooler that my dad had filled with ice cubes from our freezer.

Alejandro and I shared a backpack for our clothes, towels, and the toy bucket and shovels we'd bought at the dollar store the week before. We put the coolers, the backpack, two folding chairs, one umbrella, and an old comforter into the trunk of my mom's Toyota, and the four of us were finally on our way from our home in Bell Gardens to Santa Monica.

Mama Melda had been out of town visiting some relatives, and it was probably one of the reasons why we'd gone that day in the first place. Not only did she dislike the beach; she also wasn't a fan of the sun.

It seemed like forever before we finally arrived. So, as soon as we'd found a spot on the sand to unload our stuff, I begged to go into the water. My mother wanted me to help her unpack everything first. My dad, as usual, gave in to my whining.

He walked beside me as we approached the ocean. The first time a wave hit my toes, I squealed in both shock and excitement. The water was cold, but I instantly loved the sensation and the movement of the sand underneath my feet.

"Can we go deeper?" I asked my dad.

"Okay, but you can't let go of my hand," he said.

I nodded, and we began to take one step at a time farther into the water until it was above my knees. My giddiness only grew with each wave. Still holding on to my dad's grasp, I jumped up as if to bump the roll of water back into the ocean with my chest. Part of me probably should've been more scared when the bigger waves threatened to knock me off my balance. But my dad never let go of my hand, and I knew that with him holding me, nothing could hurt me.

That day at the beach was one of the best memories I had of my dad. We visited lots more times over the years, just the two of us. And when it was too cold to go wave jumping, we'd walk along the pier or sit on a bench at the nearby park and people-watch.

And that was where Oscar found me.

I called him as soon as I'd stormed out of the scholarship tea luncheon. All I said was that I needed to talk, and he just asked where to meet me.

He sat next to me on the bench but didn't say a word. After a few minutes of silence, I was the one who finally spoke.

"Did you know I moved to Santa Monica because of my dad?"

"I didn't. Did he live here too?" Oscar asked.

I shook my head. "No, but he loved the beach. And he used to bring me here a lot. I even promised him that I was going to live here when I grew up so he could visit me whenever he wanted and we could always go to the beach together. After he died, I got it in my head that he was probably disappointed that I'd ended up living out of state instead. When Jason got offered a job in Los Angeles, I told him I would only move if we found a house in Santa Monica. My dad was dead, and I was still trying to please him. How pathetic is that?"

I laughed even as I wiped away tears with the back of my right hand.

Oscar covered my other hand with his. "What happened today, Yesica?"

It took me a few seconds to find my voice again. "Apparently, my mom and I both had cheating husbands."

He stayed quiet as I recounted everything my mother had told me about my dad, his affair, and the true circumstances around his death. When I was done talking, I didn't dare look over at Oscar for fear of starting to cry again and this time never stop.

"Our parents aren't supposed to be perfect," he finally said. "We just think they are because when we're little, we need them to be. It doesn't change your memories of your dad or that he loved you."

I shrugged. "I guess. But what does it say about me that I was okay believing that my mom was imperfect?"

"What do you mean?"

"My entire life I have questioned and criticized everything my mom ever said or did. Meanwhile, I thought my dad could do no wrong. And if he did, then I somehow blamed it on her. Even now, I'm angry at her for keeping his secret, even though he's the one I should be furious with!"

I shouted the last sentence as if to make sure my dad—wherever he was now—could hear me. My mom's confession had shaken me to my core. The revelation about my dad's affair was another earth-shattering moment in my own personal disaster movie. I was furious with her for destroying what I had always believed about my dad. But I also felt guilty because I knew why she'd done it. For me.

"So now what?" he asked gently.

"I stay here on this bench for the foreseeable future," I said half jokingly. I wasn't ready to think about what would happen when I went back home. I wasn't ready to talk, especially since deep down I knew my own secret would have to come out eventually.

Oscar squeezed my hand. "Then we'll just sit. I don't have anywhere to go for the foreseeable future anyway."

I laughed and finally turned to meet his eyes. "Thank you. I'm glad you're here."

"I'm glad you called me," he said with a smile.

Warmth spread over me, and I suddenly felt a sense of peace. I squeezed his hand back and said, "Don't let go, okay?"

The look he gave me took my breath away. "Never."

CHAPTER TWENTY-SEVEN
ANA

"Am I really that boring?"

Lucas's question startled me. I blinked a couple of times, and his confused expression came into focus. He was sitting across from me at the diner, but he might as well have been in another galaxy because my mind and its troubling thoughts were definitely somewhere far, far away.

"I'm sorry," I rushed out. "I told you I wouldn't be very good company tonight. I should've just gone home after class."

He waved me off. "It's fine. I'm just joking. You might feel better if you talk about what's been bothering you. You've seemed . . . off . . . the last couple of days."

"Off" was an understatement. Everything that had happened with Yesica at the scholarship tea was still a fresh wound. She'd stayed at Evie's for two days, and then when she did finally come home, she told me to give her some space. So I stayed mostly in my room when she was home and tried not to push her into talking. Because talking was something she'd decided she definitely didn't want to do—at least not with me.

I was so bothered by it all that I almost didn't even come to class tonight. But when I texted Lucas to tell him that I had some personal things I needed to work through, he ended up convincing me that writing down my feelings would help.

Except, the only thing I had to show for my work in class tonight was a blank page in my notebook.

I took a sip of my tea before answering him. It felt wrong to tell Lucas about Benny when I had just told Yesica. It didn't matter that Benny had betrayed me—it still didn't feel right.

"It's a long, complicated story," I said. "But basically my daughter and I had a fight, and she's not speaking to me right now. I want to fix things between us, but I also know that if I do what I usually do and push her to talk, then it will only make things worse."

As I said that, a realization hit me. This was what I had been doing with Yesica this whole time. The more I felt her pulling away from me, the more I tried to hold on tighter to her. If I didn't hear from her for a week, then I'd make sure the following week to call her every day. If she told me she liked a shirt I'd sent her for Christmas, then I bought her three more in different colors.

My relationship with Yesica had always seemed hard. Could it be because I was the one making it that way?

"Look, I'm not going to win any parent of the year awards, so take what I say with a grain of salt," Lucas said. "But I can see that your kids are your entire world. And if I can see that, then I'm sure they can too. Maybe you just need to let your daughter realize on her own that whatever the reason for the fight, it's something you two can get over."

"I hope so," I said earnestly. "Otherwise, the rest of our time at her place is going to be difficult."

"Your house is almost ready, then?" he said after taking a bite of his burger.

"Supposedly. I've learned not to expect things until they actually happen. So we'll see."

"Were there some delays you weren't expecting?"

"Um, more like I decided to do a little more renovating than my contractor was expecting," I said.

Lucas nodded. "Good for you. I bet you can't wait to move back into your own house."

I was excited. Once Yesica had pointed out that I didn't need to keep the house exactly how it had been, I'd allowed myself to think of what would make me happy. And I was looking forward to not having to commute any more. Still, I couldn't help but dread the day the construction was finally over—especially if it meant leaving Yesica as angry with me as she was right now.

"All right, enough about me. What about you? How's the book coming?" I picked up a French fry and popped it into my mouth.

Lucas sighed. "I think I'm almost done. But every time I think I'm ready to send it to my editor, I read it and decide I need to rewrite the whole thing."

I couldn't help but laugh. "You always do this," I said.

"Do what?"

"Think you don't know what you're doing and then end up writing a masterpiece. It's high school all over again."

"Actually, high school was worse. At least my editor doesn't hate me like our teacher Mrs. Wright did."

We both laughed about that.

"Can I get you two anything else?"

I looked up at our waitress and shook my head, still grinning. "I'm good, thank you."

Lucas told her the same, and she walked away.

"I guess Kara isn't working tonight," I mentioned.

He took a sip of his soda and shrugged. "Guess not," he said a few seconds later.

Curiosity got the better of me. "Um, so, have you seen her lately . . . working, I mean."

"I haven't been here since the last time we came together," he said. I didn't miss the amused look in his eyes.

"Really? Why is that? I thought you loved their bacon cheeseburgers?" I couldn't help but ask, as much as I hated how invested I was in his answer.

Lucas leaned back into the booth and met my eyes. "I never said I loved them."

His gaze held mine, and for a few seconds I couldn't breathe. The space between us crackled with an unspoken understanding of what Lucas was really telling me. My face heated, and I tried to shake off whatever emotion was now making my heart beat out of my chest.

Luckily, Lucas changed the subject and began talking about what he was planning for our next class.

As I listened to him, I tried not to think about why he was having such an effect on me. I was enjoying being his friend again, so I didn't want to confuse it with being anything more than that. My problem was that I tended to overanalyze everything.

And for the first time in days, I decided to stop thinking about what was going to happen with Yesica. Whatever happened now was up to her and out of my control. All I could do was be there when—and if—she wanted to talk.

It wasn't what I was used to doing. And maybe that meant it was exactly what I needed to do.

CHAPTER TWENTY-EIGHT
YESICA

The Saturday after I found out the truth about my father, I showed up early to the group meeting.

My mother and I still weren't speaking, which was the excuse I'd needed to leave the house before she'd even come downstairs. Mama Melda had tried to act as peacemaker a few times by telling me how sorry my mom was for keeping my dad's secret for so long.

I'd kept my distance, not because I didn't believe my mom, but because I was still struggling with the realization that I'd been so wrong about my dad and her.

My mom had said I'd always put my dad on a pedestal like a hero. I'd looked up to him and always wanted his approval. So much so that I grew to believe he wouldn't love me if I wasn't perfect.

And once I'd admitted that to myself, I began to remember other things.

It's true what they say about first daughters taking on the weight of everyone's world. I thought if I kept my room clean, if I got straight A's, if I behaved like a good daughter should—then my dad would never be mad. Because if he wasn't mad, then it would be a good day and he wouldn't disappear.

Memories I'd kept long buried had risen, and now that they were out, they wouldn't be ignored any longer. Like the times my dad would come home well after dinner, or the awards ceremony he missed because he'd supposedly had to work late. Or when I'd caught him walking through the door after two in the morning and later asked my mom if he'd gotten a second job. Back then I'd thought her blank expression was surprise. I wondered now if it was shame.

Could it be that my mind always knew he was hiding something, but my heart, as a way of protecting me, refused to ever find out what it was?

The second person to arrive for the meeting was Casey. He stopped at the refreshment table first to grab a water and then came and sat down in the chair next to me.

"Good morning," he said with a huge smile.

"Hi, Casey," I replied. "You seem to be in a good mood today."

"I am. I'm not sure, but when I woke up and remembered it was meeting day, my attitude immediately brightened. I couldn't wait to get here."

I was glad that Casey seemed to be doing well. I thought about what Oscar had said the other night about reaching the other side. I couldn't help but wonder if Casey was finally there.

"Casey, can I ask you a question?"

"Shoot," he replied.

"I know you've been coming to these meetings for almost a year now. Can you tell me if you feel any different today than how you felt during your first meeting?"

Casey nodded enthusiastically. "Oh, definitely. When I first got here, I was kinda lost. It took me a long time to even see what was in front of me."

"Is there something that happened that made you begin to believe that you were going to be okay?"

"Um, I think so?"

"What was it?"

He placed his palms on his knees and sat with back straight against the chair—as if he was bracing himself for the memory. "I think it was after I shared with the group about the day my mom died. I had never told the story—the entire story—to anyone before. I think I was afraid of going back there, you know what I mean?"

I did.

"I do," I said.

"So after I talked about it, it was almost as if I had faced a fear. I think that fear had been holding me back. After that meeting, I felt like a huge weight had been lifted. And every day since then has been a little easier."

My throat tightened with emotion, so it took me a few seconds to say, "I'm happy for you, Casey."

As more people began to arrive, I thought about what Casey had said. Although I'd told Oscar about Jason and the affair, I hadn't told him exactly what had happened that day. I'd never told anyone.

"Hey," a familiar voice said.

I looked up and met Oscar's eyes. "Hey," I said back.

"You okay?"

"Yeah, why?" I said with a nod.

"I don't know. You just have this look on your face that I can't quite decipher."

"Just thinking. That's all."

"Should I be worried?" he asked.

"Maybe?" I couldn't help but laugh after his eyebrows shot up. "Just kidding. I'm good. I promise."

Oscar nodded, but I knew he was still worried. Ever since his confession outside the bar, I'd felt as if he was handling me with kid gloves. I'd tried to tell him that what he'd told me hadn't changed anything. And I'd tried proving it by continuing our flirty text exchanges and by showing up this morning bright and early.

Honestly, though, the blowup with my mom had been the main thing on my mind all week.

I wasn't sure how to fix our relationship. The only thing I'd figured out was that things needed to change in order to get better. I needed to change.

Maybe it was time to face a fear.

For about thirty minutes, I listened as different people answered Oscar's question about setting up boundaries. Then it was time for open sharing.

I raised my hand.

Oscar gave me a smile and called on me. I stood up and introduced myself like you were supposed to do before you shared.

"Hi, Yesica," the group responded in unison.

My hands wouldn't stop shaking, so I dug them into the sides of my thighs and let out a long breath. "Today I'd like to tell you about the day my husband died. Or, rather, the day I thought I killed him."

I waited for the murmurs to quiet down before I continued.

The memories of that day broke through whatever barrier I'd erected as a defensive wall in order to maintain my sanity. And it all came rushing back as if it was yesterday.

"It was the only thought that had come to mind as soon as the police officer told me that Jason was dead," I began. "In fact, I had expected that his next words were going to be, 'You have the right to remain silent.' The baby-faced, redheaded cop had even asked, 'Mrs. Diaz-Taylor, did you hear what I said?' I had heard his words—starting from 'I'm so sorry to inform you,' all the way to something about a car accident. But I don't think I really understood them. All I could focus on was the fact that Jason had died, and it was all my fault."

The dryness in my mouth made me stutter those last few words. I held up a hand and picked up my water bottle and gulped. Once my tongue had stopped sticking to the roof of my mouth, I stopped drinking and continued.

"After the realization hit that my husband had been killed, my gut reacted first. And before I could stop it, bile seemed to erupt from my gut like an acidic volcanic explosion—forcing it up my throat. I slapped my hand over my mouth and ran to our guest bathroom with just a second to spare. When I returned to the front door a few minutes later, I was surprised to see the officer still standing there. His original passive expression had morphed into something between sheer uncomfortableness and pity. It was the way he looked at me that finally triggered the anger. I knew that look. I hated that look. It was the look my husband had given me just before he told me he was in love with someone else and was leaving me for her."

I heard a few gasps, so I paused. It gave me the tiny break I needed to take another long breath and one more sip of water.

"It was hard to believe that it was less than four hours earlier when my husband had asked me for a divorce," I continued. "In that amount of time, I'd wished on everything I knew for Jason to die some horrible death so that he could feel the same horrible pain he'd inflicted on me with his ultimate betrayal. And then this young cop showed up on my front porch to tell me that I'd gotten my wish. I remember the cop asking me, 'Is there someone else here with you? Or can you call someone?' I told him there was no one. That's when I realized it wasn't all some horrible dream. That morning I had been a wife. That afternoon I was close to becoming a divorcée. And by dinnertime, I was a widow. I still can't quite believe it sometimes. It's a club I never imagined I would join. Of course, I know now I didn't kill Jason with my thoughts. If that was possible, I'd wish for him to be alive now. Not because I still want to be his wife. I've accepted that our marriage was over months before he died. But because there was a time when I truly loved him, and I know he truly loved me. So I wish for Jason to be alive just so I could tell him I'm sorry for forgetting that. Thank you for listening."

I offered my audience a quick smile and then took my seat again. As another woman stood up and began to share, I tried to focus on her words. But the blood was still rushing in my ears, and her voice and the other noises around me sounded muffled as if I was underwater. My body quivered as it released the once-roaring adrenaline, and I took measured breaths in an effort to slow my heart rate.

The worst, I hoped, was over. After the meeting, most of the group members came over to me to tell me how much they appreciated me sharing my story. Others said they hoped one day they could share theirs. And one man offered to set me up with his son.

It was true what they said about how much lighter you felt after unloading a burden. My feet never left the white laminate floor, yet I felt as if I was weightless. Finally sharing the story of Jason's death had released whatever it was that had been tying me down and making it impossible for me to move on.

After saying goodbye to the others, I stuck around to talk to one more person.

"I'm proud of you," Oscar said as soon as I walked up to him.

"I'm proud of me too," I replied.

"What made you decide to finally talk about it?"

"Not a what, but a who. Casey kind of inspired me."

Oscar nodded approvingly. "I should be jealous you didn't say it was me, but I'm not. Whatever or whomever helped you get to where you are now, I'm happy."

I smiled but then thought about my mom.

It was finally time for me to tell her the truth about everything.

CHAPTER TWENTY-NINE
ANA

I tried to fold the sheet for the third time. But as much as I tried to focus, the thing just ended up a misshapen ball.

"It doesn't have to be perfect, Ana. It's just a sheet. It's going to get wrinkled no matter what you do. Unless you want to iron it?"

I looked over at my mother, who was knitting in the armchair across the den from me.

"I don't want to iron it. And I don't need it to be perfect. But if it doesn't fold flat, then it won't fit in the linen closet with the other ones. One lumpy sheet can throw the entire order into chaos."

My mother put down her knitting needles and the blanket she was working on to come sit next to me on the couch.

She took the sheet from me and began folding. "She is going to come around, Mija. Don't worry. And don't take your frustration with Yesica out on the laundry."

I hated that my mother was so perceptive. Well, when she wanted to be anyway.

"It's been a week, Mama. We've never gone this long without speaking. She barely acknowledges me when we're in the same room, and this morning she was gone before I even came downstairs. When we moved in, I thought this was going to give us the time we needed to become close again. But we're going to be going home soon, and things between me and Yesica are worse than ever. Why did I tell her?"

My mother put the perfectly folded sheet on top of the towels in a nearby laundry basket and turned to me. "You told her because it's not good to keep such secrets between you. She deserved to know."

"Maybe. But I could've told her in a better way. I could've tried to make her understand I only kept Benny's affair from her to protect her and Alejandro."

"She knows that, Mija. Yesica is a smart woman. She just needs time to realize everything you did was because of them."

"I guess. But even if she forgives me, what if we just go back to being how we were before? I still don't know where she goes every Saturday morning."

"And why do you need to know?"

I almost didn't tell her because a mother's intuition was hard to explain. "Because . . . because I feel like whatever she's doing, it's something important. If she was just going to the gym or Target, why wouldn't she just say so? The fact that she says nothing makes me believe it's something . . . a big something. And it makes me sad that she's not sharing it with me."

I hadn't expected my mother to scoff so loudly. "De tal palo tal astilla."

"What does that mean?" I asked.

"I mean like mother, like daughter. She's not the only one keeping secrets in this house, Ana. When were you going to tell me you've been seeing Lucas Padilla?"

I froze in shock. "What?"

"You think I wouldn't find out that he's your writing teacher? I've lived a long time. It's not so easy to keep things from me. Plus, he called one day when you were in the shower, and when I saw his name on the screen, I answered it. He told me to tell you to leave for class a few minutes early because there was construction going on in front of the building."

"Why didn't you say something before today?"

She shrugged and began folding another sheet. "I figured you'd tell me eventually. Or just wait for the wedding invitation."

"Mama!"

"Qué? I told you I see everything. When you two were teenagers, I thought you would end up together eventually. Then, when everything happened with Cuca, I knew it was wrong to forbid you from seeing him, but I was hurting. Of course I know you didn't listen. Then you married Benny, and I decided I would support you, even though I knew you didn't love him—not like you loved Lucas."

My eyes watered with decades' worth of the emotions I thought I'd been hiding. "I can't believe you never said any of this to me."

"Would it have changed things? Would you have left Benny and told Lucas how you felt?"

"No, I wouldn't have," I said.

"The past is the past, Ana. The only thing you have the power to change is the present. For Yesica and for you. If you want to be with Lucas now, you will be the only one standing in your way."

It was as if someone had taken a hammer and shattered a mirror into a thousand pieces. I nodded as the tears finally spilled from my eyes, and I reached over to give her a sideways hug. She didn't like to show emotions, but I could've sworn I saw one tear sliding down her cheek.

I had always admired my mother for her strength. I realized maybe that hadn't been fair to her or me. Being vulnerable had its benefits too.

After we'd both composed ourselves, I decided to ask her a question.

"Mama, did you mean what you said about the past being the past and us being able to control our present?"

"Pues, of course. That's why I said it."

"Good. Mama, do you think you could help me with a writing assignment?"

Before I could tell her what I was thinking, the kitchen door opened.

215

Yesica walked into the den and stood in front of us. The look she had on her face scared me. I grabbed my mother's hand and braced myself for whatever was about to happen.

"I'm ready to tell you where I've been going on Saturdays. But before I do, I also need to tell you the truth about the day Jason died."

CHAPTER THIRTY
YESICA

When I was about twelve or thirteen, my dad woke me up early on a school day and announced he was taking me to Knott's Berry Farm.

Normally, I wouldn't have thought twice about ditching school to spend some time with him at an amusement park, but it was the day of a special assembly, and I knew there was a good chance I was going to be named student of the month. I asked if we could go Saturday instead, but he said his work had given tickets to all the employees only for that day. I was surprised, though, when he added that it would just be the two of us.

"Your mom has to take your grandma to an appointment, and your brother is too little for the rides at Knott's," he'd explained as we drove.

I had never been there, but I'd assumed it would be just like Disneyland. I was wrong. As we walked through the entrance, I couldn't shake the feeling that I was walking onto a movie set for an old western. Besides enjoying the old-timey theme of the park, I was also surprised to see it had roller coasters. Big ones.

We met up with a group of his coworkers and spent the first hour with them. A few of them had their kids, too, including one woman who'd brought her daughter, who seemed to be about my age. We got along fine and even sat together on some of the rides. Then the girl asked me if I wanted to go on the park's wooden roller coaster with her.

My dad answered for me and said he would wait for me with the girl's mom at a nearby bench.

It wasn't until we were almost to the ride that the nerves and shakes began. I was afraid of heights, which meant I didn't do roller coasters. It had bothered me that my dad didn't remember that before practically pushing me to get in line.

Finally, the girl must have noticed my pale expression. "What's wrong?"

"I don't like roller coasters," I admitted.

"Oh. Then why did you agree to come with me?"

I wanted to argue that I hadn't. Instead I just shrugged.

"We can get out of line if you want. Or I can just go by myself."

Although part of me wanted to, I didn't want her to think I was a baby. I also could just imagine the look of disappointment on my dad's face that I'd chickened out.

So I told her I would still get on the ride.

The anxiety and nerves I had nearly made me throw up as the coaster pulled away from the station. And by the time we were climbing to the first drop, tears were streaming down my face. I screamed bloody murder as the coaster took off. Maybe it was the adrenaline, or maybe I had fainted at some point, but the fear quickly transformed into something else. And I knew I was going to be okay.

We got off the coaster, and the girl asked me, "So what did you think?"

"It wasn't as bad as I thought it was going to be."

I'd never learn if that girl's mother was my dad's girlfriend. I never saw either of them again. But I thought of them as I was driving home after the meeting. The streets of Santa Monica were far from a rickety wooden roller coaster track, but it felt as if I was back at Knott's Berry Farm again and preparing to face my greatest fear.

I could only hope that after I told my mother and grandma about Jason's affair, I would be able to say it wasn't as bad as I thought it was going to be.

Now in my den facing them, I swallowed the nausea roiling my stomach and began my story.

"On the day he died, Jason told me he wanted a divorce. He had been having an affair, and the woman was pregnant." I ignored their gasps and continued. "We'd been trying for two years to have a baby of our own. We did everything we could—even IVF. But after I miscarried, we both decided to take a break from trying. I don't think that's what ended our marriage—we'd had problems for years. But it was probably the last straw. So this baby was Jason's chance to start over, and he was going to take it."

Both of them gasped again.

"Ay, Yesica, mi amor," Mama Melda cried and then covered her mouth with her hand.

"Oh my God." The pain in my mom's eyes made me want to stop the story there. But I knew she deserved to know everything. They both did.

"When the police told me he'd made a U-turn in the middle of traffic, part of me wanted to believe that he was coming back to the house because he'd changed his mind—I thought he was coming back to me," I told them. "Then, after they left, I heard the sound of his phone ringing. I found it inside his suit jacket's pocket. The caller ID said 'spam,' so I didn't answer it. But that's when I knew he hadn't changed his mind at all. He'd just wanted to come get his phone. And it dawned on me that 'spam' was probably the girlfriend calling, wondering where he was. I was so angry that I grabbed a hammer from the garage and destroyed his phone."

I took a step closer to the couch. "I'm so sorry, Mom, for what I said last weekend. I had no right to judge you. Then or now. I'm so sorry that I didn't want to see how Dad treated you. I blamed you for his actions. Now I see that I was so worried about not turning into you when I married Jason that I didn't realize I had turned into Dad. I should've told you the truth about my marriage a long time ago."

She reached for me, and I lowered my body so we could hug. We squeezed each other so tight—as if we were trying to get rid of decades' worth of old hurt and regrets.

"I'm sorry too, Mija," she said after we'd pulled apart. "Maybe if I told you my secret earlier, you would've felt like you could talk to me."

I wasn't too sure if I would've. Part of me still felt embarrassed that I hadn't seen what had been happening right under my nose. I could blame work. I could blame our fertility struggles. Truth was, I had prided myself on not letting anything get the better of me. And Jason's affair had done that and more.

"Maybe," I told her. "But you know how I am. I had the perfect job and the perfect house. How could I tell people that I didn't have the perfect marriage? Or that I had basically failed at becoming a mother. I was ashamed."

She was openly crying. "I wish I could've been there for you."

The pain in her voice broke my heart, and all I wanted to do was soothe it. I reached out and grabbed her hand. "You were. Maybe you didn't realize it at the time, but you helped me survive the miscarriage."

Her eyes widened, and I knew she remembered. Then she hugged me again.

I turned to hug Mama Melda, but she put her hand up. "I've cried enough today. If you hug me, I don't think I will ever stop."

"Too bad," I said with a laugh and pulled her into my arms. A few seconds later, I felt a pair of arms hug my back. The three of us clung to each other, alternating between crying and laughing. It was as if something was trying to pull us apart, and the harder it pulled, the harder we held on.

Eventually, Mom left the room and came back with a box of tissues. After we'd wiped away our tears, I sat down on the armchair.

"There's something else I need to tell you both," I said.

"Ay, Dios mío," Mama Melda replied. "I don't know if I can take any more confessions."

My mom shushed her. "Go ahead, Yesica."

"It's not bad—but it's important that you know," I explained. "The reason why I leave every Saturday morning is because I've been going to a grief support group over in Malibu. I didn't voluntarily take time off from work. Damien made me because he felt like I wasn't dealing with my anger and grief issues, and it was starting to affect my work. Oscar—the man you met at dinner at Damien's house—leads the support group meetings. Going to the support group meetings was Damien's, um, suggestion."

"Oh," my mom responded. "That's good, Yesica. Really good."

"Qué therapy? You tell our business to strangers?" Mama Melda said.

"Mama," my mother warned.

"It's okay. I was just like Mama Melda when Damien first told me about the meetings. But, no, I don't talk about our business. I only talk—when I talk—about why I'm so angry and sad. And it's helping me. It really is."

"Well," Mama Melda said. "If it helps you and you are going to be happy again, then it's okay with me."

I laughed. I didn't need her approval. But it was a welcome surprise.

"I'm proud of you, Yesica. I wish I had been brave like you and found someone I could talk to after your father died."

"You talked to me," Mama Melda argued.

"It's not the same, Mama."

I knew what my mom meant. "Maybe you can use your writing to work out those feelings now, Mom? Oscar says it doesn't matter how we face our emotions, just that we don't keep them bottled up inside us."

She smiled at me, and I ignored her curious eyes. "Oscar sounds like a very smart man. He's very handsome, too, if I remember."

"All right, that's enough confessions for one day," I said as I stood up. The day had ben emotionally exhausting. Unloading decades' worth of pent-up feelings and regrets was not for the weak. I knew our lives were going to be different now. It was a good thing. But first, I needed some time to absorb it all.

Like the roller coaster, I was glad I'd gone on the ride. It didn't mean that I wanted to do it again, though.

CHAPTER THIRTY-ONE
ANA

"I'm so happy for you, Ana."

I looked over at Lucas, and I knew my smile must have gone from one ear to the other. I had just told him how me and Yesica had fixed things between us for the moment.

"Thank you. I know we still have a lot of work to do on our relationship, but for the first time in a long time, I feel like we're in a good place."

He had invited me out to dinner to celebrate the fact that he'd finished writing his second book. I even told my mom and Yesica the truth about where I was going. He picked me up from Yesica's house and drove us to the restaurant. It felt nice not to worry about hiding anymore.

Lucas raised his glass of champagne. "We should toast to you and your daughter."

"We should toast to your new book," I said, and I picked up my glass too.

"How about we toast to both?"

"Cheers," I said, and we clinked our glasses together.

"Thank you for coming out tonight and celebrating with me. Writing is such a solitary act. It feels nice to celebrate this with a friend."

I shouldn't have been disappointed by him using the word "friend." After all, he'd never given me any reason to think he ever wanted more than friendship. I blamed my mother's admission about her thinking me and Lucas were going to end up together.

"So when are you going to write a book?" he asked. I almost choked on my champagne.

"Me? I'm no author," I said.

"Sure you are. I already told you your detective stories were my favorite."

I waved my hand as if to dismiss the idea of me writing an actual book. "And I already told you those stories were just for fun."

"Fine. So write something new. You're talented, Ana. I wish you could see what I see in you."

I had been about to take a bite of my steak, but my stomach's flip-flops made me put the fork down. "And what is that?"

From across the table, I could see his expression change from neutral to serious. "I see a beautiful, talented woman who deserves only the good things in life. I see someone who is important to me and whom I'm enjoying getting to know all over again."

Suddenly, it seemed as if the temperature in the room had risen by twenty degrees. The glass of champagne had nothing to do with my face feeling as if I was on fire. I didn't know what to say to him. I barely trusted myself to speak.

"Thank you," I squeaked after a few seconds.

The rest of our dinner conversation stayed in safer territory. We talked about my job and how sad I'd been to learn that the nursery was going to be sold. But the new owners had already asked me to stay on. Lucas showed me new photos of his grandbaby and even said he'd mentioned me to his mom.

"And what does she think about us reconnecting?" I asked.

"Oh, she's happy. She's always liked you, Ana. In fact, part of me thinks she kind of wanted us to be more than friends."

"Really?"

"Really."

The words spilled out before I could stop them. "My mom thought the same thing!"

Lucas raised his eyebrows. "She did? I thought she hated me."

"I thought that too," I said with a laugh. "I guess our moms are more alike than we thought."

We followed dinner by sharing a slice of cheesecake. And although I wanted to treat him to dinner as a congratulations gift, he insisted on paying since he'd been the one to invite me. The short drive back to Yesica's was quiet, and for a minute I wondered if he'd been offended by me offering to pay. But when we pulled into the driveway, he asked if he could walk me to the door.

I agreed.

"Thank you for dinner," I told him when we reached her front patio. "Next time it's on me, though, okay?"

"So there will be a next time?" he asked.

"Of course. We're friends, right? Friends take each other out to dinner. Or we could do lunch if you prefer?"

He shrugged. "Dinner is nice," he said. "Before you go inside, can I ask you a question?"

I nodded, thinking it was going to be about the class.

"When we were younger, did you ever think . . . Did you ever wish we were more than friends?"

I couldn't have hidden my shock if I'd tried. He had caught me completely off guard. "What makes you ask that?"

"When we were talking about how both of our moms thought that, it just made me wonder if they were seeing something neither of us saw back then."

"Well, that's because you thought of me as a sister."

"Trust me, Ana. I never thought of you as my sister. You were my best friend. And I have to admit there was a time when I did think about what it would be like if we were more than that."

My heart thumped so hard against my chest I wondered if he could hear it.

"You did? Why didn't you ever say anything?"

"Because I didn't want to risk it not working out and that ruining our friendship. But then I lost you anyway."

My mind was racing just as fast as my heart was beating. Everything I'd thought about Lucas back then had been wrong.

"I . . . I don't know what to say," I told him.

His expression paled, and he dragged his hand down his face. "I'm sorry if this is making you uncomfortable. It really wasn't how I wanted our night to end."

"What did you want?"

Lucas rubbed the back of his neck as he studied the ground. "I just wanted us to be together. Like we used to. I miss that. I miss you. I didn't realize how much until I saw you that day in the market."

"You've missed me this whole time?"

"Of course I have. How could I not?"

I should've been jumping for joy to know that was how he felt. Instead, it made me sad to think of what might have been. "I wish . . . I wish things had been different back then."

He shrugged. "I wasn't sure if you wanted to ever talk to me again. Then you married someone else, or did you forget that small detail?"

"Because you took someone else to the prom."

"You told me you didn't want to go." Then he dropped a bombshell. "Besides, I did try to see you after graduation. I even came to the house."

The champagne in my system, combined with everything else he'd just said, didn't let me process what was happening.

"Benny was the one who answered the door. He told me you had gone to the doctor with your mom. Then he said you were pregnant and were going to marry him."

"I wasn't home?" I asked, as if that was the most important part of the story. Not even close.

Lucas had tried to see me again. And it was Benny who had told him about me getting pregnant.

"Yesica was born the following January," I admitted.

Lucus stuck his hands in his pants pockets and stared down at the concrete floor. "I figured your life was going to be different now, and I didn't want to do anything to mess that up. So I never tried to contact you again."

I felt lightheaded. It does something to a person to learn how differently your life might have turned out because of one decision.

"The past is the past, Lucas. Why are you telling me all this now?"

He stepped closer so I could see his face under the porch light. "Because I don't want to make the same mistake I did when I was a stupid teenager. I'm so glad we're friends again, Ana. But I need to let you know that I have feelings for you. And I can only pray that doesn't scare you away and we go back to being strangers. I know this is out of the blue and you need time to process it. So I don't need an answer from you tonight."

My throat tightened as if my body was protecting me from saying anything else. But I had to know. "What are you asking me, Lucas?"

"I'm asking if there's any possibility that you feel the same way?"

CHAPTER THIRTY-TWO
YESICA

My husband's mistress was named Amber.

And she was indeed very, very pregnant.

My mom estimated she was at least eight or nine months so, in fact.

"You don't have to do this," she said as we sat in my car outside a small coffee shop called the Grindz. It was around the corner from Jason's office.

"I know. But I need to."

It still seemed strange talking to my mother about my husband's mistress. But she and I had both come to an agreement that there would be no more secrets between us. We'd wasted so much time believing that we didn't understand each other when, in fact, we had gone through nearly the same trauma.

A few days ago, she and I had been talking about how Celeste still refused to let me come visit Henry. The cousin I was still friendly with had said his condition was rapidly deteriorating. I couldn't shake the feeling that I needed to see him one last time.

"It's sad," my mom had said. "There's a part of his son out there in the world, and he's never going to know."

I had been thinking the same thing. "Am I just as bad as Celeste?"

"What are you talking about?"

"By not telling her the truth about Jason and the possibility she may have a grandchild."

"Mija, you said you don't know anything about the other woman. No one expects you to hire a private detective and track her down. You don't owe that lady anything."

"Maybe. But I owe Henry. And, in a way, Jason."

I didn't think I'd ever get over the guilt I still carried for not being able to give him a child. What if finding Amber was the universe's way of making up for that? As much as I didn't want to know this woman, I couldn't shake the feeling that I had to at least try to find her.

We had spent the last week staking out the coffee shops in the neighborhoods surrounding Jason's building. My mom would go in and strike up a conversation with an employee and casually mention if they knew anyone who was pregnant and wanted to sign up for free baby classes at the Learning Lab. We'd struck out until today, when my mom walked into the Grindz and saw a very pregnant barista behind the counter. Still not sure if she was the woman we were looking for, my very clever mother mentioned that fathers were also welcome to attend the classes. When the woman said the baby's father had died, we knew Amber was the one.

"I wonder how she found out about Jason," I said as I looked out the window.

"I don't know. But it's good that she knows, right?"

It was. Because I had been dreading being the one to break the news to her.

"All right. I'm going in," I said, and I opened the door. My mom grabbed my arm before I got out.

"Are you sure you're ready? We can come back another day."

"Oscar wanted me to wait until tomorrow so he could be there when I talked to her."

"I can go with you."

I shook my head. "I'm telling you what I told him. I appreciate the support, but I need to face her on my own."

My mom let go of me, and I exited the car and walked across the street.

I could say Amber wasn't what I had pictured. Truth was I had tried very hard the past several months not to picture her at all. She was a faceless woman, and the less I knew about her, the better. At least that's what I had believed.

She looked to be in her mid- to late twenties. Except for her protruding belly, she was a small thing. She wore her light-brown hair in a messy ponytail, and even from the doorway I could tell she was exhausted. I could only imagine how hard it must have been to be that pregnant and have to work on your feet all day.

I shook the unexpected empathy away. I couldn't be emotional. I had come here to do one thing. And it didn't involve feeling sorry for my husband's mistress.

"Hi there, how can I help you?" she said in a friendly tone as I walked up to the counter.

"Hi. Um, I'll take a medium dark roast."

"Great. Anything else?"

I took a long breath. "Yes. I was wondering if I could speak with you privately, Amber. Maybe on your next break?"

Her eyes widened in surprise. "I'm sorry. Do I know you?"

"No. At least I don't think so. But you knew my husband, Jason."

It was another twenty minutes before Amber was able to go on break and sit with me at a table in the corner of the coffee shop.

"I only have fifteen minutes," she said. I detected a tone of defensiveness. Maybe she expected me to make a scene or cuss her out.

"That's fine. I only need five." As I sat across from her, I tried to ignore the rapid beating of my heart and the way my stomach was twisting itself into a huge knot.

"Before you say anything, I need to let you know I didn't plan on getting pregnant," she rushed out. "And I wasn't even going to keep it, but Jason, uh, he begged me to and promised we could be a family."

"But then he died," I said bitterly. "How did you find out?"

Amber's face fell, but she quickly regained her composure. "Before . . . before anything started between us, he used to come into the café with one of his coworkers. When he didn't come back that day or even answer my calls, I figured he'd changed his mind about telling you about us, and he was ghosting me. Then a few weeks later, his coworker came in, and I just asked him what happened to the guy who used to come in with him. He was the one that told me about the accident. No one at his office knew about me and Jason. Poor guy probably was so confused when I burst into tears."

I wouldn't be human if I didn't feel at least a small pang of empathy. After all, I was the widow. I was the one Jason's coworkers offered their sympathies to, with flowers and casseroles. Amber was Jason's secret. And that was how she'd had to grieve his loss. In secret.

"Can I ask why you decided to keep the baby after that?" I said, making sure my tone was even and unaffected. I didn't want Amber to know how hard it was for me to talk about this.

She shrugged. "Because I'm stupid. After I found out Jason died, I had this romantic notion about how the baby was my way of keeping a piece of him with me. I thought about trying to find you to see if he had any life insurance or something. But I decided this baby was my problem, and I had to figure things out."

For being so young, Amber was more jaded than I thought she'd be. And though I thought I'd find a woman who was still reeling from the grief of losing her one true love, I was sorely mistaken. I couldn't help but think that if Jason had lived, their romance would've had a short shelf life. It was clear to me that Amber was regretting her life choices.

Again, though, I wasn't here for Amber.

I sat up straight and looked her squarely in the eyes. "So, first of all, whatever life insurance Jason had paid for his plot at the cemetery and the funeral services. Second of all, I didn't come here today to find out why my husband cheated on me with you or ask why you would sleep with a married man. I couldn't care less now about either."

She raised her eyebrow at me. "Why are you here then?"

"Because I think Jason's parents deserve to know they're going to have a grandchild. He was their only son, and his dad is very ill. Maybe finding out about the baby would bring them a little bit of happiness. And I think it would be nice if the baby could learn more about who their dad was and where he came from."

"You really think they would accept the baby and me?" Amber said. Her voice was animated—even excited.

I already knew that Celeste would be less than thrilled with Amber, but, like me, she'd put up with her to get what she wanted.

I chose my next words carefully. "Look, I can't promise that. All I can do is put you in touch with my mother-in-law. What happens after that has nothing to do with me. In fact, don't be surprised if you never see me or hear from me again."

Amber nodded. "Okay. I'm willing to talk to her."

Somehow I knew that would be her answer.

"Great. Write down your phone number on a piece of paper, and I'll make sure she gets it."

"What if she doesn't call me?"

"You're carrying her only son's baby. Of course she's going to call."

After Amber wrote her information on the back of a napkin, I stood up to leave.

"I don't know how to thank you," she said.

"I don't want your thanks. Just take care of that baby."

I held my head up high and walked out of the café. But as soon as I got into the car, I let out all the pain and anguish I'd been holding in.

And like the good mother she had always been, my mom just held me and told me everything was going to be okay now.

CHAPTER THIRTY-THREE
ANA

I was still thinking of Yesica as I walked into class that evening.

She had been so brave to do what she'd done. I couldn't stop telling her how proud I was of her. And I could finally say that she believed me.

I knew our relationship still needed some work. We had trust to rebuild after so many years of secrets and assumptions. I wanted us to be open with one another. I didn't ever want to feel like my daughter was a stranger. And if that meant holding her while she cried after meeting her husband's mistress, then I was happy to do it.

Seeing her go through that pushed me to face one of my own fears.

It was because of her that I raised my hand when Lucas asked who wanted to be the first to read their essays to the rest of the class.

We hadn't texted much since the other night. When we did, it was casual. I knew he was giving me the space I needed. That didn't mean I liked it.

He called on me, and I slowly stood up and picked up the pages I'd printed out the night before. I walked to the front and met Lucas's eyes. He gave me a warm smile, which bolstered my confidence.

When I decided to tell my mother's story for the assignment, I wasn't sure if she would let me. It actually took a few days, with some extra coaxing from Yesica and Evie, for her to open up. Once she did, though, I began to have doubts. The voice in my head—the one that sounded a lot like Benny's—kept telling me I wasn't a good enough writer to tell such an important story. But when I asked my mother for the millionth time if it was okay for me to do this, she told me I was the only person she trusted with these memories.

Like Yesica, she had decided to be brave.

So I had to be brave too.

I turned around to face the class, cleared my throat, and said, "This is my mother's story, about how she and her family were forced out of her childhood home. I'll be telling the story from her point of view, as she experienced it as a little girl."

Then I began:

"When I was a little girl, I lived in the Palo Verde neighborhood of Chavez Ravine.

"For those of you who don't know the history, Chavez Ravine was named after Julián Chávez, one of the first supervisors of LA County. The small neighborhood was so different compared to the city of Los Angeles that sat just beyond the hills. It was small-town living just a few feet away from big-city life. The people who lived there were the ones who taught at the schools, preached at the churches, and even grew their own food on the land. It was common to see children playing right alongside turkeys and goats. To many outsiders, Chavez Ravine was known as the 'poor man's Shangri La.'

"Not that I knew any different. Our neighborhood was poor, but it was full of community. Our house was simple, but it was ours.

"Until it wasn't.

"I was only eight years old when I first learned what the word 'eviction' meant. My daddy had said that the city wanted to build new apartments in Chavez Ravine. They wanted to build a new community on the land and call it Elysian Park Heights. I told Daddy I didn't want to live in a new apartment or in a place with a different name. The only world I'd ever known was Chavez Ravine. I didn't want to leave. Ever.

"City officials started to hold meetings promising all kinds of things, like new schools and playgrounds. Daddy and his friends would go to these meetings, just to come back and say all kinds of bad words in Spanish about the men who worked for the city. He called them all 'mentirosos.' Liars.

"But some of our neighbors believed what the city was telling them. One by one, my friends left Chavez Ravine. They promised they would be back when the new apartments were ready.

"It turned out, my daddy was right all along.

"The new apartments and schools were never built. But it was too late. Most of the people were gone, and most of the houses were torn down or burned. Chavez Ravine looked like one of those abandoned towns where they said ghosts lived.

"Daddy swore up and down that he would never leave our home. Our family was one of about twenty who stayed in Chavez Ravine. My friend told me that the city wanted to build a baseball field for a team called the Brooklyn Dodgers. I didn't know who they were, and I asked my daddy why they couldn't build the field somewhere else.

"'I don't know, baby,' was all he said.

"I didn't hear anything more about the baseball field for a few weeks. I had hoped that meant the city had changed its mind, and all my friends were going to move back to Chavez Ravine.

"Then, on Black Friday in 1959, the bulldozers and la policía came.

"I didn't understand why a man was yelling at us to get out of our home. I hid under my bed and covered my ears. I could hear my neighbor Aurora screaming at the top of her lungs and more voices shouting at her to shut up. I found out later that the police had taken her to jail.

"When a hand reached under the bed and grabbed my ankle, I screamed as loud as Aurora. But it was Mommy. Her face was wet and streaked with black mascara. She gave me a pillowcase and told me to fill it up with whatever would fit. It was time to leave Chavez Ravine.

"'But Daddy said we were never leaving,' I cried.

"'Daddy is staying. Me and your brothers and sisters are leaving.'

"Of course, I didn't understand why we couldn't stay with Daddy. But I was an obedient child, and I knew whatever was happening was so bad that it had made my mom's mascara bleed. So I did what I was told. I grabbed a few T-shirts, a pair of pants, my pajamas, my favorite doll, my backpack in case I had to go to school on Monday, and my toothbrush. My mommy grabbed my hand and led me out of the bedroom. As we passed the kitchen, I noticed the book where she would write down recipes for our favorite foods. I ran back and stuffed it into my pillowcase.

"When I walked out of our house, I couldn't believe what I saw. My beloved Chavez Ravine looked like a war zone. But instead of smoke, the air was filled with dust as the houses around us were bulldozed to the ground.

"Someone, I still don't know who, picked me up and took me to a waiting car. My mommy and siblings piled inside after me. I placed my forehead against the window in the hopes of seeing my daddy.

"It wasn't until we were driving away that I finally saw him. He was sitting on the ground with some of our neighbors. His hands were behind his back, and his head was bowed. I screamed for him, but he couldn't hear me.

"I never saw my daddy again. Mommy said he got in a fight when he was in jail and had to stay longer. She promised we would go visit him one day, but we never did.

"Two days after the Dodgers played the Cincinnati Reds at the brand-new Dodger Stadium, my daddy died in prison. I didn't know it at the time, but he'd been sick for a while.

"I don't like to talk about what happened that day in Chavez Ravine. I don't like to think about all the families who lost their homes and their community.

"Instead, I hold the memories of the good times in my heart. And sometimes, in my dreams, I go back and visit my Shangri La that used to exist just beyond the hills outside the city of Los Angeles.

"It will always be my home."

I wiped away the tear that had slid down my cheek and lowered the last page of my essay. The class clapped, and I walked back to my seat. I didn't dare look at Lucas for fear of bursting into full-on sobs. Not because I was sad for me, but because I was sad for the little girl who'd grown up to believe her home could be taken away from her at any moment. My hope was that by having me share her story, she would have the freedom to finally let go of the ghosts from her past.

When the class was over, though, I waited in my seat until the last student had left. Only then did I stand up and walk to his desk and hand him my papers.

"I know I already emailed it to you," I said. "But I was hoping you could read it and make your notes on the hard copy instead. It's easier to see. I don't like that track changes mess in my Word document."

He nodded and put the pages inside his leather satchel. "Did your mom read it?"

"No," I said, and I sat on the edge of his desk. "She said she didn't need to because she's already lived it. Yesica read it, though. She even made some edits that I thought were helpful."

"You should be proud of yourself, Ana."

"Thank you. I'm actually thinking of writing more firsthand accounts. Maybe even turn it into a book. Who knows?"

"I think that's an excellent idea. You know you can count on me to help with whatever you need."

Lucas stood up and picked up his bag. "Well, I guess we better go before they lock us inside."

I got off the desk and grabbed his hand. "Wait. I need to tell you something."

He squeezed back. "No, you don't."

"I do. I want to. My daughter did something very brave today. She inspired me to do the same."

"You did. You read your essay out loud in front of a group of strangers."

"I did. But what I'm about to do scares me more."

Then, before I could think twice, I moved closer to Lucas and kissed him on his lips. When he didn't kiss me back, I began to pull away. Panic shot through me. Had I gotten this all wrong? Then his arms wrapped around me and brought me back against him.

This time, he was kissing me.

His lips were soft—so much softer than I'd ever imagined. His breath tasted like mint, and I knew it was from the Life Savers he always kept in his pocket.

Someone cleared his throat behind us, and we jumped apart.

"Um, sorry, we're about to lock up for the night," a red-faced man said before closing the classroom door.

We looked at each other and laughed.

"Well, that was . . . um," I began. Heat warmed my cheeks from both embarrassment and a lingering desire.

"Unexpected? Long overdue?" he said with a smile.

The glint in his eyes made me feel safe. "Nice. And those other two words."

He reached out to grab my hand. "Are you sure about this? About us?"

"More than I've ever been sure about anything else."

"Me too. Shall we?" he said as he pointed to the door.

Class was officially over.

Me and Lucas, however, were only just beginning.

The next morning, I decided it was time for another fresh start.

"Are you sure?" Yesica asked. "You still can change your mind."

We were at her favorite salon, and I was seated in the chair facing a large mirror. Her hairdresser, Nikki, stood next to my daughter, holding a pair of scissors.

With my fingers, I combed through my long dark-brown hair, which fell at least two inches below my shoulders. I'd given up on the box dye for a few months now, and gray hairs were beginning to invade the hairline above my forehead and the roots along the middle of my scalp. I'd had the same boring long layers since my twenties. Most days I wore it up in a clip or messy bun. My hairstyle was dull. Brittle. Tired looking. Just like I had been. It was time for my outside to match what was happening with me on the inside.

"I need a change," I told them both. "I'm sure."

Three hours later, I couldn't believe what I saw in the mirror. Neither could Yesica.

"Holy shit, Mom. You look at least ten years younger," she said as our eyes met in the reflection.

"Is that a good thing?" I asked hesitantly. Honestly, Yesica's shocked expression had me doubting my impulsive decision the night before to chop off my hair.

"Very good," Nikki said as she continued to style my new look with some gel and her fingers.

She'd given me what Yesica had called a pixie cut. My long locks were now on the ground—chaotically scattered in pieces all around the chair. I felt lighter in more ways than one. The grays were gone and had been replaced by a vibrant auburn color.

I looked so different. I couldn't believe it.

In a way, my long hair was the last hold Benny had on me. He would've absolutely hated everything about my new look. He believed women should only have long hair, because that was more feminine. And I'd been so desperate to make him happy that I'd agreed and only trimmed a few inches every couple of months.

Well, I was done living as if Benny was still controlling my life.

"Do you like it?" Yesica asked.

I looked at my reflection and nodded. Unexpected tears filled my eyes, and I reached for my daughter's hand.

"I love it."

CHAPTER THIRTY-FOUR
YESICA

Celeste finally answered the fourth time I called.

"Yesica, hello. So sorry, I'm on my way out and—" she began.

"I want to come visit Henry tomorrow."

"Tomorrow? Oh, I'm sorry, dear, but tomorrow is not a good day. How about I call you later this week so we can find a day that works better?"

"Sorry, I misspoke. I should've said, 'I'm coming to visit Henry tomorrow.'"

"And I already told you that you could not. Now, I really must—"

I took a deep breath. "Celeste, if you don't let me come visit Henry tomorrow, then I will never ever tell you about the woman who is about to give birth to your grandson."

She gasped. "What?"

"You heard me. I'll see you tomorrow at eleven."

I hung up before she could say anything else, and I didn't answer any of the several calls she made throughout the day. I knew Celeste. If I talked to her again, she would try to manipulate me into giving up the information and then find an excuse to not let me visit. But if I just showed up at her door, I knew she'd have no choice but to let me inside.

Because as much as she probably hated me, I could give her the one thing she wanted most in the world now.

A piece of Jason.

I showed up at my in-laws' home in Calabasas half an hour before I was supposed to. So, instead of pulling into their driveway like a normal person, I parked down the street and waited. The only thing Celeste hated more than people showing up earlier than expected was people showing up five minutes later than she'd told them to.

As I sat in my car, I sipped on the lukewarm tea I'd picked up from Starbucks before I began the thirty-minute drive up the 405 freeway to their home. They'd bought it when Jason was thirteen, just so Celeste could enroll him in the prestigious private Salinger School. Henry had once confessed to me that Jason didn't pass the entrance exam on his first attempt, but after they'd made a generous donation, he was allowed to retake the test and had miraculously passed the second time around. After we were married, we donated regularly to the school over the years, always making sure to support their annual auction fundraiser and booster program. I still got letters from the school reminding me of the next big event to support. But now I just tossed them in the trash.

The families who sent their kids to the Salinger School were some of the most elite and wealthy in all of Los Angeles County. I figured the institution would survive without my measly ten grand every year.

My iPhone's alarm beeped, alerting me that it was time to finally head over to the house. I was proud of myself for timing it so that I was ringing their doorbell at exactly five minutes before eleven.

Celeste herself opened the door about a minute later.

"Hello, Yesica." She nodded curtly before waving me inside.

"Hello, Celeste," I replied, just as coldly.

As soon as I stepped inside, I was greeted by a large portrait of Jason sitting on the table in the middle of the foyer. Emotions I hadn't expected threatened to overwhelm me, and I gripped the sides of my coat as if to brace myself. The photo hadn't been there the last time I'd visited with Jason—a few weeks before he'd died. But that wasn't the only thing that seemed different about the house. Or rather, about the woman who ran it.

I couldn't help but notice that Celeste looked like she had aged in the past several months since I'd seen her last. She'd boasted often about her expensive skin regimen and the spa treatments that had kept her skin looking smoother and brighter than most thirty-year-olds'. New streaks of white and silver threaded through her usually perfectly colored auburn hair. And most noticeable was the way her sweater and slacks hung loosely on her body. Celeste had always had a nice fit figure. Now she was thin. Too thin.

Part of me wanted to ask how she was. I knew better, though. Celeste didn't want my compassion or my concern. She only wanted what I dangled in front of her. That was the only reason why she'd opened the door.

So, I went straight to the reason why I had shown up in the first place.

"Where's Henry?" I asked.

"Don't you have something to tell me first?" she said with a raised eyebrow.

"I said I would tell you after I visited Henry. So where is he?"

I could tell she didn't like my answer or my tone. But I didn't care.

Celeste walked past me without saying a word, so I assumed that was my cue to follow her. She led me through the foyer and down the first hallway on the right. She stopped at the closed double doors, which I knew belonged to the library.

I took a step forward, but she held out a hand to stop me.

"Henry's dementia has gotten worse. He doesn't always remember that Jason . . . is gone. I would appreciate it very much if you didn't say anything about that. The doctors can't say how much time he has left. I want to make sure he's comfortable and peaceful for however long that is. Do you understand?"

I nodded, mostly because I didn't know if I could get out any words because of the knot of emotion in my throat.

Although she seemed skeptical, Celeste also seemed to accept my unspoken promise. She placed her hand on the doorknob and then looked back at me. "Also, don't be surprised if he has no idea who you are."

Of course the woman had to toss out a gut punch like that. I pushed down my feelings and put on a smile. It nearly fell off my face, though, when I saw my father-in-law by the window, sitting in a wheelchair.

"Henry, dear. You have a visitor," Celeste sang in her fake saccharine tone.

He looked up from his newspaper. For a second, I could see the confusion cross his face. I gulped down my heartbreak. But then his eyes brightened, and a huge smile beamed from cheek to cheek.

"Yesica!"

I brushed past Celeste and quickly made my way across the room to him. He opened his arms, and I happily leaned down to give him a hug. Henry squeezed me tight, and tears wet the corners of my eyes.

"It's so good to see you, Henry," I said sincerely.

"You too," he said after we'd pulled apart. He looked past me toward the door. "Is it just you today? Is Jason working?"

My heart sank, and I tried to sound light. "Yes, he has a big project he's trying to finish. He says he'll come visit tomorrow."

"Good. It's nice, though, that it's just us. We always have a good time together, don't we?"

I smiled. "We sure do."

"Are you going to stay for dinner? It's Sunday, so we're having pot roast. Afterward, we could go get some gelato at that place downtown. What do you say?"

I remembered what Celeste had said, so I stopped myself from correcting him that it was Wednesday and that the gelato place had closed over a year ago.

"I wish I could," I told him instead as I sat down on the couch. "But I'm on my way to meet some friends. I just wanted to stop by to give you something."

I reached into my purse and pulled out the reason I'd been both wanting and dreading to see Henry again. I handed it to him.

Henry's bushy gray eyebrows furrowed at the bundle of white tissue paper in his hand. Slowly, he began to undo the layers with shaky hands. But his face brightened when he found what had been wrapped inside.

"It's my train," he said. "Why do you have it?"

I cleared my throat. Unlike the dinner question, I wasn't sure how to answer.

"Oh wait. I gave it to Jason, didn't I?" Henry said.

Relief washed over me. "Yes, that's right. You let him borrow it, and he wanted me to give it back to you." My voice broke on the last word, so I coughed to try to cover it up.

"I wanted him to give it to his first child one day."

I stilled as I met Henry's clear blue eyes. The clarity of his tone caught me off guard. It took me a few seconds to choose my words.

"That's right. But now he wants you to be the one to give it to . . . to your first grandchild. He thought it should come from you."

Henry looked down at the train and seemed to examine it. "My father gave this to me when I was eight years old. I gave it to Jason when he was seven."

"I know," I said, trying so hard not to let my voice break with emotion again. "He told me that it was the first train he ever had and that you gave him a car every birthday and every Christmas until he had the full set. He doesn't remember what happened to the others, but he held on to that one because he knew it used to be yours."

"I told him, even when he was little, that it was an heirloom, even though he had no idea what that word meant. But somehow he knew it was special to our family."

"That's right. It is special."

And Jason had every intention of keeping that tradition of giving it to his first child. But since he wasn't here, I was going to do it for him. Not out of some sense of love or guilt. In fact, I wasn't doing this for Jason at all.

I was doing it for Henry.

It didn't matter if he knew or remembered that his son was gone. It didn't matter because nothing could change that fact. But I had the power to change this one thing for him—to give Henry the chance to not just see his first grandchild, but to carry on the tradition that meant so much to him.

We spent a few more minutes talking about trains. But I noticed the more he talked, the more he became confused or lost his line of thought. Eventually, he just stopped and stared out the window. I knew it was time to leave.

I took the caboose from his hand and set it on the table next to him. "Would you like to lie down for a little, Henry? It's okay if you'd like to rest."

He turned to face me. "Yesica, when did you get here? Where's Jason?"

My heart broke. "Oh, he's in the other room, talking to Celeste. He says he'll come see you after your nap, okay?"

My father-in-law nodded and returned to looking out the window. I stood up and wrapped my arms around him. "Goodbye, Henry. I love you and I'll see you soon."

He patted my arm. "Bye-bye."

A sense of peace overwhelmed me. I didn't get it with my dad, and I didn't get it with Jason. But at least I'd gotten it with Henry. I was finally able to say goodbye to someone I loved.

I took one last look and made myself walk away. Celeste was waiting on the other side of the doors.

I handed her the napkin with Amber's phone number on it. "She's due at the end of the month," I said, wiping away the tears from the corners of my eyes before they became more than I could control.

Celeste took the napkin and nodded. Before I took a step, I said, "Despite our issues at the end, I truly loved Jason. He was a good man, and, in your own way, I think you were a good mother to him. I hope you'll be as good to his child as you were to him. But you're not this baby's mother. And if you treat Amber the way you treated me, there's a good chance you will never be a part of the baby's life. Then you really will lose Jason forever."

And for the first time in all the years I'd known her, Celeste was at a loss for words.

CHAPTER
THIRTY-FIVE
ANA

I was home.

That's what I immediately thought as I walked through the front door of my house. The pungent odor of fresh paint and new flooring welcomed me, my mother, and Yesica.

"Oh wow. I can't believe this is the same house," my daughter said as she walked inside the living room.

The 1970s chocolate shag carpet and dingy white walls were gone. The flooring underneath our feet was now a light-beige tile, and the sun creeping through the large bay window cast a warm glow on the light-gray walls. Even the popcorn ceiling had disappeared.

"I thought the damage was limited to the bedrooms and bathrooms?" she asked.

I couldn't help but smile as I looked around for the hundredth time at my new living room. "It was. But I took your advice and decided, since the other areas of the house were getting a makeover, why not just do everything?"

"Yesica, come see my room," my mother said, and she grabbed her hand. "It has heated floors!"

Yesica met my eyes with what I took to be an impressed look and followed her grandmother down the hallway.

I rolled my suitcase toward my bedroom. It glided easily down the tiled path, which ended at my door. Instead, I'd opted for a dark laminated wood floor and bright-white walls inside the room.

My floors were heated too.

A few minutes later, I was joined by Yesica. "It looks so much bigger in here, Mom," she said as she walked around my bed to the other side of the room. "Wait. Where's your big dresser that used to be against the window?"

"I sold it on Facebook Marketplace," I answered. "I have a smaller dresser inside the closet instead now."

"I thought you hated Facebook?"

"I still do. But Lucas said the dresser would sell fast on there, and it did."

She laughed before walking into my adjoining bathroom. "Love the tile in here, Mom. Did you pick it out?"

"I did. You don't think it's too . . . much?" I'd had reservations about the colorful backsplash behind the sink and in the shower. I'd originally picked out a similar pattern for the kitchen but chickened out using it there. The bathroom—a lot smaller canvas—seemed like the perfect way to get the colors I wanted without having to make such a big commitment.

Tiny steps.

Yesica walked back into the bedroom. "The house looks really nice, Mom. They did a good job. Actually, you did a good job handling all of this."

I couldn't help but smile at the compliment.

"Come with me," I said as I reached for her hand. "I want to show you one more thing."

I led Yesica back down the hallway to the first bedroom closest to the living room. I motioned for her to open the door. She gave me a confused look but followed my direction. The gasp she let out was worth it.

"Oh. My. God."

I followed her as she made her way inside the room that had once been her brother's bedroom and then, after he'd moved out, had become Benny's office. It had the same white walls and dark-gray laminate flooring as my room. But unlike mine, every single piece of furniture and wall hanging was brand new.

This room was now my new office.

A sofa with a pretty floral pattern and a white wooden five-shelf bookcase were against the wall to the right of the door. A beautiful desk, matching the bookcase, sat underneath the room's large window.

Yesica pointed to it. "Facebook Marketplace?" she teased.

I laughed and shook my head. "IKEA."

It was quiet between us for several seconds, and a familiar anxiety began to build in my gut. Perhaps I'd been wrong about showing her the room. Perhaps she was upset that I'd made such a drastic change to this space. After all, I really had basically removed all trace of Benny.

"You don't like it," I said softly.

She spun around to face me. "What?"

"You're upset because this room isn't his office anymore."

Yesica shook her head. "No, I'm not upset. I admit that it's a big difference. But I promise you I'm not upset."

"Then what? I can tell something is wrong."

She walked over to me. "Seeing what you did here just made me realize something."

"What?"

"That I need to do the same. It's time for me to do something with . . . the room. You know."

I did know. Yesica was talking about the room that was supposed to have been a nursery.

"Are you sure?" I asked. "There's no reason why you can't wait some more if you're not ready."

"It's time," she said after a long sigh. "I don't know. Maybe I'll turn it into a home gym, or even an office like you. I'll figure it out."

I smiled and nodded. "Actually, this isn't just an office."

"It's not?" she said, and she looked around the room again.

I walked over to the couch and sat down. "This is a pullout," I said, and I patted the cushion. "So this is officially your room—or Alejandro's—for whenever either of you want to come visit and stay with us."

Yesica walked over to the couch and sat next to me. "This is a very nice room, Mom. I would love to stay here."

"See, I told you she would like it," my mother said as she came into the room. She took a seat on the other side of Yesica.

"No, you said she would be fine with it . . . after I said you couldn't switch rooms."

"Mama Melda! You just got done telling me how much you love your new room," Yesica said with a laugh.

"I do love it," my mother insisted. "But this room is a little closer to the kitchen. You know sometimes I need my snack in the middle of the night."

I shook my head as if I couldn't believe what she had just said. Although I definitely did.

"Well, I only see one problem with this room," Yesica said.

Worry tightened my chest. "What?" I said, looking around to find what she could be referring to.

"Me and Alejandro fighting over who gets to sleep here when we both come to stay for Christmas."

The worry turned to warmth. Having both of my children under one roof again was a dream I hadn't let myself have for a long time.

"That's not a problem I mind having," I admitted with a smile.

The three of us sat there in silence for a few minutes. My eyes scanned the room, and it was still hard to believe how different it looked compared to just a few months earlier. But I knew it wasn't just the new floor or new paint or even the new desk.

The ghost of Benny had haunted this house for five years. Maybe he hadn't played with flickering lights or made doors slam shut, but his presence had prevented me from living my life the way I'd wanted. And that had also haunted my relationship with Yesica.

But it wasn't all his fault.

Truth was, I'd had five years to fix things between us, and I'd chosen to not do anything differently. I would probably always feel guilty for being so complacent about so many things for so long. I was done blaming others, though. This was the only life I had, and it was about time I took ownership of it.

Clearing out the office and making it a guest room for the kids was my way of showing Yesica that whatever happened to us, it wouldn't be because of what her dad did or didn't do.

This was our fresh start in more ways than one.

And now, the three of us could say we were all finally home.

EPILOGUE
YESICA

Two years later...

Oscar and I arrived at the book signing about fifteen minutes before it was supposed to start. I had taken my last meeting via conference call while he weaved through rush hour traffic to get to the independent bookstore in Hollywood. It had been almost a year since I'd taken over Damien's position at the firm, and I had no qualms about using conference calls and Zoom meetings whenever I needed to. I knew some of the partners raised their eyebrows over the fact that I wasn't in the office twelve or fourteen hours every day. But the last few years had taught me that life was too short, and there were more important things to do than work.

Like attending a book signing on the other side of town.

"Wow," Oscar said as we entered the store. "It's packed. I bet you there're no more seats left."

I scanned the room, but I wasn't as worried as Oscar. "Mom said Lucas told the bookstore to reserve some chairs up at the front for us. Mama Melda is already here, so I'm sure she's guarding our seats liked a rabid Doberman."

We made our way through the maze of people and chairs and eventually spotted my grandmother seated in the first row.

"Finally," she said as I bent down to kiss her cheek. "I almost had to start whacking people with my cane to stop them from sitting down here."

Although Mama Melda had initially been resistant to the idea of using a cane once the arthritis in her knees began making it difficult and painful to walk some days, I'd noticed she'd been using it more. Sometimes I'd get a little sad, thinking the cane was just another sign of her getting older and more frail. But then she'd threaten to use it as a weapon, which comforted me in a strange way.

Mama Melda was still a force to be reckoned with—especially when it came to saving seats for her family.

Oscar took the seat next to her, and I told them both I was going to let my mom and Lucas know we'd arrived. After being directed by one of the store's employees, I found them in a back room. Lucas was standing and appeared to be reading from a piece of paper in his hands, and my mom was sitting down next to him on a metal folding chair.

"You made it," she exclaimed as I walked over to her. She stood so I could give her a hug and a kiss on the cheek.

"I told you I would," I said. "Although you probably should thank your future son-in-law's video game driving skills for getting us here on time."

I was still getting used to the idea of calling Oscar that. Although we'd been dating for two years already, we'd only been engaged for a few weeks. He'd proposed on my thirty-fifth birthday on the beach during a weekend getaway trip to Santa Barbara. Then he'd taken me to a beautiful Italian restaurant for dinner, where I was surprised again. My mother, grandmother, Lucas, and Oscar's mom and dad were all there, waiting to celebrate with us. It was one of the best nights of my life.

I gave Lucas a hug next and asked, "How are you feeling?"

"Good," he said with a nod of his head. Then added, "Maybe a little nervous."

"Why are you nervous?" I scoffed. "Aren't you a pro at this by now?"

My mom put her hand on his left shoulder. "That's what I keep telling him. If anybody should be nervous, it's me."

I reached over to grab her other hand. "And are you?"

My mom took a deep breath and tightened her grasp. "Yes," she admitted softly. "Part of me still can't believe this is happening."

"Well, believe it. You are officially a published author."

My voice nearly broke on that last sentence. Like Mom, I, too, could hardly believe it. Not because I doubted her talent as a writer—I'd read enough of her short stories over the past two years to know this was what she was meant to do. I was more surprised by just how much her life had changed . . . for the better.

After taking Lucas's class, she'd enrolled in community college and was just a few units away from finishing her associate's degree. In between classes and work, my mom and Lucas had begun writing a book together. *The Day the Bulldozers Came* was a collection of interviews and essays featuring former residents of Chavez Ravine. It had taken them six months to finish it, and then it was another six months before it was bought by a small independent publisher. Today was the book's release day and Lucas and Mom's first joint book signing.

And besides their professional relationship, they were also dating. It was strange for me at first, and I realized it was strange for Mom too. I began noticing she'd shirk from any show of affection from him when I was around. When I'd mentioned this to Alejandro, he said it was probably because she wasn't sure how I would feel. Truth was, I didn't know how I felt about it. After learning the truth about my dad, I'd tried to separate my feelings about him as a father from how he'd been as a husband. My memories of my dad were just that . . . mine. And my mom's memories of him were hers. That didn't mean that either was wrong or right. So I had to accept that my dad didn't treat my mom the way she deserved. And now she had found a man who did. Who was I to take that away from her? So, one day I sat her down and told her that if Lucas made her happy, then that was all I needed, and she didn't have to hide her feelings for him anymore. After that, Lucas kind of just became an unofficial member of the family. He was there for dinners and holidays and wherever else my mom wanted him to be.

To my surprise, Mama Melda immediately accepted him. She still considered Cuca Padilla her mortal enemy—but she could see that Lucas was not his mother.

I knew Lucas had wanted to make things more official for a while now, but Mom had told me she wasn't ready. She liked her freedom and the fact that she didn't have to listen to anyone. Well, besides Mama Melda, of course.

"Lucas isn't Dad," I'd told her.

"I know he isn't," she said. "But I got married at eighteen and was a mother by nineteen. My entire adult life has been spent putting others before me. I want to know what it feels like to put me first for a while."

And Lucas, the very patient man I'd come to know, said he would wait.

As the three of us stood in that little back room of the bookstore, waves of emotion overcame me. But instead of fighting them, I just surrendered. Another lesson I'd learned over the past couple of years was that holding back feelings didn't do anyone any good.

Through tears, I reached for my mom and pulled her toward me into a warm, tight embrace. "I'm so proud of you," I whispered.

She buried her face in my shoulder, and I felt her body shake. "Thank you for saying that," she said after pulling away to look at me.

"I'm sorry I've never said that before," I confessed.

My mom reached up and touched my cheek. "I thought we promised to let go of our regrets."

"We did. But this was long overdue."

We hugged again for another several seconds. Then my mom let me go so she could dig into her purse for tissues.

"This was supposed to be a happy day," I said with a laugh after blowing my nose. "I can't believe we're standing here crying like a couple of chillonas."

"Um, what did I miss?" a male voice not belonging to Lucas asked.

I'd been so focused on my mom that I hadn't realized my brother Alejandro had walked into the room.

"Nothing. Just some mother-daughter bonding," I said.

"Well, if you're done, I'm being told to bring everyone out so the book signing can start," he explained.

I turned to Mom and said, "You might want to go to the bathroom and fix your makeup. You don't want Mama Melda pointing out your raccoon eyes in front of a packed bookstore, do you?"

"It's packed?" Lucas asked.

"Standing room only," Alejandro answered.

My mom covered her mouth with her hand and gasped, "Dios mío."

"You're going to do great. Both of you are," I told her. "Now go do what you need to do, and we'll see you out there."

Then Alejandro and I left the room to go back to our seats. He'd gotten into town the day before and was staying with me and Oscar at our condo in Santa Monica. I'd sold the Sunset Park house a few months earlier, and we'd moved in together right after. He still ran the grief support group on Saturdays, and I was still a member. I hadn't missed a Saturday in over a year.

Grief, I'd learned, didn't have a finish line. It was an endless journey. Some days the path was easy, and other days you'd be running perfectly fine and then, out of nowhere, you'd stumble, and the pain would come roaring back as if your loss had just happened. Group, in addition to my therapist, helped me accept the fact that I was always going to grieve my dad and Jason and, even, Henry. He'd passed only a month after his grandson was born. I took comfort in the fact that he'd been able to meet the baby at least once. Well, that's what I was told by Jason's cousin. I hadn't spoken to or seen Celeste since my last visit with Henry. I didn't even go to the funeral. I'd said my goodbye, and I was at peace with that.

I took my seat next to Oscar, and Alejandro sat in the chair beside me. When my mother and Lucas emerged from behind a tall bookshelf and the entire room erupted into applause, I grabbed Oscar's hand so I wouldn't leap out of my seat like I was courtside at a basketball game.

Excitement and sheer joy accelerated my heart rate, to the point where I wondered for a second if anyone would hear it thumping once the room grew quiet again. I felt giddy. And hopeful. Not just for my mother, but for me and Mama Melda too. We'd traveled alone in the dark for so long because our secrets and pride had kept us from realizing that we were on the same path all along. Once we let our guards down, we were able to finally see each other—really see each other. And together we took our first steps into the light.

As I watched my mother beam with pride as she talked about the book she'd helped create, I was so grateful to be in this moment with her.

And I couldn't wait for all the other moments we would share in the future.

It didn't mean that she had suddenly turned into the perfect mother. And I was still far from a perfect daughter. The difference now was that we knew we didn't have to be in order to love and be loved.

I closed my eyes and released one long breath. My heart calmed, and I let go of Oscar's hand.

I had finally made it to the top of the mountain. And for the first time in years, I wasn't afraid of what was on the other side.

RECIPES FROM THE BOOK

Mama Melda's Frijoles Charros

Ingredients:
>1 pound dried pinto beans
>1 onion
>1 jalapeño
>2 roma tomatoes
>4 hot dog wieners
>9 ounce package of pork chorizo
>half a pack of thick-cut bacon
>*Optional:*
>cilantro
>cotija cheese

Directions:

Rinse the beans and remove any split ones or debris. Soak them in cold water for about an hour. Boil in 6 cups of water with salt and half an onion until the beans are soft—usually takes about 2 hours.

Dice the bacon and slice the wieners. Fry the bacon until cooked (but not crispy), then add the wieners to the same pan. Once the wieners are browned, add the chorizo sausage and break it down into small pieces. Cook everything together for about 5 minutes until the chorizo is well mixed in with the other meats. Dice the tomatoes and jalapeño (remove stem and seeds) and then add to the meat mixture and fry everything together for about 5 minutes. Pour the mixture into the beans and stir. Let simmer for 10 minutes. Serve hot and top with cilantro and crumbled cotija cheese if desired.

Ana's Entomatadas

Ingredients:
>10 corn tortillas
>4 roma tomatoes
>half an onion
>2 jalapeños
>2 cloves of garlic
>shredded cooked chicken
>shredded cheese or crumbled queso fresco
>½ tablespoon of chicken bouillon
>*Optional:*
>avocado
>Mexican crema or sour cream
>chopped white onion

Directions:

For the tomato salsa, boil the tomatoes, onion, and jalapeños in the same pot until everything is soft. Remove the stems and seeds from the jalapeños. Transfer cooked ingredients to the blender, along with 1 cup of the water. Add the garlic and chicken bouillon. Blend until well combined. Taste and add salt or more chicken bouillon if needed.

Heat 1 tablespoon of oil in a frying pan and pour the tomato salsa into the pan. Let simmer for about 7 to 10 minutes.

Warm the corn tortillas and then lightly fry them in 1 tablespoon of oil. Afterward, assemble your entomatadas by adding the chicken and cheese to each fried tortilla and then rolling into a cylinder shape. Pour the cooked tomato salsa over the entomatadas. Warm in a preheated 350-degree oven for about 10 minutes if needed. Before serving, top with more cheese, chopped onions, Mexican crema, and avocado if desired.

AUTHOR'S NOTE

As a Mexican American author, I sometimes struggle with a sense of obligation to use my stories to also weave in pieces of our history that have been either forgotten or purposefully hidden. It's that part of me that wants to show others that the Latine/Latinx identity in the United States is about more than just immigration. Generations and generations of Mexican Americans were planting roots on this side of the border long before there was talk about building walls.

Not many people outside Los Angeles know the story of what happened at Chavez Ravine. Unfortunately, it's not that well known to the city's residents either. I only learned the history as an adult, and it both shocked and saddened me. I wondered how an entire town—an entire community of people—could be erased, and I wanted to learn more. And then I wanted others to learn too.

So when I was thinking of the characters in this book, I knew I wanted to share the history of Chavez Ravine through Mama Melda.

When I first thought of the idea of writing a story about three generations of widows, I knew I didn't want it to be all about grief. After all, I'd tackled that theme in my last book, *Too Soon for Adiós*.

Instead, I wanted to focus more on the mother-daughter relationship, and how it can shape our experiences and beliefs as adults. Yet I had no idea just how stubborn these particular women were going to be.

It took longer than usual to finally pull their stories out of them. They'd held on to them tightly—as if they weren't quite ready to face their truths.

And maybe I wasn't quite ready either.

Because you can't tell a story about mothers and daughters without reflecting on the women in your own life and the lessons they've handed down from generation to generation.

Especially the ones no one ever wanted to learn.

My great-grandma Welita became a widow at age forty-six.

My grandma Chayo lost my grandpa when she was eighty-six.

And my mom was almost seventy when my dad passed away.

I'll never know why the universe decided they should all belong to the same club—the one no one ever wants to join, yet they have to pay the highest price in order to be a member. And even though the three of them weren't widows at the same time like the characters in my book, all have been examples of strength and enduring love.

They will always be my inspiration.

It's not a surprise, though. They're mothers and daughters, after all. Each learned from the one before how to carry on. It's in their nature.

That's the story I really wanted to tell, and I hope I've done it and them justice.

Thank you for reading.

ACKNOWLEDGMENTS

As always, I am grateful to everyone who continues to help make this dream of mine come true every day.

First, I'd like to thank all the readers who have messaged, emailed, and told me in person how much they've enjoyed my books and how much it means to see characters who remind them of their own families. It's because of their support that I'm able to write more stories.

Second, I want to thank my agent, Sarah Younger, for her constant advice, guidance, cheerleading, and wisdom.

Huge thanks also to Maria Gomez, Charlotte Herscher, and the rest of the team at Montlake. You all are amazing!

Special shout-outs to my circle of wonderful author friends. You inspire me every day.

And finally, thank you to my husband, Patrick, my kids, and the rest of my family. You have always believed in me, and I couldn't do this without you. I love you mucho.

AUTHOR BIO

Annette Chavez Macias writes stories about love, family, and following your dreams. She is proud of her Mexican American heritage, culture, and traditions, all of which can be found within the pages of her books. For readers wanting even more love stories and guaranteed happily ever afters, Macias also writes romance novels under the pen name Sabrina Sol. A Southern California native, Macias lives just outside Los Angeles with her husband, three children, and their dogs.